Other titles by Patrick Summers

Key Change:
An Alternative History of Mozart

The Prison of Time: Poems from 2023

The Spirit of This Place:
How Music Illuminates the Human Spirit

A COLLECTION
of
BREVITIES

A novel by
Patrick Summers

Contenti Press

ISBN 979-8-9876023-3-1

This is a work of fiction.

With grateful acknowledgment to Jim Luigs and Chris Gwaltney for assistance.

Design by Pattima Singhalaka.

Dedicated to the cherished ladies of my childhood who didn't get heard.

You know who you are.

ENIGMA
2010, Houston, Texas
ALTA

There is a mysterious man of late who keeps calling and imploring me to "just write a few notes in advance, since it will help you gather your thoughts." He is mysterious solely because he has phoned me out of nowhere, something which used to happen all the time but hasn't happened in a few months. There is certainly no mystery in our conversations, as he wasn't an interesting enough voice for that. For me it is all about the voice. He phones asking when he can talk to me about my son, about Joey. I always tell him the same thing, that I have a few questions for Joey myself. Joey, at least, calls a little more since Gene died, and I'm grateful for that.

Mother has crossed over into that most untenable stage of elderliness: she now chews with her mouth open and I do not know why. I point it out, of course, but she can't remember that I've said anything and three minutes later there she is again, showing us her food. Her most persistent irritants have long been with her, but this is a new one. I wonder if there is some strap I could buy to close her mouth. May my Savior, or my savior, or whoever it is, please pluck me from the jaws of this world before I begin presenting my meals to my relatives. I can't believe she is still alive.

WHO ARE YOU, STRANGE MAN? (WO WILLST DU, FREMDER MENSCH?)

2010, Sydney, Australia

JOEY

They won't give up. Even the new man in the red coffee shop this morning, engaged as he was in conversation with someone else, kept trying to include me, assuming my interest. I can't imagine he knew who I was so far out of context, but thinking about it now, he might have. Arriving home to find yet another e-mail from the publisher in New York was a hard symmetry to dismiss.

I go to the red coffee shop nearly every day, and I've never seen him before. Besides, no one has recognized me in years. When I first got to Sydney, it used to happen regularly, as I was less than a year out of it all. I don't want to take the time today to answer the publisher's letter, much less commit to writing an autobiography no one wants, or at least one *I* don't want. Why can't someone else write a book about me, if there even needs to be one? There must be tons of information out there, magazine articles, but there is no story, so what would be the point? Everyone wants a story now.

The coffee shop guy reminded me of Gene: assuming and loud, unable to imagine that someone might not be fascinated with his every fustian nuance, his whimsy in the most mundane phrases, feeling so inventive at what has been said a million times by as many people but better. I'm not afraid of a confessional book; I don't care if they know who I had orgasms with. I just don't think what I actually know will be of interest to anyone. What they all will want is an intemperate account of invented controversies. Gratitude and precision have no drama, either in life or at the piano.

I know what Mom thinks. She thinks she was denied the opportunity to live in her talent while I've squandered mine. She exists in a world where she blames everything wrong with her life on Grandma and Grandpa. Maybe they fucked her over; I have no idea. I only know I'm tired of the story. The publisher is calling her, too, but she won't talk to them until I give permission, and I appreciate that. She called last night, wondering why I don't want this opportunity, as though it's something real in itself, something desirable. She still calls me often. I appreciate that, too, but there is so little to tell her. My days are an endless da capo, which is what I claim to have wanted all along, right?

No matter what we actually talk about, which isn't much, most of our recent conversations take this tone: my life will never be remembered, no matter how much I did, as in how much I deep-down-in-the-depths did for *you*. Tell your story; it is a remarkable one. Why do you throw it all away?

After years of politesse, suddenly a new narrative has formed, that I "threw it all away." She seems to think I had some choice.

CONTESSA, PERDONO
ALTA

I always thought Texas was a place that would never run out, or at least there would always be enough of it for *me*. But my Texas has been spent; there's nothing left. I have a gorgeous home and all of the carapaces of being alive, yet somehow in these past months, years maybe, I've lost the feelings of presence that used to just feel like *me*. Yes, in case you are wondering, anonymous future biographer of my son, I am indeed the sort of person who uses the word *carapace* regularly, as well I should! The vocabulary of the world has diminished so drastically across my lifetime that it is a wonder we have words left to describe anything.

Am I now rejecting my body that has faithfully served me these seventy-one years? Am I preparing to leave it, in some faceless natural process I'll only discern at the very end? I don't feel ill; I just don't feel at all. I used to have such imagination. I could solve any problem. Every day was a list of goals and shopping lists, and I happily accomplished them all. Gene was never an issue except in retrospect, and that is the hardest thing of all for me to understand, because every other part of my life was lived in real time. But not my husband, not Gene, not the one thing in my life I should have felt as he happened, and should have long ago abandoned but before he had the good sense to die not so long ago.

I continually forgave him, or uttered the words of forgiveness at least, because that is what I was always told I was supposed to do. Forgiveness was the great thing meant to move mankind forward like no other force. All through my childhood I was told that nothing in life happened without forgiveness. That was the lore; but I forgave and forgave and forgave and it never made anything happen. Nothing ever changed. I actually *heard* his last breath, can you imagine? I've heard some of the greatest music in the world, much of it played by my son, *my son*, but I've also heard someone accept their last intake of oxygen. I can only barely touch the beauty of that in my memory now, yet on the day he died I felt about him pretty much what I'd always felt: indifference and resignation. I loved the feeling of him, the thought, but I didn't love him. Has he really been gone ten years?

OFF THE SHELF
JOEY

For most pianists the limbering exercises result in a reward of the music one is able to play because you've exercised. Not me. I love the freedom of the routine of exercise. Middle C is, like so many things, misnamed: the actual center of the keyboard is in the space between E flat and E natural above middle C, and I grew to love the energy of that tiny area. Several times a day I would slowly position myself at a piano and, first standing then sitting, find the vibration that happens between E flat and E natural, like some energetic pull from a compass, and align it to the center of my body. Everything I needed to know about any given day at the piano was immediately made known to me by that initial exchange.

If it was a performance day and that energy was difficult to find, then the performance would be have to be searched for, and playing would be a fight with myself. On other days, though, especially early in my career, that energy would come blazing out of the piano and into me, and vice versa, and nothing was difficult about those days. Hours of practice would pass so joyfully when that energy arrived, and it was the exercises, those repetitive and mechanized cracklings, easily the most noncreative and dull things in music, that renewed my creative energy every day. And I do those exercises a few times a week when the house is absolutely empty. I've never once practiced any piano music in the last ten years, but I do pull the exercises off the shelf and love every moment of them: Brahms, Chopin, Moszkowski, Hanon, Liszt, all the scales and arpeggios in all configurations.

Silent Hall

ALTA

I seem to know very little anymore, but I do know that I've spent an inordinate amount of time trying to figure out what men want.

My son's publisher, or I guess *potential* publisher, has become more insistent. His calls are the impetus to keep this diary again; for years I didn't want to record anything, afraid that someone might find it. Why? Trying to explain how it all happened is too complicated, too outside what people want to think. Joey didn't achieve what he did by the usual channels: the world's great pianists don't come from Texas, and they don't spring fully formed out of a quiet neighborhood near the museums in Houston. Our little hamlet, North and South Boulevards, obviously not burdened with great creative naming, was initially developed as a Jewish answer to River Oaks, since the great neighborhood of Houston, which has many oaks but no river, was restricted to the followers of Jesus. Oh, my fellow Christians have so much to answer for, and every year I find it more difficult to be counted in their company. Now, when I reflect on those years when Joey was first learning to play, and growing faster than I could manage to grasp, how I wish I had a written record of those halcyon days. I doubt if Joey has the slightest interest in a book, though, but I'll try to get an answer out of him shortly. I'm afraid I call him too much.

My heart cracks when I hear musicians talking shit about one another. I never use that word lightly, *shit*. I hate the word, in fact, but when it is appropriate there may be no better word in our limited tongue! Gene used it all the time and I detest it. My sons have even been known to benignly carry it into conversation with their very own mother, despite knowing my feelings about it. Musicians take so much for granted. Do they ever think of the hours of their lives they get to spend in the presence of the greatest of arts, hours that were denied to me? I can't create a false sense of it, either. My friends, and especially Mother, are forever giving me recordings, which are inherently false, and one of the many benefits of moving her to a nursing home was that I was able to throw out her huge collection of classical recordings while letting her think I'm constantly home listening to them. I only have the small battles left.

I never sang in front of Gene. Never. But when I knew he was gone, for a few hours I would inevitably go to the piano and try to find my voice again. The house on South has resounded with my soprano voice since I was a little girl. I am part of this house. My voice has seeped into its skeleton, and this is the only place where my voice has a chance to live forever, hiding in corners and resonating among the beams. I know that when I've walked into the many opera houses of the world, especially the oldest ones, and if I'm lucky enough to be in them by myself, in their silence I can sense what is hanging there forever, the voices which have resounded through the pulsations of the air. We think the sounds of live performance are ephemeral, but they last, I assure you. Every voice changes the voices that follow it. One need only to look at the wind through an aspen tree, and there is nothing on earth that projects more spiritual energy, to see that this is also true of singing: the wind erupts through an aspen, and every leaf—not the branches but the leaves—is set in vibration against the forces assaulting it, but the tree does not fight against the intrusion. It not only welcomes it; it creates something new from it, and each gust of wind lives within the tree forever, lingering in its humid interior.

When Joey would play in those great concert halls around the world, that's what I felt about him, too—that his gorgeous playing would live somewhere within them, and I believe his musicianship is there still, eternal. Often I would wait in the hall for him to greet all the people he needed to. The ushers would all leave. Occasionally janitors would silently pick up a few things, but usually that work was left for the following morning. As the hall gained silence, air conditioners turned off, I could sometimes drink in that glorious moment. My *son* had just played a piano recital twenty minutes before, an entire evening of the greatest music ever written, played with a brilliance that joined him to the ages. My *son* did that. And I could inevitably hear him still in those moments, just in my thoughts. The sounds he created, or re-created, were always there. Now, through his decisions, he has taken away my choice in the matter: if I'm going to ever hear him again, it may be *only* available in my memory, and that will someday come to an end, and then what?

GRAND PAUSE
JOEY

Mom is the reason I haven't responded to the publishers, because the story they seek is actually hers, and while it wouldn't remotely bother *me* to say that, it is not the narrative they want. I had no brilliance except to absorb hers. My creative life was sedate next to what she did. I never heard a violent word emanate from her until recently, and now I fear she will turn violence on herself. The joy in which she used to live each moment has turned into fear of everything. She used to fill my own life with comfort and catharsis. Now I dread the buzz of my phone in the early morning or late night, knowing it will likely be a cloud of darkness and supposed controversies, none of which would have bothered her former self. When I try to engage her about music now, she quickly changes away from a subject she has enormous knowledge about and which gives her a unique access to a type of joy cut off to most people. She used to question me about my life. Now I hear about nothing but hers: her minor health issues, her friends at church, her incredulity that she has accomplished so little, as though her life is nearly over even though Grandma still lives with some energy in a little nursing home south of Houston.

The hotels were a blur, but even all these years later I remember a found day, an unexpected day off, in the Hotel Bel-Air in Los Angeles. I woke early after a recital the night before. The morning was misty, which was rain to the Angelenos, and strangely chilly. It must have been summer. I descended into that glorious oval pool and drifted over to the deep end. When I turned around and started treading water, the hills to the west were a particularly vibrant green from the wet morning, and other than birdsong, there was not another sound. Most hotel pools were impossible places for me because of the screaming children, always so indulged and cute to their parents, and so endlessly irritating to me. But on that morning, with a chilly dew dropping from the hills, I treaded water for what must have been two hours. Inexplicably, those few quietest hours of my life were in the middle of the most luxurious of hotels. The Bel-Air was, is, otherworldly—no beds were so crisp and clean, no floors more marbled and perfect, no problem that the staff couldn't solve. It wasn't real, of course, but that morning in that perfection of a pool put me on a path to buy a small home in the Bel Air hills, even though I eventually settled for a quiet Westwood apartment, simply so I could re-create that silence. I bought the apartment, put a piano and a bed in it, and spent a few fitful nights there trying to practice. It sat empty most of the time, along with most of the apartments in my building, which were used by movie stars a few weeks a year. The Bel-Air would always let me come and swim, bless them, so I'd often walk over from Westwood because I loved the walk through UCLA.

But that original morning there could never be re-created: I would inevitably start swimming in silence, but soon children would arrive and come crashing through the peace. I always liked the restaurant there, too, so whenever I could I would walk over for breakfast. Thinking back on it, I spent a lot of time in Los Angeles even though it wasn't much of a classical music town, despite all their boasting. Once at the Bel-Air, a single fly was slightly perturbing me as I awaited a frittata, and two handsome young men were dispatched to my table to capture it and take it elsewhere, specifically instructed by the maître d' not to kill it, as that would be unsightly for the guests and possibly upsetting to my artistic soul.

I can't imagine what I spent on hotels in my career—undoubtedly hundreds of thousands of dollars, as it was always assumed by my presenters that I desired luxury, when actually all I needed was silence, a strangely expensive commodity in hotels, considering that they exist solely for one's rest. I think it is hard for people to imagine the endless noise of most hotels, unless you spend as much of your life in them as I did.

But oh, what unimaginable noises I dealt with in the thousands of hotels in which I had to rest and work: vacuums, leaf blowers, ice machines, elevators, drunken youngsters, screaming babies, traffic, trash collecting at 5:00 a.m. the day of a recital, trees being trimmed (it seemed they always needed to be shorn on the only day of the year I was scheduled to stay there), slamming doors, rooms next door being renovated (did no one think of that before I checked in?), water leaking, thump-thump "music" from the bar (with a concierge incredulous that I wanted to move far away from "the action"). "I have a recital tomorrow," I told him to no response.

In various articles that appeared after I stopped performing, I read that I had a reputation for eccentricity and was "famously passive-aggressive." This was news to me. I made demands on hotels because I *needed* silence in which to fully work, and I was always surprised at what passed for quiet in some of these establishments that were charging a thousand a night for the privilege. In the busiest year of my career, I spent more than 250 nights in hotels, and yes, there was eccentricity in trying to find silence. I'm sure the small concierge community talked about this quirk of mine, this profound need for quiet, and a reputation developed. But can this really be counted as either passive or aggressive? I would heap praise and generously tip those who made my silence a priority, and those who took care of me. I insisted on maximum peace. So should we all.

PANGEA

JOEY

So much of the career happened in Europe. My mysterious piano career that started so long ago is murkier in my memory now than I imagined it could ever be. I stopped playing and no one is sure why, which hasn't stopped everyone in my life from fostering their own reasons. What I remember now, strangely, are European trains. Why the hell don't I ever think of Texas? It's as if I didn't grow up there, but I did. Texas was that foggy word: *home*. In my career I traveled through Europe by train, almost never by plane except for the long journey over, and the trains never lost their allure for me. Mom traveled everywhere by train, but by the time I came along, we didn't ride trains very much in the United States, especially in Texas. Here in Oz I used to take a train up to our Blue Mountains house, just a couple of hours from here. I never tired of climbing our way west into what felt like the innards of Australia, though actually it isn't far inland at all. Men go west for adventure, don't they, in both of our countries? I've never been anywhere else in Australia by train, even after a decade of living here. How can it have been ten years already?

Trains never bored me the way planes did, though I logged a lot of miles in the air. Somebody somewhere probably knows how far I went, since my agents were forever putting together statistics of my career, for reasons I still cannot fathom. But now I understand, in this time when the calls to know more about me are getting more insistent.

I had a train routine in Europe that never failed me: I looked for rabbits. For some reason rabbits congregate in the European countryside around train routes, and I considered their appearance some kind of talisman; whenever I saw them, my next few days were lucky and my concerts better. The glimpse was always momentary, a little quivering energy on the outskirts of a field as the train raced by, perhaps a moment of seeing a quickly rotating mouth devouring something. Birmingham to Cardiff was a beautiful route because it was slow. Istanbul to Vienna many times, and tons of rabbits there—I even once saw a whole family of them dart into their holes before we crossed the Danube. Moscow to Berlin was one of my favorites. I always wanted to go from Beijing to Moscow by train, even if it took weeks, but I never managed it. It is unlikely to ever happen now.

Trains allowed me time to study music, and study was always in short supply, but mostly I just enjoyed the scenery, even if I found a lot of it inexplicably sad. I've always found beautiful things sad because I want everything to be beautiful. Throughout my career, in every interview, I kept talking about what a joyous person I was, but was I, really? I recognize a huge number of retroactively joyous things about my life now, but I don't know that I felt that joy deeply within myself, at least not as it happened, so what is the good of feeling it later? Was that joy mine, or someone else's, perhaps just a phantom, a thing about a thing?

I had—have—a life that anyone would consider joyous: I had a world-wide career at the summit of my profession, and I was paid exorbitant nightly sums for 90 minutes of playing the piano. Of course, no one knows that to achieve those 90 minutes I probably practiced and studied for 10,000 hours. That number isn't so hyperbolic: practicing 8 hours a day amounts to 2,920 hours of practice in a year, and my career was 25 years, which is roughly 73,000 hours of practice. That's a conservative estimate, as I often did more than 8 hours in a day, and it was rare for me to miss a day unless I was flying somewhere throughout it.

I also got to know specific portions of the great cities of the world, and there aren't many professions which invite that. I really *knew* Paris, London, Vienna, Berlin, Amsterdam, Istanbul, Tokyo, New York, Copenhagen, Barcelona, Moscow, Rome, Milan, Honolulu, Hong Kong, Los Angeles, Madrid, and so many others; and I knew them solely because

I bathed every day in great music, because I worked to be good at what I did. I owned a townhouse in Manhattan on East 49th Street, right up the block from Katharine Hepburn and Stephen Sondheim, and close to my favorite Indian restaurant in the world, where they would make whatever I wanted and bring it over. I had a country house near Hudson, New York, that I utterly loved and regret selling. How I wish I were there now, given all that has happened. I kept the apartment in Westwood for a while, until I realized I hadn't been in there in eighteen months. I had an apartment in Honolulu for a while, too, at the tip of Diamond Head, and I used it a lot when I was traversing the Pacific. I spent so much time traveling between Asia and California, or between the U.S. and Australia, that I often could sneak in a few nights in Honolulu. I loved my piano there, difficult as it is to keep a piano in a tropical environment. I never bought a London place because I always stayed with Paul and Mary, even after Ben and I met.

But none of it ever felt like it was mine. I accepted the talent, and I did and do love the ability to make music happen, but there was some version of *me* that wasn't me at all. I didn't escape it because I wanted to; I escaped because I had to. I reached a point, in those few weeks before that last London recital, and it was *final*, when I couldn't proceed. But now I don't know what has replaced it. How often can I reflect on something that wasn't fully mine to begin with? The reflections fill every day now.

Why do they need a book? That's what I ask myself as their calls get more insistent. If anyone is interested, this diary might be around and should be enough, though I can't imagine anyone caring enough to worry about it. The industry, that awful word, has gone on just fine without me, as it always does. I read the trade magazines for several years, I guess to find out if I was still mentioned. There were dozens of articles that first year, speculating on all of the possible reasons why I stopped performing, some even retracing my steps from the Royal Festival Hall that last night back to The Savoy hotel. The Savoy, now in leaner times, named some hilarious weekend package deal after me for a few years, from which they undoubtedly made nothing. I understand the hotel has been remodeled and the old charm is gone. No doubt it needed the overhaul.

Not that the precision matters, but I didn't go back to The Savoy that night for many hours. The public received only a couple of weeks' notice that it was going to be my last recital, and the ticket demand surprised even me. So we decided to add a second recital the night before. The British musical press, always making pedantry vie with viciousness, took this as profligate populism, a plea for funds, and they soundly criticized adding the recital the night *before* instead of after. They seemed unable to believe what it actually was: an attempt to allow as many people in as possible, especially the patrons who had long-purchased tickets, to authentically attend my *final* recital.

Only a few weeks later, one person actually wrote of the event as what it was: the unexpected self-silencing of someone they thought they knew. "We've grown so accustomed to following the next sensation that we have forgotten what artistry is supposed to do: it is supposed to mature and change along with the artist; we are supposed to share in the joy of that artist discovering the breadth of repertoire throughout a life, and through the lens of life's experience. Why he has made this decision is anyone's guess, but the world is less rich for it. Perhaps he will be back."

And perhaps not.

HOME

ALTA

Though I've been destined to be in Houston for my whole life, I've never really felt at home here, which is just another thing I don't want to have to admit to my son's biographer, since I am surrounded by people I love. I inherited my parent's house on South Boulevard, ensuring that every day I am reminded of them; and once Gene and I moved in there, I was tied to it. One might agree that I was cushily imprisoned. We could have sold it and moved to River Oaks, which probably would have been better for Gene's business, or, better yet, moved to Los Angeles or somewhere with some culture, but we settled into the comfort of the house. We settled continually, both of us. Gene liked the house much more than I did, even though I grew up there, and I didn't feel like going through the process of a finding another one and moving with him. That would have meant discussing what we were looking for, what was important to us. In the end it just seemed better to stay in my childhood home.

But Houston has never felt like a fully real place, never my home. It feels imposed on the land against its will. There is no aesthetic beauty beyond what has been created, yet not far out of town there is geographic beauty and peace beyond the imagination, so one is always left wondering if Houston couldn't feel like that as well without such powerful impositions inflicted upon it. One must love trees to love Houston, as they are the sole feature in our utterly flat and faceless topography. And how lucky we are with trees on our beautiful South Boulevard, where every block is encased in a vault of oaks.

We are a community of gigantic utilitarian grids randomly placed across huge tracts of land, occasionally marked by accidentally diagonal streets, and muddy bayous crowded with litter meandering through the assumed order. The freeways are new in my lifetime, and they are an absolute horror, filled with aggression and disbelief that another car could possibly be vying for that space. Only the wealthiest parts of town have buried their power lines, so much of the city has ugly poles plonked down in the middle of sidewalks, and violent clumps of power lines strung everywhere. It is a dystopian nightmare.

SET FOOT

JOEY

I sat in Farm Cove today and wrote for a while. It was a beautiful, masculine day. Every man who passed seemed to be on the violent edge of orgasm. This is the Sydney I love when I remember to think about the place at all: the *almost*-home feeling of it, and the liminal quality it has. Sixty seconds do not quite equal a minute on this continent filled with otherness. I sat on a little blanket by a lovely old wall embedded in the earth. As the light shifted, I noticed words etched into the wall that I'd never noticed before, though I'd been here many times. Inscribed in the stone, difficult to see: "At this spot on 3 February 1954, Queen Elizabeth II became the first British monarch to set foot on Australian soil."

Some group of civic leaders in the not-so-distant past thought it necessary to raise funds, design, and place a permanent marker on the place where a fellow human being once walked onto this continent for the first time. That such a time even existed is an amazing thought for this day. Her Maj is still with us, and if a biographer ever wanted to structure a book simply on her appointments, not on their content, it could easily be done and people would be interested. A thousand years from now, on this spot in Australia, people will be able to read a weathered commemoration of where she was on the 3rd of February in 1954, and presumably everything else she did that day.

But Sydneysiders do not bring flowers or rub their hands on the nine letters of the monarch's name. I doubt many of them even know the monument is here. Joggers fly past it constantly, and unaware families picnic nearby. This is not, nor presumably will it ever be, a place of pilgrimage, not like the real monuments of the ancient world. Still, I love that it is here, and that I am here with it.

I am a secular pilgrim in this land, because I came here to search for what could only be called my spirit. I'm ashamed to say that when I first arrived, I wandered around in amazement that Australia was here at all. Where, I wondered, did they get all of the building materials? Who planned their cities? I made every clichéd cultural assumption about Australia, that it was some kind of temporary colony and someday it would all revert back to what it was. It is a typical American diversion from having to feel that way about our own country. In both the United States and Australia, we usurped the land from people who had occupied it long before we arrived, all in the name of progress, and we treated the indigenous people horrendously. It is a permanent wound in both nations, and it comes out in strange ways, as in my fascination that a societal infrastructure exists at all outside of the U.S. I live in one of the most privileged neighborhoods in the world now, Vaucluse, in a city so beautiful that it often doesn't feel real. There is, however, a quality in Sydney that I've never felt anywhere else in the world; and whatever else might be said about me, it can be said that I've seen the world. One can imagine Sydney *not* being here, that it is all an illusion, that native eyes are watching you from behind dark trees on the hot summer nights. There are still and distant fires.

Thou Art Translated

ALTA

I'm sure I'm the only member of my family who reads poetry. But I always read foreign novels and poetry in translation, because I need words that have been thought about. I want to know there is someone trustworthy standing between me and the thin layer of a poet, sparing me the extremes of joy or pain that occur when I read poetry in my own language. I want someone to write words that serve ulterior motives. If the translator is a prude or judgmental toward his subject, then I will sense that and move on to another. I can just bear the Greek and Roman poets and playwrights only because they are so far from me, so interpreted on my behalf, like the Bible. I try always to find translations by women, for I trust that they will spare us the numerous political agendas created by generations of men, always men, who have tried to control what we thought. We are all translations of something.

Gene always complained about how much firewood I used. "We live in fucking Houston, Texas. Who needs a fire?" he would bellow. I needed fire then, and I still build one any morning below sixty-five degrees, letting it rage away in my little den off the living room. I can sit and watch that fire for hours, drinking my tea and reading poetry.

Particularly after Joey left home, the house was so quiet, and those fires were my most precious memories. I could sit there as the day arrived, as I was always up very early, and sometimes even hum some melodies to myself. Sometimes I stare into the living room, where my parents forced me to marry Gene. Looking back on it, I didn't put up much of a fight.

Why didn't I? It's so easy now to think I could have made a living, or Giuseppe could have at that moment taken me into his apartment in New York. We were so young. Living together was not much done in those days, even in a big city. I've stuck with my religion, but look at what it has cost me: if I'd had no religious misgivings, maybe I would have just run away, but memory manipulates me.

I always imagined myself having the deepest possible human life, one of introspection and knowledge, joy and passion, yet I've actually lived never fully knowing the consequences of my actions. I trained my son to have the life I was denied, and now my son has freely chosen to close it down.

OUTSIDE OF MUNICH

JOEY

I looked over some of my old scheduling diaries today, back when we used to keep them by hand. Twenty years ago right now I played a week of concerts in Munich and one full recital. It was an unforgettable week that taxed my stamina: four concerti in four days, all of which needed multiple rehearsals, of course. It is unimaginable to me now that I could ever physically manage it. Rachmaninoff two, Beethoven five (or was it four in Munich? How can I forget that?), Mozart twenty-four, Brahms two…I remember an absolutely hopeless set of conductors, and I can't for the life of me remember any of them individually. The orchestra was very good, but they seemed out of sorts over the fact that these concerts all ended with my concerti, as I was the focus of the week. They wanted, naturally, to close each concert with a grand symphony, and they resented that they couldn't. In the following week their lives were no doubt back to normal, and they wouldn't have to play background to a flashy American pianist. Oh, there are things I don't miss!

On my only day off, I was so tired that I didn't get out of bed until nearly noon. The glorious Mandarin Oriental, one of my favorite hotels of many, had a car and driver for my use so I decided to have him drive me into the Bavarian countryside before it got dark in the late afternoon. I spent so much of my career in cities that I treasured any opportunity to get out.

He drove me around Munich for an hour or more before we headed south for the countryside, but we never got out of town. I noticed a sign for

Dachau. I had never before felt the need to visit any of the concentration camps from World War II, but I asked him to stop. Suddenly, faced with an actual place, something as benign as a road sign and not just a name in a book, I had to see it. I paid admission to the memorial site, and the woman there told me that almost no one had come that day because the weather was so cold. The driver waited, though I offered to pay his admission. He said quietly that he didn't need to see it.

And it was cold. I wasn't dressed right for the weather, but I *needed* to be there. I walked in silence for a long time, seeing no one. Near the back of the property, at least what was available to the public, there was a barracks and I went inside. It wasn't heated but it felt slightly better than being outside, so I walked through the various large rooms. Ahead of me I heard muffled sounds that drew me toward them. As I came around the corner, and even now I cannot believe I saw this, a woman was bent over, balancing herself on the window pane, while a man stood behind her, fucking her. In Dachau. I wanted to flee, but there was something mesmerizing about it, something completely nonsexual. They weren't making love; they were fucking. The man was driving into her violently, pulling her hair, and she was murmuring toward some distant image that only she could see. I stood in the cold and watched them. When they finished a few minutes later, they pulled up their clothes and I fled.

What, I still wonder, were they doing? Did they plan to go to a former concentration camp that day and have sex, or was it a spontaneous impulse? Did they wander through the horror of the camp and suddenly have an urge to purge the place with a loving act? If so, why were they so rough with each other? Did they want someone to find them so that the evils of the place could be replaced with this incongruous memory? I've chosen to turn it into a beautiful thing and not an act of disrespect for a sacred place. I've chosen to remember that it was their only option: to take a short and violent journey outside of body and mind in order to reconsecrate a place of such horror.

LULLABY

ALTA

I hate all of the invented saccharine sentiment of Mother's Day and Valentine's Day, as they each serve as annual reminders of my two great failings: my husband and my mother. It has been my destiny to have my mother with me still, approaching a century of life. I hear people all around me giving thanks for having so much time with their mothers. That isn't at all how I feel; I am cursed to never be rid of her. It is difficult to write that down, because it sounds like I didn't love her. I did. But I never liked her much, and she remains totally impossible. She wrecked my life, and the worst part is that she still has no idea that she did. I have plenty I will have to carry with me to my end, but it was worth lifting all of it. Joey has to agree to this book. I need our story to be told at least once.

I think I could have handled Gene cheating if he'd just been honest about his feelings for me. But perhaps I was never honest with him: surely he knew I always loved another man. Not that I ever told him, but a lie never lasts for long; you just can't conceal the truth over two lives together.

I remember one warm summer night…it must have been in the 1960s, when Joey was a toddler. We just had window air conditioners then, and I had ours on upstairs, but I still heard Gene's car pull onto South Boulevard and into our driveway. He might even have turned the engine off at the end of the drive and pushed the car, but I couldn't be sure. I stayed in bed the whole time. I knew where he'd been. It was probably 4:00 a.m. I didn't hear him come in the house; he was always very quiet about that. He knew exactly which steps creaked—especially that loud third one from the top—but on this particular night he miscounted, or was too drunk to remember. I heard the creak, yet it still took him ages to get to the bedroom. He went slowly into his dressing room and took great care to take off his clothes in complete silence. He crept into the bathroom and just put on a trickle of water to brush his teeth. He seemed to think if he brushed very fast I couldn't hear it.

He inched his way into bed, glacially slipping under the sheet. It was a hot night. I let a few minutes go by. When I finally heard him let out a relaxed sigh, secure in his secrecy, I took a slow and silent breath, the kind I used in singing.

"Good night!" I shouted, making him levitate.

He always tried to get away with whatever he was doing, yet he would never just talk about it. Friends would tell me what was going on, of course. As if I didn't know! I always knew what Gene was up to; so why did I remain totally in the dark about my son? How could I not notice? Did I just want to ignore it? Was it motherly blindness that didn't apply to a wife?

SELFISH DREAMER
JOEY

Mom didn't get the life she wanted, and that finds its way into my thoughts often these days. She sits in Houston right now, just as she has for her whole life, the love child of George Bailey and Amanda Wingfield. She longed for a life like the one she thinks I had. Art in all forms is what she lived for, and it's the only relationship she's had that has held meaning for her. She never loved Gene, whom I should call "Dad" but can't, yet she kept throwing loving acts at him hoping he would love her in return. It never happened.

Gene was the type of guy I ran into all the time in the classical music industry: an entitled narcissist who used to be handsome, with the morals of an amoeba, so into himself that he was sure you must be, too. "Every time I play, it is history," a colleague once said to me. That's how Gene felt about his cock: every time it spewed his DNA, he thought it had meaning. He seemed to have little interest in anything beyond keeping up appearances with his wife and hunting down the highest number of orgasms with the least number of consequences.

But Mom kept trying to project meaning onto both Gene and Perry, my cousin who lived with us, kept trying to find love where it simply didn't exist. Gene had no love for her, nor for any of us. His interests in life were solely his own. It never once occurred to him how his actions might affect anyone else. Mom kept pushing the visual arts, literature, music, theater, and opera, but neither Gene nor Perry had interest in any of those, never once accompanied her to a performance, never engaged in a conversation about her feelings for the arts. Her wonder at artistic expression has never stopped. But Gene denigrated her for it, as if he was having the "real" life while hers was a fantasy.

I worked with every major musician in the business for decades, but I never met a better musician than Mom. What a sentence to write down!

Smiling Liberty

ALTA

This little writing tablet has been following me around now for months, since the man first called, but it is most challenging for some sentences to realize themselves, particularly remembering distant moments like my trip to New York City with Millie, which was another lifetime ago now. Incredible, too, that Millie and Mother, heroine and amanuensis, are still with us in varying states of elderly decay. I can't imagine life without Millie, even as I've endlessly tried to envisage life without Mother. Even now, after the passage of more than half a century, I can still feel the excitement of boarding the train that would carry us to New York City. My parents relinquished control of me for the first time and let Millie take me to New York for a *week*. Naturally I was excited about going to the city and everything we would see, but mostly I was breathing in the feeling of first freedom as Houston receded on the rails behind us. "Come, ever-smiling Liberty"! All of the greatest emotional references were written by Handel!

I wish my parents had hidden more of their decisions and ideas from me. Every night of my childhood, our dinner conversation revolved around some idea they had about what I should be doing but wasn't, how I should be behaving and never would, what sort of man I would eventually marry no matter what I felt, about who would inherit my daddy's jewelry business—with never an uttered thought that I might like to do that myself. I didn't want a jewelry business, as it turned out, but there was no way to know that then. I could have at least been presented with choices, but that remains the story of my family: no choices.

They liked it when I sang at parties as a child because it gave them an ignition for conversation they wouldn't otherwise have had, but they expressed no interest in my *actual* voice, and were never visibly moved by it. I could swear Daddy tried to be. Sometimes, even all these years later, my heart aches for having lost him so young. How one's impressions change as the years pass and as cherished people like Daddy are silenced. Looking back on it now, it feels like he was never fully in the family, like he didn't belong there; and that was our truest kinship. But he never spoke up against Mother. He might have supported me if he'd known my true heart, but Mother always smothered him, which over time one must conclude is what he wanted. Whatever she thought became what he thought. I hate thinking that about him because it might also be true of me.

My older sister, Sally, could play the piano well and accompany me, so we were a picturesque little set of blondes. Sally, as far as I knew, never wanted to pursue music. Will we ever know what happened to her? I still think Mother knows but won't tell anyone. My parents were always dubious about me having more advanced training as a singer, always expressing that they thought it best not to "overexcite" me—a favorite word in my mother's lexicon, as though too much excitement was somehow bad for the world. But I persisted in wanting to study, and my parents finally agreed that I could take private voice lessons with Millie Selford, whom they trusted. They knew her because she organized and sang in the choir of our very wealthy church near the museum, just a few blocks from our house on South. It was never *character* that my mother trusted or distrusted; wealth was the only sign of accomplishment to her. So because Millie was from New York, married to a wealthy oil man, and lived in one of the finer River Oaks homes, they entrusted me to her. Had she been poor but possessed of the same talent, they would never have relented. Daddy might have, had he been blessed with a longer life, but he always subsumed himself to Mother.

And had they the slightest interest in getting to know Millie, they would have discovered a woman much deeper than what they were satisfied to know. Millie had willingly forgone her own singing career to move to Houston with her husband in one of the boom years just as the war was starting, planning to be there for a short time before going back east, but they never left. That sums up many a Houston story. Millie was young, just a decade older than I, and she is the person who truly raised me because she's one of the few people in my life who let me have my voice. Millie had been one of the final Juilliard students of Anna Schoen-René, one of the only direct links to the last golden age of opera. Despite great promise for a singing career for Millie, the might of the mighty oil business brought her to Houston, and she seemed content not to pursue singing in order to support her husband. Millie found joy in running a household, much more than I ever did, and she loved teaching singing. Those were years before there were formal voice departments in the area schools. Her studio at her home in River Oaks was filled with young ladies who would learn the basics of singing for their church choirs or sororities, except for me.

I was a different kind of student for Millie. With me she could actually use the knowledge she'd acquired from Schoen-René; and even just a few weeks into our lessons, when I was still very young, Millie commented that she was learning more from me than I from her! Such a sweet thing to say, but looking back on it now, given my own experience teaching piano to my son, I have only just understood what she meant by it. After it all happened, when I most needed to hear it, she told me I was the most gifted student she'd ever come across, and the only one she had who was able to absorb what she knew. Millie knew my parents didn't understand talent, and that Mother never recognized a beautiful thing in her life. Now I realize why Millie fought so hard for that fateful New York trip the week after I graduated from high school. She thought that if she got me to connect with her circle in New York City, that if someone else besides Millie evaluated me, perhaps my parents would allow me to further my studies.

"She will get married eventually and perhaps, at the most, *teach* music," my mother continually said to Millie throughout my teenage years. Millie would always point out that the teaching of music had changed after the war, and I would require a degree to be able to work, to which Mother always, *always,* replied, "No one who taught me music had a *degree.*"

Not that she had the slightest idea what she was talking about. Music, to Mother, was something useful for the church or something ladies did in afternoon clubs, but was certainly not a career. I can hear her still: *Alta needs discipline and social skills, so we are willing to let her have voice lessons to assist in that. But she certainly is not going into such an unpredictable profession as singing and acting. Her father and I would not be in favor of something so risky.*

Oh, the depths to which I hated that statement! Daddy never contributed to these conversations; he either sat in silence or wasn't there at all, immersed in work.

Still, they did finally—and surprisingly—let me take the long trip with Millie, and only later did I realize the multiple purposes Millie had for the trip. She wanted to introduce me to the coaches and teachers she knew, and she wanted us to return from New York armed with their advocacy, hopeful that my parents would come to see the possibilities for me in a musical career. On the train, with so much time together, Millie let down the reserve she normally maintained in Houston. From her I learned the power of words, the force of naming something with precision. Millie made me aware of the stifling atmosphere I was enduring at home, and how controlling my mother was, but she did so by telling me about *her* life. She had to open every door for me to be a successful singer because she had chosen not to pursue it herself.

I learned so much about her on that journey, how she managed a happy life in Houston with her husband, despite how far it was from what she thought she wanted when she was young. I know she has long-harbored regrets about our New York trip, but she was the only person in my life to keep perspective on it. In fact, she kept perspective on everything: she went to the opera and symphony in town, tons of plays of all varieties, and always found something in them to love. She never indulged in the lazy cynicism of many artists. She found an artistic life in Texas that I only grudgingly acknowledged. The great music I needed was provided by only two souls: the extraordinary musician who was my only love, and by my son. They were the only sources of beauty I could bear without pain.

Millie introduced me to the opera *Rusalka* by Antonín Dvořák, an opera I never saw in performance, not simply because it is rarely done, but because I could never have contemplated being in the same room as that music as it was being performed. The story is so simple: a water maiden wants to marry a prince, but she has to become what she isn't—human—to do so. The music, which Millie used to listen to on her record player in that huge River Oaks living room, became part of the forever-music of my life, along with the great pieces Giuseppe and Joey used to play. The courage hidden within that music, and the glorious longing lyricism of it, seeped into my soul. Rusalka is the woman I wanted to be, and the poetry I wanted from my life and only found at the very moment I was told I couldn't have it.

I imagined myself at some moment near the end of my time on earth, which is obviously much closer now than when I first heard that opera, which would *be* just like great arching phrases near the conclusion of *Rusalka*, where she confesses her love to the man she can never have. That a composer could feel this, craft the expression of it, and take the time to write it down is a joyous wonder to me that I find almost impossible to comprehend. It is a feeling captured and shared across all generations and borders, and seemingly intended precisely for me. I recognize this feeling as irrational and out of step with everyone around me, but it is who I am. I am not some creature put together from the ether of a writer's mind, like Aurora or Blanche, as Joey sometimes teases. I am solely, and with soul, myself, a self I've come to know only now, viewed against what I've lost.

Big and Little Ben

JOEY

I've gone from being gay, single, and retired, to being a surrogate father to a child with my lover's twin, in the span of less than a decade. When I stopped playing the piano, the last thing I expected in my life was a child, particularly a child I fathered with Ben's twin sister, yet Ben is now gone and she and Little Ben remain here with me. Claire doesn't understand what happened and she thinks it is temporary. I hope she's right but I doubt it.

Little Ben is a wonder. I heard him picking out tunes on the piano the other day. He is such a beautiful boy, and he looks at me with such need and expectation. I'm impatient with him because I'm impatient with myself. He looks like me. I should have been a father years ago but I was too selfish and too absorbed in a huge career. My life on the road would not have been good for a child, and I was alone in those years. Raising a child isn't something to do alone, either. Claire is an enormous help, and she is everything I'm not to LB; but such is fate that it is me he most often turns to since Big Ben left. Claire and I don't often agree on how to raise the boy so I invariably defer to her, mostly out of terror that he'll grow up to be a murderer and will cite some long-forgotten decision I made as the catalyst.

I wanted him to learn Ben and Claire's native Cantonese, but they would not accept this. When they emigrated to Australia, they left everything about China behind them. Ben's visual arts career is highly influenced by China, which he will readily admit and talk about, but he will not answer questions about their living conditions when they left, nor the fate of their parents, nor how they got out. I've tried and I no longer ask. They've been here since they were in their early twenties, and Claire's English was such that she handily became a barrister in Australia. That is particularly impressive considering it isn't remotely the system of law in which she grew up. But being a barrister also means she works extremely long hours, so now that Big Ben is gone I have most of the responsibility for our little guy.

I never expected that. I was a virtuoso at only one thing, the piano, and I definitely am an amateur father. Big Ben was the pro of the household. Claire lived with us from the start in this ridiculously huge Vaucluse house. I took most of the corpus from selling my other properties and put it into this place. Ben set up a trust fund for our son, and Claire and I have both been contributing to it, as well. He'll be just fine.

Little Ben is a great kid. He is, like Claire, quiet and unassuming. When it feels like he needs a lot from me, it is because I feel so inadequate in raising him. I need Ben here beside me to do this, and he took away that choice.

During my career I did almost no "new" music, never had a concerto or sonata written for me, because I simply didn't have time with all the other demands on me. I regret it at a one level, but there's nothing I can do about it now. After a certain amount of notoriety, one is faced with the halo of a reputation, and as it glows all around you, you get further away from where you started, and that's when the harshest critics begin. To see and hear beauty in music, one must first be able to see it in others; and—another layer of that statement, like arteries to capillaries—to see and hear beauty in others, one must see it in one's self. There are few things in life that are as irreversibly true. My newness now comes from our son, who is greater than any sonata, and much more challenging.

The Echo No One Hears
ALTA

"I am an echo no one hears," Rusalka sings. Had I pursued the great unknown life I might have had as a singer, how could I ever have sung those words? *The echo no one hears.* Might I no longer be an echo?

Though opera is obviously meant to be a fantasy, the only real emotion I've felt in my life has been inspired by opera. The nights I used to spend all over Europe when Joey was playing—so many wonderful nights of opera in those gorgeous little theaters, not the monstrous opera houses in the United States. Opera used to leave so much room for fantasy, and one certainly never sought it out expecting reality. I loved when opera sets were more obviously sets, and back when people didn't worry so much about their looks and weight. That delicate line between the performed world and the effort to achieve it was not so blurred in my younger days. Nothing about opera was effortless except the singing—how I miss those effortless Joan Sutherland high notes, the great radiance of Pavarotti, Jussi Björling, Tebaldi, Crespin, and so many others. Now, on those rare occasions when I hear singers live, I'm so constantly aware of their effort, while they compensate by trying to make the rest of their struggle invisible. Something very literal has taken over the world now, and the distillation of poetry and the magnet of beauty are its victims.

My mother still looks at me through her gray and dull eyes, and she manages never to see loss in me, never sees any of her own failings. She lives in a world where she thinks did a fine job raising me, that I've been happy all this time. No amount of her knowing it isn't true will convince her otherwise. I visit her every two days or so in Sugar Land. Never was a place more inaptly named. I go even on the days when she no longer has any idea I am there. What is remarkable is that our relationship hasn't changed: she never did know who I was, and the only difference is that now her behavior is said to be a pathology by those who didn't know her before. She did say to me the other day that she missed Daddy, and it was the first time she'd mentioned him in years. I asked her if she knew when he died, and she named the day and year as though nothing was wrong. She spooked me, too, but I'm sure it was one of her demented illusions.

"I slept with a gorgeous pianist who might be your daddy," she said, clear as a bell.

"You what? What did you say? Mother?"

"That man. My parents were furious. But he was beautiful."

Something about me had gotten tangled in the tapestry of her mind and it came out in first person. But still, it was a horrifying thing to hear. I want her to be comfortable, of course, but I also wonder why I go so often. I am ashamed that I hate her so, as someone in her late nineties should not have to contend with hatred, but there the hatred sits between us, like a great border river, and it is her fault.

THE CHOICES

JOEY

My choices were taken away, yet now I'm blamed for making them. I still have no one to mourn with, not even Claire, who can't figure out what to say to me about her own brother. He stopped communicating with her, too. None of our friends know where he is.

It isn't how I envisioned my life, wandering mindlessly down the little street full of shops by the train station in Sydney, where one can buy schnitzel and cucumber salad, as I have on this chilly day. I spend hours overhearing the conversations of others. I am in a woods without a path, which means I am surrounded by love and protection but it can't show me the way out.

My life was large, and I played a huge amount of music. But aren't we all searching for something purposefully *not* large, a tiny shelter? I'm trying to shrink here in the Antipodes, but my life keeps enlarging. Ben, in some parallel place there is a version of us where none of this happened. And I know this universe exists because I lived in it until that day I picked up your phone. Are you back in China? Are you sick? I actually do care about those things, Ben. You used to trace the lines in my hands and imagine what the piano felt like when I played it. You used to talk about that, remember? You were my home. I don't dream anymore. I just relive what was between us, and now I'm being forced to relive my playing life. Pieces of piano music I haven't thought about in years are coming to me in dreams, complete from beginning to end, with specific fingerings and pedaling challenges. They are all in there somewhere.

My life is mystifying to me, like *Kreisleriana* always was. As much as I loved it and as often as I played it, I never could understand it, the misplaced inflections, the muscular internal quality of it encased in an expressive surface.

What if I never manage to actually get over this, Ben? What will you do then? What if we both wake up every day wanting each other but not knowing how to move beyond wanting? What if I keep waiting for a sign that never comes? At the moment I'm transformed and translated into something else, which Mom thinks is meeting God and someday seeing all of our dead relatives, but what if this has been false from the beginning? What if you were my forever but I wasn't yours? How do birds stay in formation? How do they know? Mom told me something about lobsters once, how they march underwater depending on the one in front of them to guide them. I'm lost, Ben.

I wonder how much I am in your life now. Do you think of me every time you hear certain music, or do you avoid the music in order to avoid me? How many times a day do I pass through your thoughts? Music makes me both forget and remember everything.

I don't think I want to be remembered forever within the pages of a book that can only mean what it means at this moment. In a hundred years it will have no meaning at all. And it has no meaning to me now without you.

WALKING INTO A DREAM
ALTA

Some memories are fuzzy, but not this one. Millie got noticeably more excited by the trip once we changed trains in Chicago and were headed firmly east. We tried our best to get some sleep, but I don't think I fully fell through the veil that night. Arriving at Pennsylvania Station in those years was like walking into a dream. The grand hall with the light streaming through was like nothing I'd ever experienced, so different from the bland and dusty Union Station in Houston. Millie and I stayed at the Algonquin Hotel, in a single suite with two bedrooms, which was the condition my parents had made to let me go—that Millie would be standing guard.

The first night there we went to a show, a new musical everyone was talking about, *West Side Story*, which I loved, and we had dinner afterward with her oldest friends, all singers and people who worked at the Metropolitan Opera and on the sidelines of Broadway shows. We'd wanted to see *The Music Man*, but tickets were impossible to obtain. We saw *The Entertainer*, and I was actually in the same room with Laurence Olivier, can you imagine? Such a sad play.

We saw Marcel Marceau, whose performance Millie strangely claimed to not understand, but it was so gorgeous that I remember whole stretches of it even now. He was so funny, so universal, and his unexpected finale was "the creation of the world," in which that man, alone on stage, with just a large cloth, depicted the very dawn of humanity, from our rise out of the seas and movements out of the savannahs into greater lands. With not a single word, it was all there to be seen. I was mesmerized. Shows don't normally affect people so much but they do affect me. I take them on; I live with them forever after I experience them.

I'd wanted to see the revival of *Carousel*, as I'd loved the first act of it so much, from the first moment I heard it I played its cast recording endlessly, in all of its youthful joy and the wonder of love. I lived that first act for a few weeks after our trip, but I would never live it again. The second act of *Carousel* never lived with me, and I never liked it, as I could not accept that I would never walk alone. It never felt true to me.

At least now, unlike then, I am at a point where I can utter the words, "I don't think I like my mother very much," which is the more polite way of saying I hate her. There—I've written it down. It's official. I hate my mother. I hate her inability to say who she was and what she wanted. She defined everything by defiance, by refusing precision, by refusing to see me instead of just seeing a daughter, into which she tried to fit me. She worked so hard to "be no trouble" in my life, yet she made decisions that undermined my happiness at every turn while thinking she was doing the right thing. She was not malicious; she just wasn't *there*. She sits now in a nursing facility with everyone assuming that her vacant stare is something new in her life brought on by age. It isn't. She suffered from a complete lack of imagination: she could not begin to imagine anything outside of her own experience, which meant she should never have been a mother. Maybe some unspoken trauma silenced her before I came along, but why should these things be perpetuated? When I started taking these notes in preparation for Joey's book, I swear I wanted to keep the entries about Mother at a minimum; no one wants to read about her, and I certainly didn't want to spend any portion of my life writing about her, but there is no way to tell Joey's story without telling mine. If I don't live to speak to his biographer, at least a few things will be here for reference if they want it.

The second night in New York, I attended my first live opera, after all of the years of reading everything I could find about opera and trying to learn all about it. I'd listened to so many of the great operas in Millie's living room, most especially the opera we attended that night, *The Marriage of Figaro*, and Millie had taken a lot of care to prepare me. All through the train trip, we read the libretto, playing all the roles. Such fun! I was even able to see *Figaro* again, years later, in the summer of 1976, and there was the same Countess I had seen nearly twenty years before. Amazing. Imagine being able to sing that glorious role even once, much less for two decades!

By the time the second act began, I knew what I wanted to do with the rest of my life. The opening of act two was beyond belief for me; it presented the private music of my own heart, which I knew even at that age, and I had to spend my life with it. Millie and I ate at Sherry's before the performance and at intermission, but we barely spoke. She saw many friends but I just wanted to absorb the experience. And I never wanted it to end.

After the performance Millie and I walked back to our hotel near the Met. She could tell what I was thinking, that I didn't want to go back to Houston with her. She knew me so well, so much better than my own parents. My mother actually said to me years later, and she meant it, that they gave me permission for the trip because they were so sure I would hate it in New York, and the experience would make me more sensible about trying to have a singing career, something they thought was just ridiculous. She was impenetrable. I spent a lifetime trying to get her to truly hear me, to understand that my passions for singing and music-making were real. I knew it would take something seismic to get her to listen.

Then there was a single day, the next day, which would be the day around which my entire life would turn. I've relived that a day a thousand thousand times. It is my always time.

COLD SUMMER
JOEY

How did I get to this cold June day? I feel rather like Sydney itself: a heady and flashy area surrounding a harbor, but once you step away from the water, from the reason the place exists, it's all run-down and ordinary. I long for Ben's story to move on, but there it sits every day. I wonder if I will ever travel again; I think I will be carried out of Sydney as ashes.

You know one of the weird things I miss? Those in-flight hot towels. They arrive just before takeoff and feel as hot as nuclear fusion when you first hold them, then they cool down as you wipe your face with them, get rid of the dirt of the airport. Why in the world would I miss something so ordinary? I guess it is because no one would do that at home. Has anyone ever put wet towels in an oven in order to freshen one's face? It is an affectation of travel, and I've thought about it often lately.

Softened Memories

ALTA

The memories of those few dozen hours in New York City all those years ago have been the joyous center of my life. Millie took me to sing for her old friend James, and I'm embarrassed that I never knew his surname. Why do we never hear the use of *surname* anymore? It was common when I was a girl.

We walked from our hotel toward the park then over to Broadway; the neighborhood was very seedy from Columbus Circle up to 73rd Street, where James lived in the Ansonia. He was a vocal coach, a term I'd never heard before, so I assumed he was something like Millie. But he wasn't. Millie taught me how to produce sound, how to breathe, how to place and free my voice. She spent some time teaching me my notes and languages, to the extent that she could, but James was an expert in those technical qualities of singing, and in a single morning he opened up a whole world to me. I sang several of the pieces Millie had taught me, "Caro nome" from *Rigoletto;* "Je suis Titania" from *Mignon;* "Care selve" from *Atalanta*—which was always my favorite thing in the world to sing; it still is—and I even sang the big aria from *La Traviata* for him.

James was a very nice fellow, fastidious in speech and manner. His apartment was immaculate; and when I sang, facing him at the piano, I had a view down Broadway, the area we'd just traversed to get there. It looked much nicer from up high. Everywhere I could see the tops of tenements and water towers, beyond which stood the great buildings of midtown forming into their singular canyons I would come to love so much.

Of all the things I sang, James seemed to like "Care selve" best, and he gave me inventive little ideas about it, like "Sing through these decorative notes a little faster, so they sound improvised" and "What is the most important word of the sentence, Alta?" And I was able to tell him, "Vengo in traccia del mio cor"—and the way I was able to spin those notes together around the word "traccia" was just the way Handel seemed to want it, as if for that word to last forever. "I come in search of my own heart," it means; and "traccia" is the search. I thought it was the most beautiful thing I'd ever learned. I still do. How I wish I knew then what I know now—how I could infuse that phrase with the life it is longing for!

"You need some work on your languages, my dear, though they are advanced already for someone your age. If you can manage to stay in New York, I will tutor you. We need to be sure you gain entrance into the Juilliard School, which should not be a problem. I will call them immediately."

"Juilliard?" I echoed, never dreaming of such a thing for myself.

"Of course. You have one of the most extraordinary voices I've ever heard, my dear. You need to be trained properly, of course, but rest assured. I know what I'm talking about it. The rest is just finding your path."

Millie had a look I'd never seen on my own parents' faces. Not just pride, but expectation; a special joy of seeing someone about to do what they are born to do. I had enough presence of mind to experience it as joy, something I've rarely been able to feel since. We were invited back that evening for a party. This had been her plan all along, I knew.

Millie suggested I walk back to the hotel alone, so she could reminisce with James a little longer in private. I agreed, of course, but inside I was petrified of being alone in New York City. But I was buoyed by the thought of my mother's horror. Finally I had a moment of my life that neither she nor Daddy could control. It was the first time I was ever alone anywhere, and she would never know about it.

Instead of walking back down Broadway, I decided to walk over to Central Park and go back to our hotel that way. On the way—and it still embarrasses me to write this down—I stopped at a corner store to buy a pack of cigarettes, the thin lady-cigarettes that were so popular at the time. Then I walked into Central Park by myself. The day was so beautiful, and I had just been given a new outline of my life. James loved my voice. More than that, James thought others would love my voice. I would be heard. I imagined life as a singer.

I found a lovely bench in the and smoked my first cigarette. All around me women were doing the same, many with baby carriages. Quite a few couples were walking arm in arm, as it was lunchtime, and I pictured myself a few years hence, fresh from Juilliard and starting my career, doing the same. This day was proof of what Mother relentlessly warned me about: that the precise discharge needed for a birth could arrive when you least expected it. Though I'd seen the marvelous performance of *The Marriage of Figaro* at the Met, preceded by *West Side Story* the night before, nothing prepared me for the events of this day. In just under an hour, my entire life changed and a new future was presented to me. I'd never felt such gratitude.

I sat in Central Park and smoked for several hours. Most people report that their first cigarettes make them sick. Not me. I loved every one of them, and they didn't make me start smoking. That was the only pack of cigarettes I ever purchased, and once I was back in Texas, I never smoked again. Cigarettes meant joy and freedom to me, and those were not qualities I felt much longer after that day.

Millie and I got back to the hotel about the same time. "Quite a day for you, my dear!" she said. I didn't know how to respond. "We will just have to figure this out," she said, reassuringly. I told her that it all seemed too good to be true.

"I needed to be sure that what I was hearing was right; it is so easy to be fooled in these things by affection or dreaming or both," she said.

I asked her if she was sure now. She said she was.

We dressed and retraced our path to the party that evening. I guess it was my first cocktail party, though I suppose my parents had had cocktails parties. James introduced me to several of his friends, all men who were incredibly handsome and polite. Before a big buffet dinner was served, James introduced a Juilliard student of his from Italy, Giuseppe, who was going to play the piano for us. The room got quiet, reminding me of the Christmas party years before in Houston, when everyone was silenced so I could sing. Giuseppe started the low C natural octave of the first Chopin *Ballade*, a piece I would later come to know as well as my own touch, but this was the first time I'd heard it.

Meeting Giuseppe, you would not think him an incredibly handsome man, but when he played, some supercharged energy overtook him, an energy that seemed to be not him but something that inhabited him through his hands. I've never been so transported by a piece of music, before or since. Every possible emotion was in the *sound* of his playing, and the most amazing journey ensued, from that tenuous opening note to the sweet tenderness and slight sadness of the little undulating waltz that comes so soon after the beginning. He played the great soaring melody with a powerful joy and almost unimaginable energy, driving inexorably toward the end, by turns playful and driving; the final moments hurling themselves into an angry elation. I couldn't believe what I was hearing. The room went mad. I could barely breathe.

James joined him in front of the piano to congratulate him. He silenced the room, reminding me of our Christmas parties when I was a girl in Houston. He said, "I'm so thrilled to welcome Millie back to civilization. We were terrified by her abduction by cowboys; we thought we would never see her again." The audience laughed and he went on. "She brought along a very gifted student of hers, Alta, and I wonder if she wouldn't mind coming up and singing for us? Giuseppe can play for you."

I was stunned and petrified. We hadn't rehearsed. James hadn't said a word about it before. The room was applauding. Millie was motioning me to the crook of the piano. The room fell silent. James put the music of "Caro nome" in front of Giuseppe, who smiled and began. I know I sounded tentative on those first few notes, but by the time we got to the aria itself, I had relaxed. I just sang and "lived in the words," as Millie always told me to do. Giuseppe played it so beautifully. I had never been around someone who could play so wonderfully with no rehearsal at all. My voice filled the room and beyond. I finished and the room went even crazier than it had for Giuseppe playing Chopin. I was elated!

Giuseppe played one more piece, something I'd not heard before, a transcription about the life of an artist. I didn't understand it that night.

When the miniature performance was over, Giuseppe approached me. "*Che bellezza! Che voce!* You were amazing. We must have vino together," he said, offering me a glass of wine. I took it. It must have been my first glass of wine.

Millie was enjoying her old friends while Giuseppe and I found a quieter corner of the huge Ansonia apartment and talked about all the mundane things strangers talk about when they meet: where we are from, how we got interested in music, our teachers, our parents (I lied about mine), our ambitions, what life might look like. He was only two years older than I was, but he was so much more accomplished. Nothing took very long with Giuseppe; he embraced learning things about me and immediately accepted them. He did not live his life in a waiting room the way my parents did. He was eager to talk about so much and tell me about his life growing up in Italy and being led to the piano by his grandpa, who *knew* Verdi. Imagine. He was so full of life that night, and I remember it like it was yesterday instead more than fifty years ago!

I'd never experienced a conversation like that with anyone, not even Millie. I felt free to express my joys and disagreements with him on anything, and the conversations always ended in comfort. We talked and teased and sparked each other until the party was starting to clear out. I asked Millie if I could go to dinner with Giuseppe, since he'd asked me, and she said yes, but to never tell my mother.

We went to an Asian restaurant somewhere below Times Square, full of noodles. I'd expected Italians only to eat Italian food, but not Giuseppe. He treated me to my first Asian food, as my parents would not have dreamed of such a thing. In all the years I've been back to New York, I've never been able to find the place again, so I hope it isn't gone. I looked for the place a lot over the years, trying to retrace the steps of that breathless day. I was drunk—not on the wine, but on the feeling of being with Giuseppe by myself in New York City. We talked long into the night. I knew my train back to Houston was leaving the next afternoon and Millie would start to worry about me if I didn't come back. I called the hotel to try to reach her. No answer.

I can still hear Giuseppe's words: *Come home with me for a while. I know we've just met, but you are safe.* Until then, I realized, I'd never really felt safe before. But with him I knew I was. So I followed him.

As we walked the twenty or so blocks from our restaurant to his small apartment, we held hands; another new experience. We passed the Algonquin, where Millie might be getting ready for bed, but I kept walking with Giuseppe, unable to let go. His building was not terribly nice outside, and his apartment was so small that there was nowhere to sit except the bed. He walked every day from there to the Juilliard School on East 52nd. While I was scared to be there with him, I was more frightened not to be. He kissed me. I wanted his kiss to never end. Those hands that had caressed Chopin were now touching *me*, in ways no one had ever touched me. My joy was unimaginable. This sort of thing happened in those days, but no one ever talked about it; it was much worse to talk about it than to do it.

I gave myself to him completely.

Lucia

ALTA

I don't remember a lot about the train trip home except that Millie and I did not talk about what happened, even though I know she knew. She had a sense for things like that. I didn't get back to the Algonquin until breakfast time. Millie was asleep. Maybe it didn't occur to her to check on me, but I doubt that. We talked about everything else from the New York trip, especially what my entrance into Juilliard would be like, and all the things I needed to do over the summer to prepare. She was so renewed by seeing James and all of her friends as well as being excited for me.

There was a wonderful limbo of a few weeks before I was marched into our living room, where Daddy sat in silence while my mother screamed at Millie, "You let that predator seduce our child!" She must have said that dozens of times that day, just in the next room from where I'm writing now. And Mother kept insisting I was raped that night; she needed to believe that, I guess, unable to face the fact her daughter wanted a man. Millie protested; I protested. Dear Posterity, if you are out there: I wasn't raped. Everything Giuseppe did to me that night was wanted and welcomed. I knew it was wrong to give in to a man I'd just met, but I also knew what I felt in that moment, in that single day when my life was placed before me. I let Giuseppe enter me not because he forced himself on me. It was the opposite: he was the reticent one. I wanted him inside me and I wanted him that day and the next day and the next. Nothing I said or did would convince my parents, especially my mother, that he was not dangerous.

She decided what she thought happened, and that was all she would hear. Unfortunately, whatever she thought became the truth in our household.

Mother must never have known his name or not put the ideas together, otherwise she would never have allowed me to name the baby Joey. I was forbidden from seeing Giuseppe again, and any hope of marrying him was completely blocked. Gene was available, convenient, and a friend of the family, so with what feels now like incredible simplicity, they made me marry him. I still can't believe this happened, but they sat me down in the living room I'm sitting in right now, and told me that Dad's reputation in business was on the line, and they couldn't have a pregnant and unwed daughter. "Not in those days," as my mother has said in recent years, as though those days were so innocent. My own parents forced me to marry a man I absolutely did not love while carrying the baby of the man I did.

I didn't want the child; I wanted to be with Giuseppe. His parents reacted badly, too, just not quite as badly as mine. The distance from Italy helped, as they couldn't have the control over him my parents had over me. I investigated various ways to abort, but it wasn't easily done in those days, and was virtually impossible to do safely. I'd had several school girlfriends die in the process. It was clear I was going to have and raise a baby, as adoption would have been admission that I'd had sex, and my parents wouldn't allow that, either. Any of my desires for the baby or the direction of my life were blocked from that day. My singing career was not "on hold," as Millie suggested. It was over before it began. My parents were willing to terminate the dreams of my entire life, but not that of an unwanted baby.

I'd known Gene, as he lived a few blocks away, and I'd never given him a second glance, though he was a fine-looking young man. There was a hasty meeting of the parents. Gene, I'm sure, didn't want me, either, but we both sat there while our parents worked out a deal. It was hopeless and I was helpless. Most people would never believe that parents would do such a thing, thinking these things only happened in the nineteenth century, but my parents did it.

Gene's father said, "My son is always in trouble, and this marriage could settle him down, right, son?" Gene hesitated before shrugging his shoulders and chuckling. In just a few weeks, I had traveled from the heights of what my life could be to this. I was imprisoned.

I screamed. Mother screamed back. We all cried. But there was no escape. Nothing helped.

I thought of the big vat of cyanide in the back of Daddy's store that they used for cleaning diamonds. I pictured him finding me dead one morning when he came into work. Would he feel anything then about what he silently allowed that day? I knew the entire plan was Mother's; she had to punish me for getting pregnant, for feeling pleasure, for following my heart, for knowing a beautiful man when I saw one.

Prompted by his father, Gene asked me to marry him at the end of the meeting, in front of all of our parents. I said no.

My parents both stood up. "She says yes," they said firmly. And that was it.

My daddy was not a bad man, really, and I don't think he liked this solution. But I inherited his weakness; he let himself be controlled by her, and I let her control me. He didn't live much longer. I think the wedding of his daughter to a man she didn't love, and the mysterious loss of my sister shortly after, was too painful for him to live with. That part of life passed so quickly that I barely remember him. I hate that I sometimes have to get out a photo to remember what he looked like. Yet Mother lives on.

LE NOZZE DI
ALTA

We had a small wedding a month later, and Joey was a long pregnancy, so as far as I knew, there wasn't talk. I threw up the whole morning before the wedding, sure I would never be able to walk down that aisle into a life with Gene. But I did it, dazed and sad, trying to look happy for our friends. Gene had his funny moments, and I enjoyed those; he was funny about the wedding and all the getup. He had a good sense of humor in those days, though it was the first thing to disappear in our life together. It usually is.

We drove to Pensacola for our honeymoon, and my new story began. I detest Florida.

Giuseppe and I were prevented from speaking for a long time. Although his parents allowed him to stay at Juilliard until he finished, they made him live with a bunch of Italian priests. How he must have hated that! He was the most spiritual person I knew, but he couldn't bear the church. He completely rejected Catholicism. As I reflect endlessly now on everything Giuseppe and I have talked about in our lives, the religious conversations were the most confusing. Before Giuseppe, I'd never heard anyone speak badly of the church, and his doing so made me uncomfortable for a long time. But even as I eventually came to agree with him, I turned more and more to the church and to many a holy man to try to figure out why my life turned out the way it did. I've lived inside so many lies, yet I'm not a liar. I've had so few choices, yet the choices I made were sinful. Giuseppe never agreed with me, never wanted me to talk to priests or ministers about it at all. "What expertise do they have besides belief in someone who is completely made up? You trust your life to someone who tells fairy tales?" I know he was right, but I cling to it, anyway. I absolutely have to believe that there is some power at work that I can't know about. Without that, my life and my choices will all feel false, and I'll have no possibility to ever redeem myself. And I have a lot to redeem.

PYTHAGORAS

JOEY

Anton Rubenstein made $40,000 in 1872 for 215 recitals; $186 per concert, with tickets priced at a $1 for halls seating around two thousand people. What would those monies be now?

At the height of my career, I earned $50,000 to $60,000 per recital, and $20,000 for a concerto appearance, usually times three for a typical orchestra week: Thursday, Friday, and Sunday afternoon, which means in orchestra weeks I often had interesting Saturday nights. Those made up for earning half of what I made if I worked alone. Generally, like Rubenstein, I played in halls that sat around two thousand, with people often paying around $200 a ticket. Yet presenters were constantly having to raise more money to have me play—and not just me, but any classical artist. Why? It is common psychology to assume that if a concert sells out, everyone makes money, or at least breaks even, so what's the problem?

The problem is, a sold-out hall doesn't remotely pay for that performance, not in classical music, not any longer. There is no such thing as low-cost *live* music, though there is plenty of free music now on the Internet—including all of my recordings, which used to have to be paid for but are now available to anyone who can click a computer mouse. For the many smaller halls I played for many presenters, with capacities of one thousand or less, they had to raise a lot more money than the big cities, proportionally, for their communities to have live music.

Wealth is a huge hidden part of the classical music industry, no matter how hard we work to erase that reality. The only reason there are classical music concerts, and thus classical musicians at all, is because wealthy people are generous enough, and love the art enough, to be given tax breaks by the U.S. government for supporting us. There isn't a classical organization in the United States that survives on ticket sales. The sad reality is that ticket sales are poor. Less than one percent of the population regularly attends classical music performances, down from two percent at the height of postwar attendance, and solo pianists have the lowest attendance of all. I sold out a lot of concert halls and theaters, though certainly not all; but for the financial reality, it didn't matter. I sold more tickets than any pianist of my generation but it *didn't make a difference*. I didn't "pave the way" for anyone because there's no way left to pave. Live classical music in its postwar guise is dead, not because the musicians aren't there but because the world has moved on, far away from the traditions that sustained the art for centuries. Don't blame television or the Internet. Blame the forces that really severed the lines: the people who brought war and famine to the twentieth century. Blame Hitler, Stalin, Mao, and Pol Pot. They treated culture as a political chess piece wrapped in their love. Hitler only loved Wagner because he could project himself onto him; he hated the type of genius Wagner actually had because he couldn't own it. The autographed score of *Die Walküre* that went up in flames in Hitler's bunker was in his possession not because he viewed it as art, but because he had to have it as an acquisition. It was given to him by sycophants, which is somehow worse than actually wanting it.

As a successful classical artist I was expected to create the old European world order anew with every recital. I was expected to be rich and to be surrounded by the wealthy. I was collected by donors all over the world, fed hundreds of thousands of dollars' worth of food in their homes and in the finest restaurants of their cities. I played at the weddings of their children at Saint-Jean-Cap-Ferrat and Martha's Vineyard, not because I knew them or loved them, but because they offered me $100,000 to be a showpiece for their friends. And I took every dollar. What I wish I could do, really and truly, is make a ton of money from some other art, from painting or writing, something that comes solely from me and does not depend on me being a re-creationist. I'd love to go back through those thirty years and add up whatever I was paid from every organization and give it back to them. I would, too. I would just start writing checks. Imagine the good that might be done if I put tens of millions of dollars back into the art form instead of just contentedly taking it away.

I'm not one of those right-wingers who don't understand why artists don't work out of love. We do love. But that love needs to be paid for. I extracted more from the industry than I deserved to, and I want to give it back. Mom wants me to sell the paintings I did when I was in Houston, which were just a pastime for me, and I even talked to Paul and Mary about it before everything happened. But what do I do now? I certainly don't have to use Paul and Mary, and I wouldn't. But I don't know where to begin with a painting life. Painting was always something I could do to escape my real art, to forget the piano for a few hours and make it better once I got back to it. I don't really want painting to be something I have to be good at, and I don't want to have to engage with critics again. I never minded being criticized by the ones who knew what they were doing, but I definitely *did* mind all of the mindless opinion that passed for criticism.

Critics must believe in, explain, defend, and create values. Otherwise, there is no point in having them. There either are or aren't timeless artistic principles at work in great performances. It can't be both. But what are those principles, and who is going to both decide and tell us what they are? The principles and standards aren't up to the critics; they are up to the composers and performers, and, hopefully, a few gifted ears will be equally gifted writers. It is a big thing to ask. Great critics want to circumvent any oversight (they never want to be wrong) by claiming that they never, ever have a hand in deciding the artistic fate of a composition or a performance of it. No, they are only observing, they insist, which excludes them from ever being wrong, and assumes they possess the encyclopedic amount of knowledge required to be able to profoundly judge a profound performance. But for the entirety of my playing life, one thing was superbly true: if one gathered together a hundred critics and a hundred performances and asked the critics what new compositions of the previous twelve months would pass the test of time, each group would have agreement among their own tribe, but very little common ground between them. History has borne this out.

What a total fraud they are, almost every one of them. I treasured the few greats, all gone now, whom I got to know enough to be able to talk with about music. They knew what they were doing. But the ones working now? Forget it. It wasn't what they criticized I object to, it was what they praised. The ridiculous, fawning, obsequious, nonsense things that they praised—things that were not unusual or outlandishly virtuosic, but which they praised in me as if they were something special. Like trying to make Donald into some profound creature, when he was their complete creation. And the things I've read about myself since I stopped…

Oh yes, they are all a bunch of fakers.

PADRE ADORATO
ALTA

How can Joey's story be told without talking about his father? But how can I talk about my son without spilling the details of my life that I thought could be buried forever? When I was young we didn't know things about people the way we do now. Millie knew, along with the six parents, plus me, Gene, and Giuseppe. Ten people knew the truth, and we all know ten people can't keep secrets, but these ten seemed to be able to. Over time, the ten quickly became six, and now it is just four of us who know. Soon, no one will.

I hate secrets, but my life has been defined by them. Giuseppe was a secret I obviously couldn't keep, and my family made me pay for it forever, and with such cruelty that I never told them anything again. All that will be remembered of me is that I taught music; that's the only thing I had to myself. I want my son to allow this book, because who will ever remember me if he doesn't? I had a whole secret musical life with Giuseppe that even Joey doesn't know about, and it is time he did. How I managed to pull it off is still a wonder to me, and is the greatest thing in my life.

Temperament

JOEY

Bach was, *is*, will always be, music to me. Bach is the essence of everything, just…everything: space, time, love, darkness, light finding its way through trees, Pythagoras, birth, death—everything. I memorized all of his forty-eight preludes and fugues when I was fourteen. Though this is treated as a commonplace thing now, it was rare to memorize them when I was such a youngster. I loved recording them, even though that recording was the subject of endless fights with various number crunchers in my recording company, each of whom had a different view about whether the LP, later CD, should be titled in German or English. The opinion culture was exactly divided on it: the more established and conservative people felt that *Das Wohltemperierte Clavier* lent the recording dignity, whereas *The Well-Tempered Clavier* felt pedantic and scholarly. I felt we should step outside of what was, after all, a very enclosed cultural box and just call them what musicians call them, the *48 Preludes and Fugues,* which felt both accurate and gave the novice something to hang on to, but not a single executive would accept that. I never found the time or place to play them in one recital as I wanted to, because once I had the knowledge of what they were, or felt the depth that is hidden within them, I could no longer remember them. I've always planned to dig out a copy of my recording and listen to them, but I never seem able to get that done. I recorded almost all of Bach's keyboard music, the French and English suites, toccatas, partitas, *Italian Concerto*, and I don't know if I can bear to hear myself play them again.

I know I will be asked, because it has happened all my life: what do I think is the greatest music ever written?—as if such a question can be answered! How does one move beyond the *St. Matthew Passion?* There can't be any single work of art that surpasses it. *The Ring,* maybe? All of the Beethoven piano sonatas? It is too big a question, like asking what your favorite mountain range is, or your favorite sunset. But I know what music has kept me sustained through all of the years of trying to make it, and I know what music I will turn to when I'm able to count my remaining breaths. I will turn to Bach, of course, and to the Handel arias I used to overhear my mother singing, and I will turn to the trio from the second act of *Fidelio,* which is probably, for me, the single greatest piece of music ever written. There. I answered the question.

Fidelio unfolds simply enough, just intoned octave E naturals that invite two other notes before Florestan sings of a better world: "Euch werde Lohn in bessrer'n welten." *Fidelio* is opera's greatest idea, though it is far from the genre's best; but the ambition of a work, what it tries to say, must be factored in, for surely the scale of a mountain is as important as whether or not we succeed in climbing it. That trio has unquestionably changed the color of my soul forever. Every time I play it on the piano or hear it performed, I am different. This is where art, religion, and science all intersect. I know Mom used to understand this, because how could I if she didn't? That trio gives us a strange mirror to peer into and see something in ourselves we couldn't otherwise notice. It's not a case of us knowing this music, because this is music that absolutely, unequivocally, knows *us.* And it will always know more about us than we about it. I wish Mom could understand this about art and music in the way she used to, before her Jesusfreakdom.

But there is no way to talk about the greatest music ever written without trying in vain to explain the slow movement of the Debussy *String Quartet.* There is no more beautiful music written. Ultimately, you can apply every theory or principle to music and all roads will miraculously lead you back to the Debussy *String Quartet.* It is perfect, and the slow movement, the third, is the most perfect of its perfection. It lingers in the air as it lingers around just a few notes, trying to find a center; never before or since has music expressed longing with more clarity. I didn't understand it until I lost Ben.

How I hate hearing musicians say certain music is "like a wheat field" or other music is "like climbing a mountain." Music isn't *like* anything except itself. And why should music only be relevant or useful if it resembles some more tangible thing? Great music illuminates emotion; only mediocre music depicts it. I played the Debussy *Préludes* and *Images* a few times each, and it was hell to learn them as they are almost impossible to memorize, but I never loved them like I did the *String Quartet*. I toyed with transcribing it for piano, but every time I tried—and I tried a lot—it strangely sounded like bad piano music. How could something so beautiful for string quartet sound so ordinary on the piano? But that is the genius of great music: you can't move it out of the composer's mind without cheapening it. It was conceived for string quartet and that is how we must experience it. We must be as true with ourselves as we are with our creations. We can't be translated.

Ces Lettres

ALTA

Eventually I had a special post office box neither Gene nor Mother ever knew about, just for letters from Giuseppe. He concertized a bit in Europe, but never to the extent that I thought he should. He just never took off, never seemed to have the ambition. He said he needed me beside him, but I didn't believe that. Both of our hearts were broken, but we never completely parted. I was forced to marry Gene just because of a baby. Giuseppe never married anyone, and he was never with anyone else. When his parents died, he moved back to the U.S., and used his middle name as his first. He managed to land a piano-teaching job in College Station and another in Austin, so decided to live in between them in Brenham, to be near me. This gave me the perfect alibi, because my family had a ranch in Chappell Hill, and Mother hated it up there so she never went. I would say I was going to the country, and she would believe me.

I wanted him to teach piano to Joey, but of course it was impossible. So I devised a way to teach Joey myself, through his father. I had enough talent on the piano that I could get some benefit from Giuseppe's teachings, and thanks to Millie I had a real feeling and ear for music. Giuseppe could sing things to me, I could sing them back, and teach them to Joey. Giuseppe had incredible ease with the teaching of technique, with precision of scales and finger weight, and though I couldn't execute them myself, I could articulate them to my son. And Joey had incredibly gifted fingers, like his father.

Did Gene's parents even tell him that I was pregnant when we got married? I certainly never said anything. It is too impossible to think he didn't know, but it is not anything Gene and I discussed at the time, incredible as that seems to me now. We did sleep together on our honeymoon, at least once, and I'll bet Gene thinks Joey is his son. Our parents knew, so they must have talked about it, but I have no idea if Gene ever knew. I suppose I could have used it to hurt Gene, though nothing I did seemed to have any effect on him. He was as impenetrable as Mother.

MALEDIZIONE
JOEY

I heard very few pianists during my playing years because all the busy ones were usually playing somewhere on the same nights I was. The only reason I heard Donald so often was that we happened to be booked into London around the same time each year, and we shared an agent who wanted us to get along, for some reason. Donald, like me, had good fingers, but he was, unlike me, completely a product of the piano establishment: Juilliard Prep, Curtis, competitions all over the world, and everyone talking about him from the time he first walked across Rittenhouse Square.

Donald was a master publicist for himself. He knew exactly how to garner news, even as the news changed over the years. He was also gay, but refused to live out loud. He was much more clandestine than I, but I'm sure he was no less active. Practically every gay man I knew in the industry had slept with Donald, and that was another place we parted ways. I never slept with people I might work with. There isn't a single notch in my belt that belongs to a conductor or anybody in the industry. Not a single musician in any orchestra could ever say I came on to them, and I rejected all of their advances. Until I met Ben, nearly all of my sexual experiences were with strangers who were not in the business, and I'm proud of that. True, I also had a stable of rent boys in all the big cities, and I'm not going to be shy about saying that to a biographer, because that is the reality of people who live their lives on the road. Donald paid for his share, too, but no one will ever know about it because he won't admit it. The community of rentals, even in a vast city like London, was small, and they all knew most of their colleagues' regular clients—yes, I think colleague is the right word, because they were some of the best guys I ever knew. Funny, here in Sydney, where there is a huge collection of men for rent, I don't know any of them now. It isn't something I do anymore.

For a long time, I was not given credibility by the classical music establishment. They had to justify their privileged existences, and I didn't arrive via the traditional channels since I didn't attend a conservatory. I was taught by my mother, a woman who was, in their eyes, just one step above an amateur. When I started, most of the clucking academics kept asking how any pianist taught by an elementary music teacher could learn the Chopin ballades. "She couldn't possibly have the depth of knowledge for that," was something we heard a lot, at least for a while. It never stuck to me for long, because I was working so hard and so much that there wasn't time to focus on other people's perceptions.

BEGOTTEN, NOT MADE

ALTA

I knew well before he did that Joey was gay, and many of my church friends comforted me at that time, as if he had died. It would have been a miracle if he *hadn't* been gay, and the religious don't know what to do in the face of that. He wasn't *made* gay by some external force. No one is made gay that way. He was always gay, and I knew it from very early on. My church friends were incredulous that I didn't have a religious problem with it, as they certainly did. I heard them tell me he could be "fixed" with faith, that the feelings he had for men could be exorcised in some way. Joey's relationship with Gene didn't change with his coming out; Gene ignored him before and just continued doing so. My boy didn't need fixing. His desires were more honest than theirs.

If religious beliefs don't help you engage deeper into the world, what are they for? If they don't help you feel what others feel, what are they for? And if they don't make you more accepting and open to knowledge, what are they for? I only know my view of this, which is that I turned to religious faith because I needed to fill in a gap in my life. Why I couldn't see that I was continually choosing a life I didn't want, and that I *could* have changed it at any point, is beyond my comprehension. But religion isn't what taught me that; rather, it was Joey's rejection of faith. Thinking back into the incoherence of my childhood, I should have been a devout Presbyterian, and I have continued to take on the outward symbols of that tradition, but I don't share that sect's belief. I've gone to synagogues and mosques, at least the ones they would let me into, and I've gone to every possible denomination of Christianity that I could find, which in Houston is quite an assortment. I've searched through every religion to see if one made sense to me, and none does. Still, I go to the Presbyterian church that I grew up in and keep searching, keep hoping that something will dawn on me.

But there is so much I have to atone for now, so many wrongs I've committed. I maintained an adulterous relationship with a man through my whole marriage, and no one knows about it. Gene cheated on me endlessly and I punished him for it, but what I've done is far worse, because I actually *loved* another man. Gene didn't love me or anyone. He had them all just to get off, for a few seconds of discharge. He couldn't help himself.

If the Christian religion is such a deep truth, why are there so many denominations? Are we so unable to agree on the small points that we require all these separate sects to figure it out? The differences are so small, each sect thinking they have access to truth. They all end up alike to me: unable to give me any comfort for what I've done, and yet I cling to the search, the journey, because the search feels like me now. I lived my whole life in just a few individual days separated by decades. I have to find a way to atone for all of it, for what I feel about my parents, for Gene, and for my confusion about Joey. In my own inability to understand any of it, I have left him unmoored and separated from the artistry he should be deepening and living in for the rest of his life. He should be in his happiest times right now, yet he has retreated to Australia, into some version of his life that isn't real, and he learned how to do that from me.

Worship has always been about money, especially here in Houston, but now it is big industry. A congregation here has converted an old stadium into something they call a church, but it is a circus and sideshow all in one. Their "pastor" lives in a mansion in River Oaks and they preach a gospel of prosperity, that Jesus Christ *wants* you to be rich. Their services are on television, like a sitcom, and they treat our profound human spirit like the lightest of entertainments. There is nary a mention of spirituality or the inner self, just a collection of righteous platitudes that wouldn't be out of place on a bumper sticker. The church of my youth was an escape from the world; the churches today seem to want to mimic it. And the singing! Wretched pop singing, all chest voice and four cheap chords per song. Where is the nobility of music in these services? And where is the creativity? We used to have music arrive at precisely the right moment, and the tone and feel of it was never forced or inappropriate. We raised our voices to the Lord and tried to be sure that our voices were worthy of the journey.

We now have music that appeals to the basest and least discerning parts of us, that appeals only to surface emotions (and barely that), never striving to be something deeper. How I used to love going to the old Presbyterian church in Houston, especially on cold and wet winter days, the type that northerners don't think we have in Texas. I loved those gorgeous gray mornings when I was a little girl, when we would sing the great hymns with some part of ourselves that is missing now. "I Love to Tell the Story," and "In the Garden," and "How Great Thou Art"—how I would send my voice soaring on those days! The cold seemed to cry for the warmth of singing. We sang as one, but we no longer do that. In those days the feelings were real and the hymns made me cry. They still do.

I don't believe in religion at all. In fact I think it has done a great deal of harm in the world and will undoubtedly do much more. But as usual with my life, I live differently from my beliefs: I go to church, I support the church with money, and I keep up an appearance that I share people's beliefs, if they have them. I don't feel it is any of my business how others behave, and certainly not what others think. You cannot punish people for what they think, but it seems to be such a time of escalation, as though we are fomenting a new era of fundamentalism. Something dangerous is growing in the world that we are powerless to stop.

QUIRINIUS
JOEY

I'm done with my mother's bullshit Christianity. I know she doesn't believe a word of any of it. That's one of the reasons I moved to Sydney, so I could get away from the God-botherers, as they are wonderfully called here. Immaculate conceptions, transfigurations, transubstantiations—a message of *believe in me and all of my teachings or you will burn in an eternal fire*—no way Mother believes that. The Christians still talk about the census of Caesar Augustus, which wasn't true; Quirinius was not governor of Syria in those years…the list goes on and on. Who are the fucking morons in the United States, more than half the country, who believe the story of Adam and Eve is *literal*? That the human race descended from their two *sons*? Hello! Do we really live in a time when parthenogenesis needs explaining or justifying? And do these creeps who want to force their fairy dust on all of us *really* believe a virgin had a baby?

I Want My Moon

ALTA

It never mattered to me that Joey is gay, but I can't understand why he hasn't shared my religious faith. I know all of the arguments against it, and Giuseppe and I always disagreed on how to bring him up with faith. I haven't lived my faith very well, but I think it is important to try. Not only does Joey not try, he denigrates it all now, like his real father. He spouts on about geography and evolution, both big passions of his. I love hearing his passion, but down in the essence of me, at the level of blood and cell, the things underneath the things underneath, I don't care about his facts. I want my poetic explanations. I want my moon. I want to look at the stars and be ignited. I feel no wonder in the knowledge that they are gas and matter. I fully know we have evolved over the eons, or at least some of us have, and I imagine we go around several times, but I don't want to be burdened with having to figure it out. Christianity has done that for me and I'm fine to leave it there, letting me get on with life and feel other things.

In My Flesh

JOEY

Mom, not me, is the great musician of the family. And if affection and ambition were talent, she'd have been the greatest singer in history. I haven't heard her sing since I was a child, yet I can always hear it, that effortless beauty and power. The air of the living room would vibrate so completely that I used to imagine the house coming down, not from volume but from the pulsations entering me from inside of her; the joy of it seemed grander than a house. Gene was so horrible about her singing. If I didn't hate him anyway, I'd hate him for that. She has plenty of faults, of course, but her singing wasn't one of them. He belittled her in front of us, the asshole. And imitated her. I still can't believe that. I can't forgive him for that.

She loved a lot of music, but particularly Handel. My childhood was filled with "Dank sei dir, Herr" and "Dove sei, amato bene?" and "I Know That My Redeemer Liveth," and she sang them so beautifully, for an audience of just me and the neighbor kids. I can't begin to describe the beauty of that sound, the incredible life force of it, and when that sound was applied, like a paint brush, to certain words. "And though *worms* destroy this body, yet in my *flesh* shall I see God," but with the repetition one would hear it differently: "And though worms destroy *this* body, *yet* in my flesh shall I see God." It changed every time. She seemed to slightly elongate certain words, yet she never seemed to breathe. I always tried like hell to create that sound on the piano, and the attempt nearly killed me, but it was also the only thing that kept me going as long as I did.

TALL SHIPS
ALTA

Gene must have shared my awe of Joey, because he so completely ignored everything about his musical life. It was no fairy tale. It was as real as it is now over.

Shortly after that Bicentennial summer when everything took off for Joey, after Tanglewood, Gene's car business boomed. Everything in Houston boomed. He had little room left for caring about his son's musical career. The boy with whom Gene used to play and swim in our backyard during the 1960s now packed the Concertgebouw and Carnegie Hall. Joey's tours of Asia drew the largest crowds in classical music except for Pavarotti and Vladimir Horowitz, who created the classical music phenomenon that allowed for Joey's career. When Joey began, writing about him was the usual hit or miss, mostly miss, but by 1989 the few remaining skilled and knowledgeable journalists and critics were trying to describe Joey in a direct line of historic pianists from Beethoven: Padrewski, Liszt, Leschetizky, Schnabel, Rubenstein, and Horowitz. They knew he was in the pantheon of giants; they just couldn't figure out how he got there.

There was also an entire "other'" school of thought coalescing around Joey by 1989, which was that since he didn't emerge from the traditional classical institutions, and no one really knew his pedagogical parentage, he must be some sort of "fake" musician. The story was that his mother taught him, but musicians in academia thought this to be nonsense. There is simply no way a musician of his scope and technical accomplishment could emerge out of nowhere, without their knowledge. To them, an elementary music teacher was as good as nowhere. By 1989 others accused Horowitz of having taught the boy, particularly since Horowitz always steadfastly refused to teach, saying it ate too much of his concentration. That Joey played nothing like Horowitz, and his technique didn't remotely resemble the Russian master, dawned on very few. Joey never met Horowitz.

Rudolf Serkin was drawn into the discussion, since Joey slightly shared physical characteristics with him, but Serkin was a profoundly famous teacher in classical circles, and all of Serkin's many exemplary students would either have seen Joey with their teacher at some point or recognized aspects of his teaching within his playing, and neither was true. Adele Marcus at Juilliard launched a quiet campaign of many years to find out who really had taught Joey and how he'd gotten his break at Tanglewood. Other extraordinary teachers—Marcus, Pressler, the Lhévinnes, and others of the major postwar school—expressed admiration for his playing, one even saying to the press, "We should be celebrating such pianism whenever and however it arrives. This search to find his pianistic lineage is unseemly." But of course, *unseemly* never daunted anyone, especially in music.

If the truth about Joey's musical family tree was difficult for people to discern, it was even more so for me. I was present for every moment of his life, from the first time his tiny hand found its way to the keyboard to the day I overheard him playing *Moses in Egypt*. I watched him absorb the slightest technical challenge faster than I could put them in front of him. I studied the lexicon and consulted with Giuseppe at every opportunity, and I made sure to maximize those opportunities. But Joey's growth was so rapid I could barely keep up with him, and eventually I wouldn't try. I let him sail at his own speed, which felt to me like the speed of light. It was not my imagination that as Joey gained in pianistic strength, Giuseppe at our every clandestine meeting was more and more passionate and ravaging of me. He took me with such force in those years. I can never forget that.

That 1976 Tanglewood *Emperor Concerto*, the 5th Piano Concerto of Beethoven, would remain a mystery for everyone, because from their standpoint Joey did come out of nowhere. The *Emperor* was to be played by a highly esteemed pianist, scheduled years in advance as a type of apotheosis to his long postwar career. When his health deteriorated in the early summer of 1976, a number of potential substitutes were brought forward. Little Joey and I were in New York when this was all going on, though we initially knew nothing about it. Giuseppe, having waited for a break like this for twenty years, was among those considered to play it. The list was long—twenty-five pianists at least—and the obvious symbolism of playing it in the Bicentennial season at the country's most distinguished summer music series made it a particularly coveted opportunity.

The Boston Symphony Orchestra chose Giuseppe with no mention yet of little Joey walking into such a rare moment. Giuseppe called me with such excitement. It was just a few days after the tall ships had sailed into New York for the Bicentennial. He came to the Algonquin to teach Joey more lessons. As the reality sank in that in just a few short weeks he would be in rehearsal with the Boston Symphony for a Beethoven concerto he had played his whole life, for this was the break he had been seeking, the nerves began. I watched fear overtake him, like some mythic monster. Of much more concern, I could hear it. Joey would take rest breaks—he was still just a boy after all—and Giuseppe would practice the *Emperor*. Those treacherous opening scales, which I'd heard him play thousands of times in Brenham, were insecure and tentative. The long sequence of the first movement, which he knew better than he knew himself, was inspiring memory slips.

I could feel Giuseppe retreating, and to this day I can hardly believe what he did. Giuseppe knew the major administrator of the Tanglewood Music Festival, who had even been in attendance at "my" party all those years ago at the Ansonia. After Giuseppe made a series of calls, Joey was invited to the small concert hall at Columbia Artists Management across from Carnegie Hall to play the *Emperor* for a conductor and a manager, both very nice men. There were a couple of other older gentlemen there, one of whom I could swear was James, Millie's friend from all those years ago, but I didn't approach him. I called Millie for her advice. Joey was so young and even this audition I felt was too much pressure for him, but he became more and more at ease when the pressure was high. This was a sign, as Millie said, of his readiness. The representative from the Boston Symphony made the offer to us right there in the CAMI hall.

The enterprising and energetic man I met in New York nearly twenty years before, and whom I loved beyond anyone else, the man who moved to Texas to be near me, and the man who taught his own son to do what he should have done, handed his son his career that morning in New York.

I called Gene and told him we were staying in New York and tried to convey the significance of the Tanglewood opportunity, but it was completely lost on him. I suggested that he fly up for it, but he said the business was too demanding for him to leave Houston, and he complained about what the Algonquin would cost, as if that had any significance in light of what was transpiring. I could tell he was immersed in a new affair.

Giuseppe stayed in New York, too, and helped prepare little Joey for the concert. Joey assimilated his father's mature pianistic personality in those weeks in New York. I watched it. With no emotion, no excitement, and no nervousness, our little boy ascended the mountain that is Beethoven. I looked for signs that this might be too much for him but didn't see them. Had this extraordinary thing not happened that summer, it might have been an opportunity for Joey to know the truth about his father, but I could not think about adding that to the weight we were already placing on him.

Giuseppe attended the Tanglewood concert, but we did not sit together. It was all over so quickly. Joey looked like such a child in front of the distinguished white coats of the older musicians, but he was gigantic at the piano. I could barely contain my pride. That was my son. *My* son was up there playing Beethoven. And yes, my son, our son, was a direct link to Beethoven, though not in a way anyone would ever find out: Giuseppe, who was his son's highly unconventional teacher and unknown father, had been one of the last students of Artur Schnabel just after the war, when he was so young himself. Giuseppe always talked about Schnabel in the reverent tones reserved for a deity. Schnabel was taught by Leschetizky, who was taught by Czerny, who was taught by Beethoven.

The high point of Joey's career, for me, was the summer of 1989, when he returned to Tanglewood for the first time since that igniting summer of 1976. Over two weeks he played concerti, including the *Emperor* again, and two full recitals, including *Carnaval* and *Kreisleriana*. I stayed for the whole period, wrapped in the peace of the Red Lion Inn in Stockbridge, and the wondrous cool beauty of the mornings there. I was finally able to enjoy the place, as I'd had no time to do in the 1970s.

I will always remember a little hilltop just to the east of the Red Lion, where I spent each morning while Joey practiced. I must have just wandered into it, as nobody directed me there. I now wonder if the little idyll is still there, as undeveloped and dewy as it used to be. It was peaty and surrounded by bracken and old New England trees that had seen the Revolution. There was a central clearing surrounded by old foundations covered in lichen. I took whatever Will Durant volume I happened to be reading, for I never traveled with anything else, and I would sit in the clearing and read for hours. If I could manage an early enough start, I would sit in silence for an hour before reading, just me and a lovely coffee. Even in heat the clearing was cool and sheltered from any breezes, protected from the rest of the world. From there the ubiquitous traffic was silent, and no one ever gardened up there, so the screaming machines were kept at bay. I watched one sunrise from that clearing, on one of the most fortunate mornings of my life, because I had heard Joey play the Gershwin *Concerto in F* the night before, and only a dozen hours later that day he would play the Brahms 3rd Sonata for the hundredth time in public. The Brahms Sonata, which he'd learned without me in the time since he left home, is my favorite thing he plays. It is the summit of the piano literature, the summation of a century of the piano. Giuseppe taught me all of this, of course, but by 1989 he was completely in retreat from music and more and more dependent on me. The joy of his life had ebbed into silence. He still found other joys, to be sure, but I noticed that I brought him less news about Joey by those late '80s days. Giuseppe once remarked that he thought composers had retreated from the expressive possibilities of the piano after the Brahms Sonata. I didn't understand what he meant until I saw him, in solidarity, pull himself away into some kind of mysteriously symbolic solitude.

THE VALLEY

JOEY

Every few weeks now, watching the sunset over Sydney Harbour at night, there has been a fireworks display over the Sydney Opera House. From Vaucluse the fireworks can't be heard, so they seem like fake explosions, like something on television. What must we look like to the fireworks? Do they have consciousness as they are fired into the air, for those few seconds before they burst and spread out over huge crowds? Do they notice people looking at them? Do they sense when their brief arc is ending? When they burn out before they fully descend, do they know?

My life now fights with Mother's religious beliefs, which are the type of searching that arises out of some great loss or tragedy. Though she won't say it, I know she feels me as a loss. Not me losing my career, which was a choice, but she feels I am actually lost. Not hearing me play again is a death to her, as surely as if my heart had stopped. She was always going to have to cling to something that could explain the world to her, even if she knew it was all nonsense, which I have no doubt she does to this day. She is now a religious fanatic who goes through every motion of belief but she feels her feelings as beliefs. She does a huge amount of good work for the poor through the church, but it is only to have a community; it doesn't have anything to do with poverty. She is as at home now with the Presbyterians as she should have been in the company of her fellow great operatic stars, each admiring the singularity of her voice. The church doesn't give her the musical gifts it did when she was a girl, but instead of accepting that and going on she complains endlessly about it. Yet she won't give away the most precious facet of herself that might make it better: she won't sing. I haven't heard her voice in years and neither has anyone else.

When she traveled with me, she didn't attend church and never mentioned it. Even her church attendance at home in those years didn't portray any warning signs: it was solely for seeing her neighbors and being *seen* as benevolent and participatory. Something new is growing in her world, and it concerns me that she is converting her long casual habit into some version of comfort, no matter how senseless the dogma she now accepts. Either she is a different woman since I stopped playing, or I simply didn't notice her mysterious slow slide. She has taken on the words and thoughts of my grandmother, the very ideas over which they've fought for their whole lives and which Mom has regularly ridiculed and minimized. Where she used to see true wonder and embrace the curiosity of knowledge, now she attributes even the slightest unknown to God and pursues no avenue toward learning. She is newly satisfied that "some things are beyond what we should know." The mother who taught me every secret of the piano would never have satisfied herself with that.

This was a woman who in her youth could define *mutatis mutandis,* tell you about the shipwreck of the *Batavia*, who could not only find Borneo on a map but also talk for thirty minutes on the eruption of Krakatoa and its importance to the world. She could sing the kings and queens of England mnemonic song, and list all of the U.S. Presidents and their home states. She could stand with me anywhere in central Rome and give a history of where we were standing. She was able to name three hundred tributaries of the Mississippi River, while sullenly acknowledging that there were nearly one hundred thousand, so her knowledge was small compared to the actuality, which in those years gave both her and me absolute delight. She loved that paradox of learning: that it teaches you how much you could never know. Depth was what she sought and found, yet now she's content to stay on the surface. She would sketch fantasized diaries that captured a single day of Eleanor of Aquitaine's life, and they would be tens of thousands of pages. What happened to those diaries? She said they were "just folly," but what if they actually have something to them; what if she has a writer's voice that might allow her to step out of the shadow of my playing?

A single phrase of music could send her into tears of joy, something rare enough in the world, yet now she debates interpretations of biblical texts as though they were something other than Iron Age metaphorical tales. She even bothers to capitalize "Holy Bible" now in her e-mails. Theory, to my mother of thirty years ago, meant *music* theory, and so was something she *knew* was true. She required no proof of an interval or a scale, because the science of music is perfectly embedded within itself; she couldn't have one without the other.

My mother used to be a woman deeply in possession of greatness herself, as well as being able to recognize it in others. She accessed the knowledge of the some of the greatest minds that ever lived; now she seriously thinks that rules set down by people who didn't even know where the sun went at night might provide her some guidance toward happiness. Is this how we all age? If this is going to be my future, I'd rather just check out now. More and more of our conversations end in harsh words.

THE CHEAPENING
ALTA

I could never bear Joan Rivers, Don Rickles, Frank Sinatra, Dean Martin, or Foster Brooks, and you could not turn the television on from 1970 to 1985 without encountering any or all of them. Rivers and Rickles were both contemptible, making careers out of the misfortunes of others. This is not something that should be put out into the world, as it will only create worse in the future. Where is our promotion of beauty and intelligence and class? My Joey's career was made larger by Johnny Carson, but I do not think Johnny should have promoted Rivers and Rickles so much. He should have refused them airtime on his show. And Frank Sinatra: he is completely made by his arrangements…I could never bear the idea of a great arranger like Nelson Riddle creating a sonic tapestry into which *anyone* could sound wonderful. Nelson Riddle should have been the star, not Frank Sinatra. And has there ever been a greater waste of public time than Don Rickles?

I realize just how fully "belief" governs our lives. I've believed these things about all of these entertainers, but there are other people who don't remotely believe the same as I do. Who is right? And why would Frank Sinatra care one whit what I thought of him? We are all encircled by our beliefs. I believe my son is one of the greatest musicians in the world right now, and I believe he has made an enormous mistake to hide himself from a world that needs him. But I may well be wrong. I've come to believe that Jesus Christ was the Son of God. I know that Giuseppe and certainly Joey will skewer me for this belief, but I've come to it after a life of debate with myself.

THE FLANEUR
JOEY

How could we be so fundamentally different? I mean, all of us. The incredible polarity in the world is old news to musicians, because we've had polarized conservatives and liberals for generations before they were so well identified in politics. No one outside the field could imagine how conservative a classical musician can be, how wedded to the constitutional text of the printed score, how devoid of imagination and creativity, how frightened of innovation or any deviation from the traditions they believe are the sole spiritual impetus perpetuating the art. And the preaching from the conservatives...O, Christ, bleeding, on, the, cross...they will fulminate endlessly on the fading away of the great movements of music, on the severing of the arc of history, as though creativity can be contained in any generation.

But there are also, more rarely, the classical music liberals, for whom everything is relative and there is merit in every tempo that is too slow, in every ignored dynamic marking, in every eccentricity masquerading as profundity, and in giving power to every minor critic who randomly has been given a mouthpiece.

No one asks questions anymore. I know this because it became true in my playing life, and anything that trickled down as far as classical music must be true. Players like Donald appeared, well into my own career, and they had fingers. They could play. But something shifted somewhere, into something cheaper and thus less necessary.

I'm a flaneur, really: someone who just roams the city without really living in it. The world lost me, and I seem to have reciprocated in kind. Anything overused is a cliché, except for Beethoven, of course. But even old Ludwig had no choice but to reinvent himself: those last piano sonatas are brilliant and daring beyond anything written a hundred years on either side of them. There is an urgency to art created later in life, and I'd hoped to fashion a year of recitals all around music written in the last twelve months of a composer's life, a time when it is evident that there is a newly unsustainable level of perception at work, something only visible in hindsight. Irresolution is instinctively accepted and allowed to unfold without the editing that the full life force brings on. We reimagine our lives when we have no choice but to do so, as I am experiencing every day now. No biographer will be interested in an invented life of mine; they are right to expect the real thing. But I don't see any possibility of having access to it now. I am too late for reinvention. I am not morbid, nor are my thoughts filled with longings for death, yet I also know I am in some limbo that is not quite alive.

Parting the Seas

ALTA

Joey could pick out notes in chords from a very young age. He was naturally left-handed but had extraordinary finger independence, that most elusive of pianistic qualities. It is something he worked on, to be sure, but it was something he had naturally. His ear was off the charts, like Mozart writing down the motet in fourteen separate parts after only one hearing in the Sistine Chapel when he was just fourteen. Joey could hear anything and play it. I would play a random cluster on the piano or a tone row, and he would name each note, never making an error.

I've come to view my son through the lens of a single phrase of music, and how blessed my life has been, both to have this extraordinary man come from my own body but also to know this music that has helped me define the feeling of our lives together. The whole grand coincidence, the unexpected filling out of the world, the chasing of so many dreams, have coalesced in into the short soaring phrase of the Brahms Sonata, near the end of it, a piece I worked so hard to be able to teach to him, as it was so far beyond me. But I had the ability to see it from my small place in the world, and to give it to Joey, with difficulty but with such presence from him.

How often people hear this sonata, a few of them anyway, and just hear the achievement of playing it. Do they hear what is *actually* there, the emotional cells and protons of it, what it says about being alive? Joey played it at that last recital in London and, knowing I'd never hear him play it again, I've tried to hold as much of it in my memory as I could.

I willed myself to be absolutely there for it, not to think of it being the end, but just of it being. I play his gorgeous recording of it every month or so, though it sometimes pains me to remember it.

Back around 1970, I had taken Joey through his piano exercises early one morning, over an hour of the Hanon exercises and a few of the Brahms. My piano skills were more than proficient, but Joey had by then long surpassed what I was able to play myself, and he was only twelve on that morning. My own gifts were sufficient to allow me to know what I could not do, and also to understand what possibilities there were for the instrument; I was always very good at recognizing possibilities. I knew what great technique and great playing looked and sounded like, though I couldn't do it myself. Joey was barely challenged by any exercises except the most torturous of the Brahms, which he eventually sailed through. He needed more and more summits to ascend, and it took me a lot of extra study to find the right things to teach him. By the time he was fifteen, he could play all of the Brahms exercises at tempo, something only a few pianists in history have been able to do.

Later that night I went into our backyard on South. It was still a time before the pollution made it impossible to see the stars. I always could watch the night sky all night, as I've done my whole life. I took a small glass of wine to the back patio, turned off the pool lights, and began to drink in the sensuous darkness. Gene was, as usual, likely in someone's bed, though he'd told me he was staying late selling cars. Perry was at a slumber party somewhere, and Joey was in the house quietly occupied, probably reading. My evenings were so often busy in those days with the three men I lived with—husband, son, and nephew—and their preparations for dinner and bed. Televisions were usually on and there was normally much noise. Not tonight. It had been ages since Joey and I had been alone at the house in an evening.

Ursa Major was overhead, my favorite constellation. I don't believe the stars have any effect on our behavior, as in horoscopes, which I find to be complete nonsense. But I knew, and I knew it especially at that moment, that everything I could see was related to everything else, including me. When my mind had a rare moment of quiet like that night, I could feel, even as the spaces between me and everyone else in my family began to deepen, that I was a part of the grandeur I could glimpse. A curtain of great beauty briefly parted that night, though only later would I realize what it was. The feeling was not "God" but something simply suspended, like an ember that is only briefly aflame, seen from a distance.

The sky shifted. Stars that had been over the garage apartment when I sat down were over one of the great oaks. I heard the piano and felt a thrill. Joey was going to practice some more. He never played at night in those days, and didn't know I was listening. He started what sounded like exercises, a little arching chromatic figure with his left hand, then his right hand echoed it just a measure later. Just over a minute later, he started a set of thundering octaves. I realized it was no exercise.

I didn't want to risk breaking his concentration, so I remained outside to listen. He must have been working on this piece in my absences. He stumbled at a few passages and stopped to work on them in ways I had outlined for him. I couldn't remember having purchased the printed music to the Thalberg *Fantasy on Moses on Egypt*, and I wondered where Joey had found it. The night would be a forever time for me, a moment under the stars I'll never to forget.

He worked through a few of the easier cantabile passages, but by the time he got to the arpeggios and demanding octaves near the end, he was sailing through it. From my poolside chair I could barely see his twelve-year-old head over the top of the piano, yet this incongruously mature and sonorous sound, like endless layers of vapor, was emanating from the instrument that sounded perfectly ordinary when I played it. That was the night I realized what Joey might achieve.

THE CURRENT
JOEY

Only now that I've stopped do I realize what she gave me. Hell, maybe that's the *reason* I stopped. She put her voice into my playing. As I read back on some of what was written about me, most of which is complete bullshit, the common thread is *cantabile*. The half-dozen critics I encountered who really knew what the word meant managed to understand this about my playing. Sure, anyone can know that it has something to do with singing, but they couldn't discern anything deeper than that. Cantabile is what makes a river flow. It is the force that binds music together: two consecutive notes become three, four, twenty-four, five hundred. The piano has no natural cantabile. In fact, almost no instrument does—only players can have it. It is a human interaction with an instrument.

The great exception, which I found out only by loss, is singing—but only great singing, like Mother's, or Callas, or Cigna, or Lawrence, or Ponselle, all of them singers she and Millie taught me about. She would demonstrate the spinning of phrase after phrase of Chopin and Schumann, always on nonsense syllables, or simply "ah," and it translated into my playing. I had the ability to mimic her, but I held none of the artistry myself—a horrible realization I'm coming to in these endless repetitive days in Australia. That force, that cantabile, is gone in me now. It was like blood—exactly so, in that if I was still enough I could feel it coursing through every alleyway of my body. Concentrate on the foot with enough stillness, and there is the blood, and all of the other energies created by our minds. But the cantabile force is not in the mind, as so many have written. It is in the hand and the arm, like lymph and muscle, but it flows ever onward until it is used up, as mine now is. The flow has stopped.

I never had time to read a book on pianism when I was playing, but now that I've been asked to write a book myself, I've picked up a few and read them. The main reason I don't want to write about playing, and certainly not about myself, is that none of the authors capture the feeling of it, and those who get close still mangle the reality. The physical part of pianism is, by itself, a brittle and crackling thing, not an engine that has been assembled, but something akin to bone or teeth or diamond—it breaks what it encounters. You sit at the keyboard and try to subdue the natural tendency of the instrument, which is to subdue and temper the hammer hitting the strings. You engage with the keys and you make them do what you want, which isn't remotely what they want, which is to have dominance over the hammers, and the hammers want to conquer the strings. There is so much competition built into the piano. So many needs that the player has to temper.

The exercises for agility require a brain, of course, and even depths of feeling, but the muscles alone have no poetry or song within them. It isn't so simple as trying to *imitate* song; it is actually *being* song, being a delicate endless matrix of sound with every fiber of being—that is what playing the piano is. Most playing is weak, so it isn't surprising that our words are also. Most playing isn't playing at all; it is just vertical depression of keys by ten fingers of varying capabilities. Real playing, the real cantabile, comes from ten completely independent entities that all happen to exist on two hands. The hands in their muscular silence are nothing without the voice.

Ungrateful Heart

ALTA

I went to the opera occasionally in Houston but largely I stayed away, since I saw so much opera on the road with Joey. In Houston it was often too difficult for me to hear singing, especially if it was great. Once I went to *Marriage of Figaro* in Houston, and I could barely make it through. The cast and staging were lovely, but the Countess, the character who sings "Dove sono?" had the most beautiful voice I've ever heard. I haven't the slightest idea who she was. I was never one to remember names of famous singers, never one to listen much to recordings beyond my childhood times in Millie's living room. People were forever giving me recordings as gifts and I always gave them to others. Why would I want to sit around and listen to others do what I should have done myself?

But who could imagine the pain I felt hearing that glorious soprano sing the Countess? Of course, one doesn't simply "sing" an opera role; one plays a character, or should, but this performance was too real for my own comfort. It took beauty to the point of death, and I could hardly be around that. I played the society game, walked through the opera house, politely sipping a glass of wine here and there, but it was unbearable for me, so much beauty in one moment. The people around me debated the pettiest of details, particularly how singers looked, but I was unable to return.

In Houston, even more than in most big cities, one is forced to find beauty in decay, not solely because the harsh climate forces everything to deteriorate so quickly, but also because so much of what was beautiful about the city has been ripped down and replaced with cheap monstrosities.

TEA
JOEY

Every morning I perform the same rituals, something I could never do in my playing life, and every morning I wish I could live my day as does the tea I now prepare. I place a pressed sachet of tea into an empty glass vase and pour scalding water on it. It has a moment of audible shock that is quickly drowned. Then it sits silently on the bottom of the glass, almost fearful, as it absorbs the scorching water that awakens its nutrients. As it reaches a sufficiency, as Mom would call it, the sachet of tea rises to the top of the water, going as far as it is able, before it slowly (slowly for the tea, quickly for the water) breaks into the smallest possible pieces that each descend back to where they started.

My Foolish Heart

ALTA

I can't begin to conceive of the money Joey has made and spent, but it must be in the tens of millions. But none of my grief about Joey or about anyone involves money. I didn't work for money; I worked so that I wouldn't go out of my mind in that house, and I did want to make a difference in the lives of the youngsters I taught. I hate that I never did that. I got lost in the petty arguments inside the school, constantly washed my hands of it all, and most often chose to stay away from the place. The only way you can be a successful teacher is to devote yourself completely to it, to work with the problem children after school, to be willing to be there for them, to give them the confidence that their parents won't or can't. I wanted to break the cycle of my own family by going into teaching and helping others, but the cycle had such a hold on me that I couldn't do it. I let those kids down. I am ashamed to the core of how easily I succumbed to the little things in my life, even though I spent an inordinate amount of time excoriating everyone around me for doing the same.

All I wanted for Gene, Perry, and Joey was a recognition of beauty in the world, an ability to look beyond the smallness and into the great expanse of forces that we can only understand by the beauty they create: the thin wall of protection we pretend to put up against the natural world and which we deceive ourselves for generations as real. But the more beauty I tried to pour into my boys, the more bile came back, except for Joey. He was the only one who ever understood any of it. I don't know how we accomplished that together in an environment like Gene and Perry wallowed in, but we did. And the proof was in Joey's extraordinary career.

Joey's entire career happened, and Perry never once attended one of his recitals. Can you imagine? These are the sorts of petty encumbrances I have spent my life trying to overcome and overlook. I kept a huge garden of roses in the backyard of South Boulevard, constant proof that if the unrelentingly ugly and muddy terrain of eastern Texas could give birth to beauty, so could we who were above the earth aspiring to be its master. There was something beautiful and much larger all around us to which we have constant access, and music is the greatest proof of it, but only Joey could understand that. Gene and Perry loved their cars, and I guess they managed to find their version of beauty in that, but nothing about a car, no matter how expensive or fine, is beautiful to me. A car is a man-made thing cleverly disguising a basic need. Where is the beauty in that? Obviously some cars are nicer than others, and I understand the seduction of a lovely car, but I do not understand the obsession over some constructed conveyance. The only beauty in the world is that of nature, or that which allows us to see nature with more clarity and tenderness.

It appears to have been the lesson of my life to have been shown beauty for an enticing moment before it was taken away. But I've been blessed with so much beauty, and I've let it slip away. Those long summer evenings in Brenham with Giuseppe; what bliss that was! Why were there so few of them?

The only song of my childhood that has stayed with me for my whole life is "My Foolish Heart." I first heard it in a movie—can't remember which one—and I always felt it was the one popular song I encountered that understood *me*. That's the forever thing about seriously composed music: it hears *us* more than we hear it.

Giuseppe used to love to have me sing this song up at the ranch. He would play it after dinner during the sunset. Sunset watching is so vital to us all, and it was a religious part of our days in Brenham. They were so few. When we stop noticing sunsets, we begin to chew with our mouths open.

POE

ALTA

I remember the day I knew that I wanted to sing. I was in kindergarten in the very school where I now teach music, Poe Elementary—so symbolically named—long before the bombing of course, which must have been in the late 1950s—I've blocked that out, as I think it happened while I was pregnant. Do people even know about it anymore? It was so long ago, and people shoot up schools now as regularly as rainstorms.

It was a day of sweltering and still air, the kind you can cut up in cubes. And we had a substitute teacher. I still don't know her name; I suppose they didn't keep records of things like that back then. In kindergarten we didn't go to music class, but we often sang songs with our regular teacher. When it came time to sing with this substitute, however, things were totally different. I remember holding our weathered little music books, filled with songs from many countries: "Frère Jacques," "Don Gato," "O Tannenbaum," "Song of the Volga Boatmen," and so many others. I so wish I could remember the song we were singing when I first heard the substitute teacher's voice; over the years I have come to hope that it was "America the Beautiful," but I'm not entirely sure.

I was in the row of desks closest to the window and our teacher was all the way across the room when the song began. She started to move through the aisles of our desks as the verses of the song collected. I was transfixed by her voice—such beauty and concentration of sound. It seemed to come out of her like some shimmering ray. I had never heard such beauty before, had never even contemplated its possibility. As she approached my desk, her sound enveloped me, surrounded me like a descent into soothing water, a womb of radiance. There was no fear in this sound, no strain, just effortless power and vibrating beauty. That's what it felt like to me: a vibration. I never wanted that song to end. As we neared one of the final voices, this substitute teacher—how frustrating not to be able to name her!—put her hand gently under my chin and raised my eyes toward hers. Her eyes were encouraging me to sing with her, to let my voice join hers. She encouraged the whole class to join in the final verse with extra gusto, and she put her eyes back toward mine. We sang together, and it felt like her voice was actually entering me and I was sending it back to her along with mine. There was an unseen energy in her sound.

What is a singing voice? What a mystery it is. Technically, it's nothing but undulating air, but that doesn't remotely describe the act of singing, which is filled with such colors and tones inside of tones, sounds that vibrate over the one we think we hear, hidden energies that beg to be known. Yet we can't know them: singing is an otherworldly act. I can hear the anonymous teacher's voice, and I still wonder where she came from and why she chose me from the entire class to bless and consecrate with her voice. If she had chosen another child's head to raise, would that voice have been bestowed on them instead? What did she actually bequeath to me? Or did she awaken some force in me that might have stayed dormant for my whole life without her? Gene says I imagined all of it just to have a "drippy little story" to tell, as though I needed to make up anything in my life.

That moment with the substitute teacher, a few verses of a song in which she and I intimately shared the final, is the moment for which I'm most grateful in my life, because that teacher showed me the possibilities of what I could do, of what beauty could be put into the world if we simply let it emanate from us. I had the ember in me to sing, but my fire was never given the fuel it needed. I became a music teacher because it was the only option available to me, after I'd been shown the world.

Singing is what I think about all the time, and have throughout my life. But thinking about singing is like writing about the stuff of the stars; words are useless when faced with either of them. That is what has changed so much over my life: how available people are for hearing anything. When I started teaching music, my students would actually hear me—they could repeat things I told them or sang to them even years later. Now, no one seems able to hear anything. I talk and talk, and no one listens. Everyone expects me to have this noble stance on the teaching of music, or more generally on the importance of the teaching profession. Of course, I have loved teaching at some levels, but largely it is a horrible field, not worth it, because all one does is deal with the pettiest and smallest thoughts the bureaucratic numbskulls can imagine.

Our school has been held back constantly by a single gorgon school secretary. God, I hated that woman! She ran the whole place, freeing up several generations of principals for lives of leisure. There was no interest in the wonder of what we could have brought to those children, no interest in nature, no contemplation of the beauties of the earth, particularly as exemplified in music. It is through nature that we learn beauty—and I tried to symbolize this by teaching music class outside whenever possible, under a grand oak tree in the schoolyard—how I loved those days, the late-winter days in Texas of such endless remarkable beauty, of seeking healing possibilities out in the air and the peace of the wind. I would roll the piano out there and get those children to sing, like Rusalka, to the moon.

But no, that was deemed unsafe and outside the norm, too disruptive for other classes, not equitable for the science or history classes that wanted to do the same, too much wear and tear on the cheap piano. Nameless school secretary, the pea-brained bitch, worked on that for years before finally winning the battle: "What is to become of this school if every teacher who loved the outdoors decided to move their classes outside?" I'd say rather wonderful things would happen to this school! That's what. She thought in terms of school days; I taught in terms of the vast legacy of recent musical and artistic history, the whole different world out there. To the earth there is nothing in the spans of days—there is nothing even in a millennium. How will children learn that if not through music and painting and expression?

How blessed I was to have Millie in my teenage life to teach me to sing, to teach me so much—and she got blamed for what happened to me.

MALINCONIA

JOEY

Sometimes she is so irritating. The passage of time is not "melancholy," as she said on the phone to me last night. *Melancholy*; I fucking hate that word. It is such a boring cop-out of a description of anything. Time isn't melancholy. It is decay and withering and unstoppable regret. Avoiding the fact of oblivion is infantile, and I hate it. I am hardly a poster-child for treasuring every moment, am I? I have thrown away more time than anyone I know, even when I was still playing; it is a meal I once lustily consumed that now slowly eats me. I sit here in an aging Sydney city park, as I do nearly every day, writing in my diary for a few hours, contributing words to what is just a latest obsession, yet always writing the same thing, always taking the same vows, recognizing sameness, watching the young people in the park grow into new young people the next year.

I spent years in the heads of others. Composers, writers, thinkers, philosophers, and they connected me to life for a long time. But that night in London when I met Ben, a nickel dropped. Until then I had no idea who I was. I had played a vast amount of the greatest and most challenging piano repertoire all over the world for twenty-five years, since I was a child, yet there was no *me* away from the piano. I had no choice: that night at Paul and Mary's, by that amazing pool in Mayfair (who the *hell* has a pool in Mayfair?), I knew my decision was right. My life told me clearly what it wanted, and for once I listened. I didn't make the decision because of Ben, which is just some of the nonsense I've read about my retirement in the past few months. I had already decided to retire before I met him.

DEAR DEER

ALTA

I taught Joey much more than music. I taught him how to be in the world, how to listen to nature with his eyes and ears, how to imagine the world without the two of us in it, running through the bluebonnets, as we did so often. I remember a gorgeous twilight in Brenham, where we stopped on a perfectly blanketed hillside and I asked Joey to imagine what it might be like out there at this moment if we weren't present. That wonderful little boy said, "I think the animals that are hiding right now because they are scared of us would not be scared anymore. The houses would all be gone, and probably a deer would walk up here right now and know we were once here, but not fear it."

That was my little boy. Joey had no fear. He had that extraordinary spark from the beginning. He didn't get it from a teacher like I did. Just once when I was teaching I wish I could have given someone their voice the way that long-ago anonymous teacher did for me, and which Millie honed. But Joey is the only one I've ever taught who made me feel like a real teacher. None of the hundreds of kids over decades of music teaching made me feel that way. Not one. I tried to get them interested in the world; I did not want teaching to make me feel a failure, like singing…I wanted to be the greatest teacher in the world, but I quickly knew I wasn't going to be. I wanted to be one of the memorable teachers who contemplates the beauties of the earth. I wanted the children to find silence, the silence of the great stars above. But over my teaching career, the emphasis turned to things. Silence isn't a thing, isn't something that can be acquired, though I know that we are heading into a time when even silence will become very expensive.

I didn't have to teach, given that I did have my family's inheritance, but that wasn't so much, really, or wasn't so big that I wanted to solely rely on it, and I didn't think I would be able to keep the rest of my family out of it. And, frankly, I wanted to keep it from Gene. None of that money ever felt real to me, because Mother has lived so long, and I was never fully sure where the money came from, which sounds odd.

THE ROCK

JOEY

If I'm asked to write a book about my life, I guess I'll have to include my cousin Perry, and remembering him is always so complicated. I get furious when I recall what he did to me, yet I also miss him. Fury is foreign to me: if my closest friends were polled, as they will be for this book, I would be described as docile and even-tempered, but that disappears when I think of Perry. Perry was, is, a brother figure, though he is my cousin. We are the same age. I never knew his mom, my aunt. She died in the Middle East shortly after she was married and I'm not sure anyone knows why or how. She was Mom's sister, and when whatever happened happened, Mom agreed to raise Perry, so we grew up together and most people assumed we were brothers.

I never told Ben about Perry. Ben and I knew each other's bodies more intimately than any two people who ever shared them, yet I never told him *that*. I have kept Perry completely to myself right up to this moment. I don't know why. Perry and I now do not touch at any point besides memory, and I doubt he thinks of me at all, certainly not to the extent to which he occupies *my* thoughts. In the Blue Mountains house, where I rarely go now, I even keep a small book of photographs of him, enhanced by pornography of men who resemble him. Perry is something in my life that can't be set free, but which I hate and want to be rid of. What are we to do with what accompanies each memory?

Diaries are all about truth, aren't they? Well, the truth is I loved when Perry made me feel helpless, and the deeper truth is that I sought that feeling for many years after Perry stopped wanting me that way. When I was in the height of my career and making a great deal of money, more than I could ever understand, I hired boys who could most closely re-create the feelings Perry kindled. The ones who looked like him got the most of my attention and money.

Ariel

ALTA

I think I know what went on between Perry and Joey, or maybe I just want to think I know. Perry was unstoppable, just like Gene, but of course he isn't related to Gene, so I'm never sure where he got it. It's funny that I feel more distance from Perry, who lives just a mile away, than from Joey in Australia, always asleep when I'm awake, just like when he was a boy. I wonder if they ever talk to each other. I don't believe they do. There is love between them, and I love seeing that, but there is something dark, too, that I think I might understand. I do a lot of wondering, it seems, as I have my whole life. I've lived my life on what could be discerned by others as knowledge, yet there is so much I don't know about my own family. There must be reasons they won't tell me things. So much secrecy… and that is what I cannot bear. It weighs on my voice. I'm surrounded by secrets; and secrets, to me, are just lies with an extra syllable.

Perry was irresistible to everyone. His teachers gave him a pass because he was so cute and, very quickly, so handsome and powerful; women fell all over him, and still do. He loved having control over Joey, but the control seemed to be his only joy in him. Not everyone can grow up in the same house with their cousin, I know that. But I'd promised my sister to raise Perry, and that's what I did. What really happened to my sister? That's the first thing I'd love to know.

No matter what I tried to instill in Perry, he was a machine, just like Gene. I've spent my life trying to teach them all, Gene, Perry, and Joey, about beauty—not culture, which isn't beautiful, but *beauty* itself, to get the whole family to recognize those few things in the world that aren't ordinary. Only Joey understood, almost before I could teach it to him. I would spend evenings by the fire reading Will Durant and I would drop some random wonders from those books, and I distributed them equally amid my testosterone-laden household, but only Joey would hear them. I told him about spiny lobsters in the Caribbean that migrated by holding on to each other in single file, in single-file lines up to sixty miles long, which I read in some book, and the revelation made the boy cry! I mean, who cares about lobsters and their migrating patterns? But I care deeply that my son had the rarest human gift of wonder and that he managed to keep it for so long. So many people, most people, lose that as they get older. He felt things so deeply, noticed things that nobody else did, even as a very young boy, and his cousin and his father, Perry and Gene, wouldn't even notice them. It broke my heart when they just ignored something truly luminous that he'd pointed out.

When we first started experimenting at the piano, when Joey was so young he couldn't reach the pedals, what I first noticed was not just the natural velocity and power of his fingers, but also what moved him. He lacked the instinctive narcissism of children; he was more like a benign and polite tourist who noticed everything in a way that wouldn't disturb it. He felt every contour of every melody he encountered as a boy, like a hiker who gets to know a mountain, but unlike Perry he never bragged about his abilities, never needed to demonstrate them for others to prove anything; he was satisfied simply to experience it. He felt music so deeply that he could re-create it instantly with no effort.

The human struggle to achieve some of the greatest works for the piano, those musical works that continue to connect the generations—Joey absorbed these and, without being taught the idea, aligned them with whatever brought him joy. He could sit in our backyard on South Boulevard for hours just noticing the wind in the trees, delighting in birdsong, which I would hear him re-create for himself but never for anyone else. Music was not a different wonder to him from watching the stars; for my little boy, it was all a simple and equal cosmos: Cassiopeia and Schubert were made of the same stuff. He had no expectation of fame or notoriety; he simply wanted to live in that beauty, even as a very young child. Would there ever have been a finer way to live?

I tried to live that way myself, but it was never allowed. Someone or something now has stolen Joey's joy, too, and I must get to the bottom of it, for he had choices I never had and he's throwing them away for some reasons. Despite every effort for my whole life, I was plagued with the ordinary: family, births, deaths, raising children, the household, the meals—all things meant to bring women joy, as I continue to constantly hear from my mother. "You have everything and you don't appreciate it," she dares to say to me to this day. *Everything* to her means a husband who makes a decent living, a beautiful home, and an organized and productive life. I did indeed have those things, but they were not what I find great about being alive. They weren't *me* and they weren't *mine*. I wanted little Joey's constant wonder, but I was handed instead a constant stream of humiliating distractions. I wanted art and beauty and Mozart and T. S. Eliot and Montaigne and nature and labyrinths and poetry, and instead I got grocery lists, baby showers, church picnics, and all the other mundane tasks of our gracious neighborhood. I was able, at least, to give those things to my cherished son, but now have to endure the seeming fact he has thrown them away. Families can be so ordinary, at least mine turned out to be, and the harder I tried to change it, the worse it became.

There's certainly plenty of anger to go around in this family, but the main person I'm furious with is myself. Why in the world did I allow a life with Gene? He was never the man I loved, and he knew it. But I could never bring myself to leave him. He controlled me as surely as I tried to control the rest of the family. It is something that should always leave me ashamed, but that, too, is a distraction.

THE BELL

JOEY

I played the Chopin F-sharp minor polonaise in my mind today. I opened many a recital with it, and it's one of the pieces I genuinely loved to play. It authored authentic emotion in me, not the manufactured type of posing so prevalent in classical music now. I have no idea if I ever created that emotion in anyone else by playing it. That never used to matter to me, but at some point in my career, a moment I can't pinpoint, it started to matter: I felt a gap between what I was feeling and what I could credibly evoke, like I was feeding people who weren't hungry. It's amazing to me now—time has even made it humorous—that I received some of the worst reviews of my career for that polonaise, which has come to evoke another genuine emotion: laughter. A critic in London wrote about how I dared to trot out a piece that Horowitz and Rubenstein had owned and made theirs. That was actually his lexicon: *trot, dare, own, theirs*. He wrote similar things on the two occasions I played the Chopin B-flat minor scherzo in London, declaring me an upstart with technical skill but nothing to say. Where did he get the idea that these extraordinary pieces of music need someone to "say something" about them, when they have everything that needs to be said written into them?

Of course, this same idiot praised the way I played the Wagner/Liszt paraphrase of *Tannhäuser* or the Liszt/Paganini "La Campanella," when he had absolutely no right to do so. My fingers could deliver the notes, it is true, but other pianists were infinitely greater at doing so; I could never summon the slightest emotion in playing them, though audiences would be ecstatic. What is wanted from a pianist, or any artist, is emotion in the *listener*, not in the performer. Yet that critic accused me of "daring" to play a work that others have played wonderfully before me. How dare *he* propose to know what I'm feeling in the playing of a work?

DIVINA
ALTA

One time. Only *one* time in my entire life was my mother moved by my voice. It happened at an Easter sunrise service, without accompaniment by a piano or organ, and I sang a piece I never liked much. But that morning, some combination of things hit her hard, and I wish I knew the why or how.

O Divine Redeemer!
I pray Thee, grant me pardon,
and remember not, remember not my sins!
Forgive me, O Divine Redeemer!
Night gathers round my soul;
Fearful, I cry to Thee;
Come to mine aid, O Lord!
Haste Thee, Lord, haste to help me!
Hear my cry! Save me Lord in Thy mercy;
Come and save me, O Lord
Save, in the day of retribution,
From Death shield Thou me, O my God!
O Divine Redeemer, have mercy!
Help me, my Saviour!

The words did not mean much to me then, but I can't get through them now without floods of tears. I have come to know what it means to need redemption. Was that what Mother was reacting to all those years ago? I know Joey does not understand my new devotion to Christ. But it has come across my spirit in great waves over these last few years. If I am not to be allowed the transcendence of my son's playing, not going to be allowed the overwhelming joy of long nights with Giuseppe in Brenham, with the sun helping the day and the fields going on forever—such an endless beauty!—and if I'm not to be allowed my own voice, where am I supposed to turn to be overwhelmed and humbled? The Lord is all I have left.

I was always asked to sing that horrible Malotte "Lord's Prayer," and I refused as often as I could, giving me the reputation in our church of being difficult, when really I was simply exerting the smallest amount of musical taste. That cheap and tawdry piece of music, with its fake operatic ascensions up to "Forever!" Oh, please. I always sang it in the highest available key so that the top note was a high C. If they were going to demand that blatantly insistent and manipulative attempt at "music," then I was determined to give it to them full force. So many pieces like that cheapen music and make it into something it should never be: base.

I also hated the constant dumbing down of everything over the course of my lifetime. Did everyone in the past feel this way, too? Did Maria Callas feel that the art of which she was the greatest exponent had been cheapened by her presence in it? Surely not. One reads about Callas sitting in her Paris apartment late in her life surrounded by small pieces of paper, her reviews from over the years, wondering to a visitor, "Why do they hate me so much?" I have always felt this story to be apocryphal, because I simply cannot believe that an artist of Callas's stature would be worried about what people said about her. She had conquered the greatest Verdi roles with a depth and grandeur no one had ever achieved.

I read what they wrote about my Joey over the years. How arrogant they were at the beginning, because he surprised them; they weren't able to identify him through any of the traditional routes. Suddenly, Bicentennial summer, there he was, like one of the tall ships in New York Harbor that had been hidden until it was upon you. Gradually, over his first decade, they tempered their assessments, always averring that they weren't originally wrong in their criticisms, but he was now "growing into his artistry," which was absolute nonsense. Joey emerged in that summer almost entirely the artist he is at this moment more than thirty years later. He learned a more diverse repertoire, of course, and he gained experiences beyond what any of his contemporary pianists could achieve, but that wasn't the way they wrote it.

Callas must have known this, which is why I find it specious that she would worry about the silly reviewers years later. She had communed with music in a way almost no singer ever did. How do I know this? I managed to hear her live on two nights, both in the same week, up in Dallas during one of those early seasons built around her. Millie and I somehow managed to convince Mother to keep the boys and allow Millie and me on another train. People have altered their memories to give the impression that Callas filled the cavernous Fair Park with her operatic appearances in Texas. Nonsense. There were fewer than five hundred people there, and many of them had come down from New York or Chicago. Callas's performances were astounding. She was the most complete artist in history, not only of my generation. One occasionally sees video footage of her performances, and they look and sound overdone in that medium. But to be in the same room with her *live* was another world. You were never aware of her crafting something. She just was. There was a dramatic energy as well as that enormous voice with a huge range of colors. I shall never forget it.

I was jealous of nearly every singer I encountered. I admired them so, and envied them being able to be heard. Joan Sutherland had the most divine sound I will ever experience, so much so that I couldn't bear to listen to her often. There were so many others. But I was never jealous of Callas. I knew that whatever talent I was blessed to have, unfulfilled and unrecognized as it always would be, I would never be able to do what Callas did. That didn't make me jealous. It made me humble. Callas gave the world a standard. She showed us the depths of what opera could be. I might have been able to achieve that, but I wasn't given the chance. I did it through my son, through the piano. I put one thing of beauty into the world, and now he has silenced himself.

Mayfair

JOEY

Mom was able to come over for my last recital in London, my retirement, in 2001. I know it was very hard for her; she couldn't understand the decision, and I still think she believes it is temporary, that I'll somehow "come back." She used to talk about how a single day can change your life, and that day did, but not because of my last recital. It was because of the party after at Paul and Mary's. I'd known them for most of my life, as they were Houstonian friends of Mom's. They owned a set of art galleries in London and Sydney, and an incredible one in Houston run by one of Mom's best friends. Paul and Mary didn't just live a fantasy like Mom; they led actual artistic lives at the extremely high end of the scale. I always saw them in London, and even stayed with them a few times in their former home near Holland Park when I needed a break from The Savoy. I often imagined living their life: shuttling between the few lucrative art galleries they owned in a few cities, and keeping a softer pace in life than what I was doing.

When they heard about my decision to stop playing, they insisted they needed to give a big farewell party. Mom would be staying with them anyway while I was at The Savoy. Since I'd last been in London, they had moved to a new home in Mayfair, and I was eager to see it. It was a former mews house, apparently enormous for central London. Inviting nearly a hundred people didn't deter them. Not many people besides royalty have space in London for that kind of party.

Though we never talked about it, I chose my final repertoire for Mom, pieces that I knew she would love, and which would in some way record the journey we'd had together at the piano. I wanted the Brahms Sonata to be the last thing I played. No encores; I put all the possible encores in the first half of the evening, which essentially became a series of vignettes of my musical life. For the few people who might find it meaningful, perhaps it was. Mom has never since talked about it with me, so I know it must have meant a lot to her. When that final D-flat major chord came and the audience erupted, it felt like a birth to me, and seemingly a death of sorts for her.

It took me a long time to leave the Royal Festival Hall, and I knew the party would be well under way by the time I got there. The ovation on stage went on for a while, which was lovely. I had to greet a lot of people backstage, including Mom, of course, and the various agents who had kept me going for so long. It also took a while to get to the car outside the stage door, as multiple dozens of people were waiting for autographs—many more than usual. Newspapers sent photographers to record me leaving the Royal Festival Hall for the last time. There was a lot of emotion swirling around all of us. I sent Mom off with the agents. Finally I was alone in the back of a car, heading slowly across Waterloo Bridge to Paul and Mary's place in Mayfair.

The new house, although crowded, was dazzling, far more so than their amazing home in Holland Park had been; most conversations were about what was upstairs. Lights and bookcases were recessed into dark wood walls; there were combinations of glass and mirrored walls; I could never quite tell what direction I was looking. The house was enormous, and spread up several flights. Ascending a glass staircase, I was handed a glass of champagne and congratulated by many. Various people who greeted me said Paul and Mary were "all the way upstairs." Arriving on the second floor, the third to an American, I encountered the source of all the downstairs conversations: the bottom of a large swimming pool that seemed to be hanging in the middle of the room. Through it I could see what was presumably the top floor, and more revelers standing around it another floor up. The room around the swimming pool seemed to be

Paul and Mary's personal art gallery. Each wall surrounding the pool contained a vast canvas, with a selection of sculptures between them. The undulations of the water spread across the room, filling it with a swirling hypnotic energy. I found the final staircase and was suddenly on the roof of the house, where forty or fifty more partiers were standing around the pool, and where I found Paul and Mary.

"I can't believe you are really going to stop, my dear," Mary said, Paul nodding in agreement. "I've never heard such gorgeous playing; you sounded just like you were a boy again." I thanked her for the party, and congratulated them both on their extraordinary home.

"We want you to meet someone, Joey," Paul said. "This is Ben. He's the artist we met in China who we are showing in our gallery here and in Sydney. We may try to bring him to Houston, too."

And there it was. Ninety minutes before that moment I had finished a vast piano career, historic to some, to the extent that any piano career is historic anymore. Yet it's the moment of meeting Ben, not my final recital, that has defined the memory. I relive that moment many times a day. The memory makes me joyous, angry, regretful, grateful; I've tried many times to do more than remember it, to actually relive it, but it eludes me. I can't conjure the feeling again; it is just the memory of a feeling.

It all happened quickly. Ben and I found a quiet corner of the rooftop and sat and talked for hours. Eventually Paul and Mary found us, the rest of the house having cleared out. "Stay as long as you like," Mary said. "We have to go to bed!" As they left and we all vowed to stay in touch; of all of the people in my life, I knew I would still see Paul and Mary. They'd known me since I was a child.

Ben was staying in the guest area of their house, but he suggested that he accompany me back to The Savoy. Ben was awed by my suite, and as I showed him the extraordinary view in every direction along the Thames, I noticed the janitors cleaning the Royal Festival Hall where only a few hours before I had played my last.

It had been months, as it happened, since I'd been touched by a man. I'd been too afraid, too busy, too distracted to act on anything. Sex was not a comfort to me in most of my career days; rather, it was a burden that I tended to ignore, or hire if I needed it. But sexually, Ben wasn't like any other man I'd been with. To him it wasn't about the act, wasn't about finishing; it was about connecting with me, about letting me feel what he felt. It was letting go, not an acquisition. He held me, silently, for a long time, lightly caressing my back, my neck, and my hair. Several times I tried to release his hold, but he kept me there, gently forcing my surrender. Eventually he took my face in his hands and just looked at me for a few minutes, silent, smiling, without hunger, just presence. He kissed me, gently at first, then with incredible force and passion, pushing me down on the bed.

I had no choice but to endlessly renew him, for there was no spending him. He entered me slowly, and stayed at that tempo, never removing his eyes from mine. I'll never forget his intensity that night, because it was that way every subsequent time we were together, times which now feel achingly brief. Men tend to get bored with sex quickly, but I never felt that way with Ben. When his desire deepened that night, his gaze left mine, and he turned me over. I could hear his breath in my ear, and the quietest mutterings he made as he drove into me with more passion. It was the night I supposedly gave up everything, yet I would give it all up again right now, and forever, to be with him in that way again.

WALD

ALTA

If I could have spent my whole life in Brenham with Giuseppe, occasionally coming to Houston only when necessary, I would have been a much happier woman. Gene had no interest in the country place at all, as to be cooped up with me was a dead-heat hell for both of us. The first thing I would do at the ranch, every single time, was get out for a long walk on the property. In the spring there were great vistas of wildflowers, grazing horses, deer, grouse, and a parallel world to ours of butterflies and scissor-tails dancing and giggling. The Texas hills are not the brooding forests of up north. There is little darkness to them, as the trees have endless space to stretch themselves out. It is the most perfectly peaceful place I know, and it is where I managed to acquire so much. Gene always thought I went up there and just sat. Heavens! Those days and sometimes weeks in Brenham were easily the happiest of my life. I am a terribly flawed person, more able to linger on difficult emotions than I should, and on perceived injustices and petty differences. In Brenham, I lost all of that, and the weight of my marriage lifted. There I was gracious and giddy, like the wind through the oaks.

Gene always complained about "my" music being repetitious, when of course it is anything but. Besides, I *need* repetition. We all need continuance. Gene, who listens constantly to country music, has a lot of nerve complaining about repetition. He is the man who lives his life in repetition. Every affair he's had has been almost an exact repeat of the last, and I remember them all. I still mull over whatever evidence I have.

The moment I read Gene's letter to Priscilla, I am back in the moment of it happening, more than forty years ago. Things he never said to me, promises, sexual vows. Why put myself through that? But I do. I've read that letter several times a year for two score. I hope this is not what has happened to my dear Joey. He won't tell me.

I've hired photographers in Sydney to follow him and photograph him from afar, just so I can see him. He looks haggard and unhappy, but I can't get him to tell me anything. We've lost trust in each other.

World Upside Down

JOEY

In my youth, this time of year was summer, a carefree time of heat and long days. Here in my new home all the way around the world, it is the opposite season, and leaves are blowing across the ground, or hanging on to trees that aren't native to this place, looking like blurry words. It is already 2:00 p.m. and the sun is low in the sky. If I drove right now to the Blue Mountains house, it would be dark by the time I got there.

In ninety minutes I will pick up Little Ben from school and take him home to Vaucluse, help him with homework, and put him to bed. Claire will come home long after that, tired, and fall into bed well after I've retired. I may swim in our downstairs pool—the most beautiful part of the house. When I tread water in the deep end, my favorite thing to do, I can look straight down Sydney Harbour to the bridge and opera house. Funny, I never go to the opera in Sydney, and have never been in the concert hall here. I know that various people know I am here, but I'm never invited, and in truth I don't care to go. That's all in my past now.

I don't read newspapers. How are my days being spent? I go to a coffee shop or two in Darlinghurst nearly every day, and I walk to some secluded park and write in my diary. I've done that most every weekday for years, since Ben left. Ben, what and *who* were you? Were you my Gene, or my mom? I can't figure out how and why you took me away from my life, how you got me to know myself by giving up myself. And why did you leave so soon? Where are you now? Will I ever see you again? Are you still alive?

At each departure we comfort ourselves with the belief we will be reunited; it is the only way we can bear the separation. But I fear my own truth: I think it is oblivion. I went, only once, as I could only bear its idea once, to *Tristan und Isolde* in Zurich. So many people talk about this being *the* great love story. The cast was amazing, but there was one problem: I couldn't hear my mother's voice in it; no matter the phrase, no matter the words, I couldn't hear her. It is the only piece of music I've ever heard in which she was silent.

The feeling of *Tristan*, the feeling of Wagner, was everywhere in Zurich, and it seeped into my life there whenever I visited, which was often, and there was only so much of it I could take. I played twenty-two concerts in the Tonhalle, twelve solo recitals and ten concerti, though I repeated the Brahms second concerto eight years apart, so it was actually nine. What was this *Tristan* feeling, this *Tristan* spirit? It's about the end of everything, the endless repetitive waiting for happiness, the nothingness that follows, the rest is silence. I tried many times to play Liszt's transcription of "Liebestod," the love-in-death-and-death-in-love aria that wafts the end of the opera away, but I could never do it. I could play the notes, of course, but I couldn't go in the direction of that music. I had to keep it distant.

A record producer once had the idea that I should record the entire works of Liszt. I agreed to the initial offer, except I told him I would have to leave out "Liebestod," a major omission, and that scrapped the project. Now I feel I should have just done it, because no one would have known how I felt about it, anyway, but at the time I couldn't be dishonest. These days dishonesty comes easily. There are secrets within the score of *Tristan* that we aren't supposed to know.

Eclipse

ALTA

Between Millie and Giuseppe I learned everything I've needed to know, but it was in teaching my son that I learned the most, which has always been difficult for me to understand because I didn't possess the knowledge of what I taught him. Millie and Giuseppe led me to the books I've loved. The passions they shared became my own. I now realize that Millie tried to get me to fix my life, to leave Gene and live with Giuseppe but I missed the truth of her message until it was too late. When I look back on her life, I see she tried to make me realize the extent of my unhappiness. But, as usual, I heard the words as she said them but didn't feel what she meant. How often in my life was everything completely obvious but the noticing of it took too long? Noticing something changes it: once Joey felt known, once his every movement was photographed and reported upon, his artistry changed. Is that what Joey felt when he decided to stop? He says that he got to a point where he'd had enough, but how can you possibly have enough of what you were born to do? Isn't that the same as having enough air or water? The light that is on you can eclipse the light you should generate.

Imaginary Land

JOEY

Loving Ben now feels like an imaginary land. Our time together has coalesced into one memory from our early years, long before Little Ben. The first session was long and intense, one that started early in the day with the plans, the insinuations, the enticements, the teases. Even when it began, it started slowly, with polite and small dominations when he got home. "Go in the bedroom and relax a bit," he started. His requests gradually became demands. "You will undress and wait for me for twenty minutes." Then, "You will prepare to be entered, and you will get back in bed to await my arrival."

Ben made the seductions last in those days. His quicker hungers only came later. As he slowly began kissing me, I noticed he had a tie in his hand; I assumed he'd just taken it off from the day. Then I noticed there were several, and he used them to tie my hands to the bed. Ben had, in those years, a thrilling smile, and I could feel his mischief and enjoyment that day. He must have touched every portion of my body before he entered me. At some point the necktie came loose from whatever he tied it to, and I pulled him closer to me, whispering to him, feeling his breath near mine. Then a special connection happened, for the first and only time. The light, wherever it came from, caught Ben's eye at precisely the right moment. Ben's eye and mine were gazing into each other but neither eye was ours; memory has formed his eye into a nebula, a little world. For an instant I could see it, for the smallest of moments, just before that minutest of worlds closed down and he released himself into me. Did Ben see it, too? I will always believe he did.

SPEAK, VOLTAIRE

ALTA

G ene used to say I was always in some crisis of faith, but I wasn't. I've never once had a doubt about faith; but I've had huge doubts about the people I've chosen to have in my life. I think it is absolutely false to let religion form a basis for your life, but faith is a different matter. That is not conditioning or brainwashing or any of the things they tell us now. People speak about it so freely in these millennial days, and I don't think that is right. It was good for us to have some limits to what we could say. Life was better when there were a few more boundaries around what was and wasn't talked about.

I think theology is a waste of time, but faith, the ability to see and absorb beauty one may not understand, what could possibly be more important for the world, more usable for us all? Beauty is something that can be readily spent and is always in short supply. There is no end to our need for it, yet we whisk it out of our lives with no thought or care.

You see, when I was younger and would go to a play, film, opera, or ballet, and if I really loved it, it would live with me, become a part of me. I take on an artwork's rhythms forever, not just for a few days like a fad, but *always*. I absorb its vocabulary into my own. I empathize with the characters, particularly if they are close to me, and they live in me always. This is surely what art is for; not for that detestable word *entertainment*, but to be absorbed. Did the great creations emanate from the mind of man simply to divert us from actually living? I cannot accept that. The great works *are* life.

I believe Will Durant saved my life. My passageway to him was Giuseppe, of course. Our first night together in New York, when we were in midtown having a late dinner and talking endlessly, he mentioned the six volumes of Will and Ariel Durant's *Story of Civilization* already published at that time, and he relayed them with such passion and energy that I eventually read them. I had plenty of time in the coming months, being pregnant and having my life turned into a silent prison by my parents. I never imagined that a mind could conceive of such a thing as a history of *civilization*, but how gorgeous and artistic was the prose! Oh my—those Durant volumes sitting on my shelf in South Boulevard are among my most precious holdings. Do you think I could ever engage Perry or Gene in a conversation about *Our Oriental Heritage* or *Caesar and Christ*, much less get them to conceive of the Reformation? Ridiculous. I awaited each subsequent year of publication with such expectation. The books would arrive and I would spend hours each day buried in them—and each marked a milestone in my life that I have forever associated with it: *The Age of Reason Begins*, in 1961, I read despite having two toddlers. I could only read during their naps so it took me forever but I did it, and loved it; I associate it with their growth. *The Age of Voltaire* was my favorite of the millions of words the Durants wrote, and I can't count how many times I've read it since. It is a work of beauty that constantly renews itself in my life. Voltaire was, for me, the greatest figure in history, and Giuseppe was *my* Voltaire: noble, courageous, innovative, but mine—a fighter for freedom.

BELLE REVE

ALTA

I never kept a diary, except for the fateful New York trip. But I used to love to make diaries of women I admired. All fiction, of course, and I imagine in retrospect that I could have probably made a career as a writer. The great *why* of my life is why I've only noticed things after they happen. Why was I never once able to experience something and tell the truth about it as it was happening? Not that I lied. Not at all. But I honestly didn't understand *anything* while it was happening—not Joey's successes, his early retirement, not Giuseppe's death, not even my own affairs with men, which paled in comparison to my husband's but in an important way mine were worse. Gene never loved another woman, while I absolutely did love another man and never loved my own husband.

As much as I live for the arts, and I love so much of it, I cannot bear the plays of Tennessee Williams. So many people I've known have tried to compliment me by saying I reminded them of Amanda Wingfield or Blanche DuBois…and I've even been told—with glee (!)—that I sounded like I was in *Summer and Smoke* or, God help the world, *Orpheus Descending*. I sat through every one of those monstrosities when they were new. *The Glass Menagerie* has beautiful moments, but none of them involve Amanda, and I am most certainly nothing like her. She pushes her children, but not in the way I do. And Blanche DuBois! What a sniveling nincompoop she is, a collection of lies, and I cannot bear people who lie.

SOUTH BOULEVARD

JOEY

I was undoubtedly more tired than I knew by the time I arrived home to Houston after the last London recital. It was the kind of tired that feels like a loosening of the moorings that keep death at bay. South Boulevard. Mom. All those memories shaded by live-oak trees. She was subdued upon my arrival, though it had been years since I'd been to Houston, and it seemed no less bizarre to me. It was my home, my ancestry, and most of the things I'd ever learned in my life were learned there, yet it had never felt like a *real* place to me, outside of the small few idyllic blocks where I grew up. The city has little enclaves of sweet beauty hidden in its vast flatness, but largely Houston is a sprawling nightmare of decay and dilapidation. So little aesthetic thought went into any public decisions about the city that it is easy to unfairly transfer that lack of care onto the people who inhabit it. Houston is, and always has been, an extraordinary community of artists and interesting people, and I'm sure that has been the only thing that has kept Mom alive in the place for all these years.

Mom had a big garage apartment, the size of many people's homes, where she generally lodged a university student, but she decided to put me there for a while, not knowing how long I would be around, and I welcomed the chance to be home. She thought it would give me more privacy. I accepted the idea even as it clashed with my thoughts from the end of the London concert that I would soon be returning to my childhood bedroom. The garage apartment was Spartan: white walls with no art anywhere, and so quiet. I fell into the deepest sleep I'd had in months, and when I awoke it was already dark. I took a moment I'd not taken earlier: out the window was my childhood pool where Perry and I played for entire summers; across the lawn I could see Mom in the kitchen talking to a few people, presumably Perry and his family, whom I'd not seen in months. I wasn't quite prepared for the big conversations about why I'd done what I did, so I unpacked and waited for them to leave.

My cousin Perry was the closest feeling I had to having a brother. I thought of Ben and what had happened a few days before. Perry used to take advantage of my attraction to him. Did Perry ever meet anyone, man or woman, who wasn't attracted to him? But Perry was sweet that night, actually, softened from the last time I'd seen him, which had been years. I couldn't remember how many. He actually asked me a question about my decision to stop playing, which was a big step for him.

In my little kitchen, Mom had left a bunch of food. She knew I probably wouldn't leave the apartment for a while, and I didn't. Not long after a bite, I feel asleep again and woke at dawn, when I finally ventured outside. It was an incredibly beautiful morning. I walked over to Rice University, where a few joggers were starting their day around the track. The great expanse of the medical center looked twice the size of when I last saw it. I walked a little beyond it, over the big commercial street of Holcombe Boulevard, and then a circuitous route home. By the time I got back, Mom was awake.

"So, what now?" she said. I filled her in on the various things that had happened in New York, and about my decision to sell the properties.

"Where will you live?"

I told her I didn't know yet, and that I needed some time to figure it out.

"You know you can stay here as long as you like. Surely you will want to teach piano." I told her I would probably never touch a piano again, and would certainly not teach.

"I see," was all she said that day.

"There is a show opening tomorrow night at Paul and Mary's gallery, which I expect you would enjoy, if you feel up to it. A lot of people will be happy to see you there. We could go together."

"Are they here?" I asked, since I had just seen Paul and Mary a few days before on another continent.

"They are flying in privately. They only fly privately now."

"Gallery must be doing well."

I went. I can still hardly believe the moment I walked in there. The artist whose work was being featured and sold was Ben, and there he was greeting me at the door. We'd been so wrapped up in each other in London, and all he knew was that I was flying to New York the next day; I guess I didn't tell him the rest. We'd talked about my childhood during our night together in London, but he had no idea our paths were going to coincide again so soon. We'd talked about so much that night, but we missed this strange piece of the immediate puzzle.

"I guess this solves the problem of when we are going to see each other next," he said. I asked where he was staying and how long he would be here and if he would come home and stay with me, and too many other questions. "Slow down, cowboy," he said in his wonderfully unique accent: his native Chinese mixed with full Australian brogue. "I'm here for now and we will figure it all out." He needed to greet more of the people who'd come there to buy his art.

I was already associating Ben with loss, with something that might be taken away, and though I experienced no terror about ending my career, I was suddenly frozen with it about a man I barely knew yet knew as well as I'd known anyone.

Was Ben as charming and effortless with any man as he had been with me? Would a life with him simply be wondering who was next in line? Did he subtly collect conquests? It didn't seem so, then or now, but the questions remain even in the face of clear answers. Ben was at the garage apartment two hours later, and he stayed for two days. Mom didn't seem to mind. She basically left us alone.

COUNTRY
ALTA

My parents finally accepted that I had to pursue a music education degree in order to work, whether or not I had a child, so I convinced them that I could do in the summer months at Baylor if I stayed at our family ranch in Chappell Hill. When Joey was a baby, that's what I did, and Mother actually helped: she kept little Joey for three summers. Little did she know that Joey's father had quietly moved himself to Brenham, Texas, where he was commuting to both College Station and Austin to teach piano. The secret worked.

BALLADES

JOEY

The current silence of my days has afforded me unexpected revelations. When one's world goes from chaos to silence, everything is symbolism, so the smallest things take on meaning. So much about a music career prevents it from being more successful, more rewarding, more ennobling. I'm so often unhappy and dissatisfied with things, feelings I really dislike having, but they appear. I feel now like I am in some vast waiting room, as though all of my life was leading to something, like an account waiting to be filled, used, and filled again. Is my mind so poor and disjointed, or does more mindfulness and thoughtfulness make you notice more, injustices more exposed, more possibilities sought? Surely then it must also bring more peace, more joy and laughter at the absurdity of it all, but that hasn't come. So much now feels like exhaustion, like I am winding down. My mind is not often enough at peace, which makes me not sleep, and the cycle perpetuates. I have great fears of looking back on a meaningless life. I've seen so much disillusionment, so many who looked back and didn't like what they saw.

We draw closest to us that which we most fear, yet I often wander into piano recitals here in the city, those of students. They have no idea I'm there, of course, but I love hearing them, love being in the same room as the instrument again. Just yesterday I walked into the end of a master's recital at the Conservatorium, the Chopin G-minor *Ballade*, and had a completely fulfilling relationship with it again. How is that possible? The poor student struggled with all but its least-daunting passages. I have amassed a great deal of knowledge about that *Ballade*, so why am I content to hold that for myself? I should at least be giving it away, helping unlock it for someone else. I took no pleasure in the student's attempts to play this extraordinary statement, yet my memories of playing Chopin all over the world understood themselves as joy.

I walked out of the Conservatorium and out onto the promontory above the opera house. There's a long street, Bennelong, between Government House and the opera house. It is one of my secret places in Sydney. It is surprising that there are rarely many people there, considering it is so close to such a tourist attraction. But it is fairly hidden away by stairs and it feels inaccessible if you don't know it is there. There are so many of these unforgettable corners in Sydney, and it will always be magic for me in how unexpected they are. Like passing through Rose Bay on the way to the eastern suburbs with the harbor constantly pulling your focus, and suddenly there is that turn to Bondi and the street is just sublimely warm and inviting; you sometimes can't believe how beautiful that street is, but the native Sydney people don't even notice. Or the drive down to Coogee from Tamarama, when suddenly the whole beach is splayed out in front you. What a joy.

The price of the things we desire is the display of something like truth, and that is more weighted than I imagined. I had been buoyed through life, and my thoughts never turned to those who did the lifting. I'm not thinking of Mother now, because the life I complained about was simply her dream, and even now I can't bear to talk to her about it. I have, in recent years, finally had the time to read some extraordinary things, yet what I will do with this knowledge is not yet known to me.

This morning, in a little park near Mosman, I sifted through Goethe, "Behaviour is a mirror in which everyone shows his image." I look back on years of unyielding bitchiness, hubris, and such speed; so many colleagues who were intemperate and mean. I adopted the mannerisms and syntax of the person who taught me, and that was solely my mother, so there became no way for me to separate the two. Performance brings out the best of some and the worst of others, and in a rather rudderless and searching time as ours, there will inevitably be some people of dubious quality who rise to the surface. I'd never thought of myself as one of those, but perhaps in identifying others as *other*, I am. Each of us must do our small part for integrity, and I did mine by quitting. Life is too tremulous to allow the people who mirror their worst to control it. So much in our little classical corner of the world is simply fear—of irrelevance, of not being heard—mostly just a fear of being wrong.

Verdi Prati
ALTA

Brenham and Chappell Hill were paradise for me and Giuseppe because no one knew us. In those days few people had second homes, and the few people around us in Brenham just assumed we were a married couple from Houston who were trying an experiment with a weekend home, not at all the commonplace it became later with the next big boom. Our family ranch in Chappell Hill was but ten minutes from Giuseppe's home in Brenham, so it was easy for us to be together. We spent all of our time at the ranch, and we were completely safe there because none of my family had any interest in the ranch. This always baffled me. Gene would get bored. Mother associated the ranch with the loss of Daddy, so I guess I inherited my love for the place from him. One could see no neighbors from our house, just miles of gently rolling hills of endless beauty, gracious trees, and a lively stream running alongside the house. Within, there was a beautiful piano that Giuseppe would play. I think the ranch is the one place he was never scared of.

Giuseppe's own house was modest, a couple of blocks off the town square in Brenham, a town with little to recommend it besides quaintness; but for me it was paradise, the setting of the only absolute happiness of my life. The many days we spent there gave me the perfect secret to keep from Gene and my mother. I earned that secret. Gene bedded every woman he could, yet when I said something to that effect to Mother, she would look at me like I had two heads. She never believed me, and I'm not sure why. I suppose it was because Daddy did the same; at least that is what friends used to tell me. Mother never confronted what was more convenient to ignore.

I did have my best girlfriends, especially Sally and Mary Jane, but not even they knew about Brenham. All they knew about Giuseppe was what happened in New York. Houston in those days was so small, at least in our little neighborhood, we all knew what each other was up to. Sally, Mary Jane, and I shared every moment of our marriages, so they knew all about Gene's antics. That man didn't get away with anything, but he didn't know I knew all of it. I knew the times, the hotels, the afternoons in bedrooms in River Oaks, the trips to New Orleans, the business trips, the secretaries—all of it.

But nobody knew anything about Brenham or the pure peace and joy I felt there. If only I could have found the courage to leave behind my life in Houston and just defy them all and lived with Giuseppe. But I didn't. I would have lost my young boys if I'd tried.

Joey deserves more than just spilling out my life to explain his. He didn't quit because he was weak; he stopped playing because he was just scared of it all, I guess. I can't imagine that he's happy now, but he's had more courage in his life than five of me. He got out there on that stage when he was a little boy, something I don't have the nerves for even now.

I want to help people understand Joey's talent and career, but that will surely mean revealing everything about my own life that I don't care to talk about. I don't mind my family knowing about it now, but it diminishes his accomplishment if they know that he was taught by his own father, who was himself an incredibly accomplished pianist. Joey didn't come out of nowhere, but he also didn't come through the traditional pathways, so none of the establishment, who spent years trying to figure out where he came from, can now figure out why he stopped. Even I, an insider, could never believe how suspicious they always are of anyone who comes through from outside their system. They want to own and control every aspect of every talent, from identification to success. Joey was felt by them to be somebody who slipped through the cracks of a system they had so tenaciously put together over years and years. But still, Joey rose and thrived. It was always incredible to me that he did. There will be an assumption that I know his reasons for stopping, but I don't. Is it as simple as him being handed the life I was forced to give up, and I had to give it up before I even knew if I had it?

SOUTH BANK

JOEY

That final London recital was a year behind me by the time I decided to fly back to London for the first time to see Ben again. We'd not seen each other in almost a year, and I wasn't sure what he was doing even though we talked every day. We certainly communicated a lot through Paul and Mary, whom I saw frequently, as they were in and out of Houston as well as London and Sydney, where Ben lived.

Ben had asked me something no one had ever asked: why did I choose London for my final recital? London was a place that, historically, was a great presenter of music but not the originator of it. Those cities were Vienna, Prague, Paris…but not London. Tanglewood was the place I owed my last recital, but that just wasn't practical for when I needed it to happen. Of all of the places in the world I played, London was the city of the world for me. I always felt at home there, felt a part of history, felt something greater going on around me.

I never tired of the cab ride from Gatwick or Heathrow into whichever London hotel I was booked in, nearly always the very grand Savoy or the sweet and small Milestone, near Kensington Palace. I generally stayed in the Milestone for long trips, anything more than four days, or else in The Savoy, whose staff knew me well, as I was there sometimes six or seven times a year. The beds at The Savoy were an earthly heaven. I slept a type of sleep in the embrace of those beds unlike any rest elsewhere in the world. The Savoy was, strangely, not opulent, even though it was a Grand Hotel, at least it wasn't before the renovation when I most often stayed there. It was elegant, quiet, and beautifully understated; best of all, they respected my overwhelming need for silence. They would keep the vacuum cleaners off my floor when I was there, which I particularly loved. My favorite suite there, on the northeast corner, had a staggering view of London, which I will never tire of seeing. If I sit in the gorgeous chair in my memory right now, I can see it all again: Waterloo Bridge, St. Paul's Cathedral, Blackfriars, Westminster, Lambeth, Charing Cross, the faceless National Theatre, whose architecture is entirely indoors and alive; and, most important for my life, the Royal Festival Hall.

If cruising the Thames, in the old-fashioned sense, you would not have noticed the place; it is an unimportant, uninteresting block of concrete and glass. Only a committee devoted to utility could conjure such a building, but the jewels it housed were beyond imagining: first, the quartet of great London exceptional orchestras—London Philharmonic, the Philharmonia, the Sinfonietta, and the Orchestra of the Age of Enlightenment—each of which I played with; and second, the memories of Duke Ellington, Rubenstein, Heifetz, Piaf, Fitzgerald, and Horowitz that still lingered there.

That flight back to London to see Ben was portentous. He had flown off to Sydney. I was planning to stay at Paul and Mary's for a few days of rest before joining Ben in Australia, possibly for good. I finally fell asleep several hours into the flight. We had left in the late afternoon and flown into the darkening east. I'd always loved watching the first vestiges of the day arrive, flying that direction. At that point we were still a couple of hours from Heathrow.

I didn't have any immediate panic when we hit the first patch of rough air. I had flown thousands of times, so I'm not easily undone by a little bumping around. I ordered a double Scotch, but by the time it arrived, it like the plane itself was expanding and tautly hovering over a precipice. The pressure seemed to increase, like a wire stretched with an unseen weight. The rocking forward and side to side wasn't normal turbulence; it was a lingering in midair for what felt like many minutes. Then whatever we had been unknowingly waiting for came: it felt like the gates of hell opened. It was what dying must feel like if you aren't ready for it. The plane jerked so violently laterally, then vertically, and all of the contents hurled around us. I had experienced several sizable earthquakes in Los Angeles, Tokyo, and Santiago, but this flight was worse than all of them. The violence caused many on the plane to scream. I heard people praying. I remember wondering who I would pray to. Maybe Beethoven, since he had conceived of music that felt to me like this weather, long before anyone conceived of traveling in the air. Faced with the moment of ending all of it, I thought of Beethoven. I looked out the window and could see the sun rising. We were in clear air. The shaking went on.

The captain came on several times to tell us to remain calm and stay buckled up. People began vomiting. When we finally leveled off, the sun was fully up. The captain spoke to us again, and he strained to find the calming tone pilots usually take when trying to explain something difficult. In thirty years of flying, he said, he had never experienced Category 5 turbulence, and there might have been some damage to the aircraft so he was going to have us land at Shannon Airport in Ireland. We were starting our descent there as he spoke. He couldn't tell us when or if we would get to Heathrow that day.

We descended into calmer air, and as the news dawned on everyone, the recriminations began. My seatmate, who had not said a word to me up to that point, starting cursing the airline for the meeting he was sure to miss in London. The woman behind me in first class, who only ten minutes before had been praying to her savior, loudly cursed her circumstances. My seatmate asked me what I did for a living and I didn't want to get into it with him, so for some reason I still cannot fathom I told him I was an airline pilot. I should have just told him I was a pianist, because the moment he found out I was a pilot he tried to implicate me in us landing in Ireland. "Why can't he just take us on to Heathrow, for fuck's sake? Can't you talk to him?" I was so tired and so buzzed from the Scotch that I really didn't want to get into a fight with the guy, who had turned aggressive after being docile and quiet through the flight. I gingerly offered that perhaps it was best for us to be safe than to possibly crash somewhere before getting to London.

"Bullshit!" he exclaimed. "And you know it! We're flying now, aren't we? We can fly forty-five more fucking minutes and get to Heathrow! Jesus Christ!"

My attempts to appease him didn't work. We quickly descended to Shannon, and my seatmate asked me if the landing was normal, thinking I would know. I made up some definition of the type of landing we were making, coming in faster than normal because this really was an emergency—safety has to be paramount—anything to shut him up. And then we landed without event.

It was a busy morning at Shannon, as usual, and I sought my favorite restaurant in the airport, which was nothing great but at least I knew it, in the hopes of escaping as many of my bitching fellow passengers, all of which intensified when we discovered that none of us would get to Heathrow until early evening, and we would be spending the day in the airport. All other flights to London, we were told curtly, were sold out. I settled down in a forgotten corner of the airport with a book to wait out the day, hoping I had lost my toxic seatmate for good.

As the sun we'd all seen rise that morning was finally setting behind us, we landed in London. I escaped the passport lane and customs as quickly as possible. Since this was my first trip back to London in a long time, I couldn't be sure how I would feel, so I picked up a rental car in case I needed to escape into the countryside at some point. I had always loved driving in England, Australia, New Zealand, and Hong Kong, all the "left side" places. It never felt unnatural to me, though on that particular dark and rainy night, with exhaustion burgling anything that felt like me, I took no joy in passing the sights that used to give me great joy as I entered central London: Cromwell Road, the Victoria and Albert Museum, the heady shops of Knightsbridge, where men's shop owners used to address me by name when I would enter; the old-world Goring Hotel, glimpsed just off to the right, where I'd had so many wonderful nights with friends; Buckingham Palace, of course, and the Victoria Memorial, barely noticed any longer. I drove up the hill toward Wellington Arch, pissed that I'd forgotten where I was going. Why didn't I take Kensington High Street and Kensington Road that night, along the park?

Anyway, I wearily made my way up Park Lane nearly to Oxford Street and, to my surprise, found Paul and Mary's mews road house, where the party that changed my life had happened. I entered the code into the courtyard door, which immediately and silently opened wide enough for two cars, quickly closing behind me as I drove into the enormous courtyard. I had never been so tired.

The key that Paul and Mary had given me was still in my pocket. Twenty-four hours had passed since I left Houston, twice the time it should have taken, but at last I had arrived. As I clicked the key clockwise and the door separated from its frame, a deafening alarm went off. They'd given me a code for the courtyard gate, but not the door to the house, so I had no idea how to stop it. The alarm must have been heard all over London! It was high and piercing, accompanied by pulsating lights that I could see all over the house and courtyard. Every minute the alarm would alter to something lower and louder, and then return to the high screeching squawks. I found a keypad near the door and another in the kitchen, and frantically entered the courtyard code, but the alarm kept increasing.

I heard banging on the courtyard door, but I couldn't figure out how to open it, as there was no keypad for it inside that I could find. There was a small side door which, when I managed to open it, revealed a woman in a nightdress screaming, "You must turn off that horrendous noise. My husband needs his rest! How can you be so inconsiderate?"

I tried to explain to her what was happening, and to ask for her help, but she would not be quiet long enough to hear me. As the alarm escalated, I was just about to close the door on her when I saw the police turn onto the mews lane from Park Lane. They demanded my identification, which I provided, and asked me what was happening, which I explained. The alarm continued notching itself up in dynamics and intensity.

I explained that I had not broken in and I showed them the key, which they tested in the doorway. I told them I simply didn't know the code to turn the alarm off.

"Call the owners," they said. I explained that they were hiking in Mongolia and it would be impossible to reach them. "Well, you're going to have to do something or we'll cut off the electricity to this home to shut it down. Can you call the alarm company?"

I explained that I had done that already, but they were unable to help without the code. I tried to reach Ben but couldn't.

"Are there any numbers written around any of the telephones?" the police asked. "Perhaps someone will know the code."

Good idea, I thought, and sure enough there were a number of regularly called numbers next to the telephone in the kitchen. I started phoning them. By then it was nearing midnight, so I woke the first three people I called, each of whom sleepily told me they had no idea what the code was, or "no-fucking-idea-mate-do-you-know-fucking-time-it-is?" in one case. I dialed the fifth or sixth number and an officious female voice said, "Yes?" wide awake.

"Do you happen to know the security code at Paul and Mary's house?" I inquired through clenched teeth.

She immediately said, "Pangaea. P-A-N-G-A-E-A."

I was about to ask her what it meant and why when she hung up. I hoped I had written it down correctly. I raced to the keypad, typed it in, and the aural abuse ceased. Silence. Blessed wonderful silence. The police seemed satisfied by this and left. I was finally alone in a quiet place. Luggage, I remembered. I should get my luggage from the car.

I took the car keys and returned to the quiet of the courtyard to retrieve my luggage, but a few steps out of the house I heard a click behind me. The door. I had locked the house keys in the house, along with my wallet and cell phone. The police were gone. I was alone in the courtyard. Perhaps, I thought, if I went out the small front door and keyed the code into the pad, the doors would open and I could at least drive to a hotel for the night and sort it out the next daytime. I propped the door open to try the keypad. Nothing. Did I have the wrong code? I second-guessed myself. The code was, of course, on my phone that was locked in the house. It was late. No one around. Wind picking up. No, that did not just happen. The wind did not just close the door to the street. I was officially locked out now, with nowhere to stay in London, no car, no identification, no keys. And it was cold and windy.

The Savoy wasn't too far, I thought. I'd walk to The Savoy and they would help me. After all, I knew everyone there.

I walked. It was farther than I remembered. Brook Street. Handel's house. Grosvenor Square. Berkeley Square. Rats in alleyways off Bruton Street. Hadn't I once been at a party on Albemarle Street near here? Regent Street. Piccadilly, where I felt like just another one of the indigents and, well, at that moment I was. The Haymarket Theatre, where I'd seen so many wonderful plays, and there was a memory of Handel again, though I don't think it is the same spot. I read about it somewhere. Can't remember. I was so tired. The back of the National Gallery. The London Coliseum. St. Martin-in-the-Fields…the Strand…and finally I dragged myself into The Savoy. Please, I thought, let someone recognize me. It was so late and I was so tired.

I explained my predicament to the man at the front desk. I asked him to check the hotel records, which must surely show the hundreds of thousands of dollars I'd spent there over the years. "Yes, welcome back," he said. "I see you've been a longtime client here."

I felt so relieved, but it wasn't to last long. "But sir, I'm not sure there is anything I can do without my manager and, as you can see, it is well past 1:00 in the morning. I certainly don't want to put you out on the street. Can I get you some water? You are looking a little pale."

I remember feeling faint when I heard a voice having just entered the hotel.

"Joey? What the hell are you doing here? You look awful."

At that point I must have fainted.

The next thing I recall is waking up the next morning naked in the unforgettable comfort of The Savoy beds, the best in the world. The room was still dark but I could tell it was light outside. Someone was in the bathroom.

"You gave us all quite a fright last night, there, Joey. Here I was, without knowing where in the world you were, why you stopped, if you were starting again…all of the biggies. I had just mentioned you at dinner after my recital, and I got back here to the hotel and you fucking fainted at my feet when I say hello! I mean, can you fucking believe it? The maître d'hotel (you didn't think we still used that word, did you?) told me what happened so I brought you up here. I took your clothes off but I assure you, nothing else happened."

I slowly realized it was Donald.

"Pianists have to take care of each other—and I figured you'd had a hard enough night."

I thanked him for helping me and told him I'd quickly pay him back.

"No problem, my friend! I have to run out to a breakfast meeting but I do have a surprise for you. On your bedside table is an extra key to Paul and Mary's place."

"Why do you have a key to their place?"

"They gave it to me in case I needed a place to stay in London. But this is such a quick trip for me that I decided to just slip into The Savoy. Imagine—we might have been there together! I'm amazed at all the coincidences that have brought us together over the years. No hard feelings about some of the stuff you did! See you later!"

Yes, coincidences. Before I could inquire any further, he was out the door with a quick farewell. Suddenly I was alone, again, in a Savoy hotel room. I lifted my exhausted body to the window and pulled the heavy curtain aside. There it all was, a lifetime of memories for me, associations, all just as they had been before I encountered them, unchanged by me or anyone else. It was a beautiful morning. Royal Festival Hall just across the river. I wondered what was rehearsing that day. The National Theatre flashing a sign for *As You Like It*. Westminster. Lambeth. I showered with the luxurious Molton Brown products provided, their old scents bring back many preperformance showers—suddenly music was in my head that I hadn't thought of in years. Then my mind was flooded with postsexual showers, all from a passing scent.

Famished, I ordered a huge room-service breakfast, without the slightest pang of guilt about making Donald pay for it. He'd saved me the night before, but I'd handed him his career, so I called it square.

Soon I was retracing my steps back to Paul and Mary's armed with Donald's key. There was my rental car in the courtyard. Despite thousands of recitals and concerts, perhaps the most nervous moment of my life was putting that key in the lock that day, hoping the alarm would not be magically resurrected. I clicked the lock and entered the silent house. My luggage was still just inside the door. I lifted it to go in search of my bedroom somewhere upstairs in their vast home.

I hadn't seen the place since the night of the party. There were all the familiar works of art I remembered from their other homes I'd visited. I deposited my luggage and decided I would have a swim in the famous pool on the top of the house. I relived the party again and again, particularly climbing the stairs to the level where the bottom of the pool fills the room. Even in the silence, it remained a staggering sight, seeing it for the first time in daylight. I'd forgotten that you could see all the way through the pool to the other side of the room. Something wasn't right, I thought, peering to the far end of the pool from the top of the stairs. I slowly walked toward it. At the shallow end of the pool there was a man. Stillness. Was there to be no end to what this house would put in front of me? Wouldn't a dead body float on the top, I thought? This man was crouched as if sitting on an invisible underwater throne. He wasn't moving at all. I approached the glass. I was directly behind him. There was no movement in the water, so he had been still like this for a very long time.

I stared at the man, mesmerized, and was looking to find the courage to walk up one more flight to see what was actually going on. Or should I call the police? What if I saw the same officers as last night? What to do?

With no warning, the man darted underwater and was face to face with me. I screamed—then recognized Ben. My scream turned into laughter as I ran up the stairs to greet him.

"What the fuck?" I yelled at him as he swam toward me. I leaned down to kiss him. He pulled me into the pool, clothes and all. He took all my clothes off as he kept kissing me. I kept trying to ask him what he was doing there, how he'd gotten there, why he hadn't told me he was coming, but Ben would allow no talking. He stripped himself and threw our clothes onto the pool deck. "We'll be seen," I said. He didn't care. He sat me on the side of the pool with my legs still in the water. His mouth was on me in no time, but he knew, always, how to make it be pure ecstasy, and how to take me to the edge of what I could bear.

"Have you gotten off since you left Houston?" he asked.

I told him I hadn't. I will never understand how he did it, how he could bring my body to the brink with just a couple of words. It wasn't just sensations on my cock—even a modest gay guy can provide those. This was a pulling apart of everything that could be felt as me, suspending it in midair and bringing it all back just before it might break. When I finally released after what felt like thirty minutes, I began to sob. Ben pulled me back into the pool and held me, telling me that he'd also released, solely from the pleasure he'd given me minutes before.

"I think you needed that," he said.

BREVITIES

ALTA

Anyone seriously delving into a book about Joey will want to answer a simple question: how did Gene not know about Joey's father, about Giuseppe? The truth is no less true for being quite unbelievable: he never asked. I was intimate with Gene for a short time; we were at most a collection of brevities. Giuseppe was my unquestioned extension of life, but Gene never knew about him. Then there was Tom, whom neither Gene nor Giuseppe knew about. I can't tell you how these realities fight with how I planned to live my life, and how utterly at odds my actions are with my religious convictions. Gene never physically excited me, but I always felt him *attempting to love*, almost yearning to feel something for me or anyone, in those moments before he was close to release. I loved him for the surface of his attempt, even when he was humiliating me. That he never succeeded in loving should not overshadow his desire to fleetingly try. The will to love overshadows everything. I was so unmoored through the whole of my young life that I had no one I could talk to about any of this. I could not take my problems to a priest and confess double adultery, could I? Nor could I have left Giuseppe up in the country all alone pining for me.

I envied Joey's sexual life, as I know that after he was out from the clutches of Perry I think he had quite a good time. I worried about him being alone all those years, but now he has his Ben and they certainly seemed a pile of sex. Now he has made me a grandmother of sorts, I guess. I don't know quite what to do with that information, because I was not party to anything emotional about it. I was informed, over the phone, of a surrogacy—hardly the kind of romance one needs to feel like a grandmother. I envied Joey because he seemed to love sex so much. I did, too, most of the time, but it also seemed to cause no end of problems in my life. It didn't occur to me that Giuseppe and I were having sex in New York; it sounds so ordinary. I certainly wasn't raped, as my mother's narrative constantly told. I simply gave myself to a feeling of possibility, and I loved being close to him, loved hearing and seeing him feel the kind of pleasure he felt.

I was well into my forties before I had a truly spiritual orgasm, something that caused me enormous shame for a long time. The truth is, it simply never occurred to me that there should be something more. Oh, some of the movies in those years sounded exactly like my own feelings, and a few lines could have been uttered in my own life—"It went flat when I told it to. I didn't think to ask for more" when Eleanor of Aquitaine is asked in *The Lion in Winter* if the English Channel had parted for her crossing. How I loved that. Eleanor's character was closer to me, something I wanted to scream at every moron who told me later that I reminded them of Aurora, though I had no fondness for the eccentric personality of Miss Hepburn, Katharine of Arrogance. I wasn't among the Kate cult, much as I loved so many of her movies. I assumed I would empathize with her living with someone else's husband for so many years, but I found it unseemly somehow, which has always been curious to me, for how was I any different?

Little Joey didn't seemed traumatized by Perry, even though I know Perry caused his share of horrible anxiety in anyone who encountered his sexual force. I'm not a woman who trivializes the forcing of sex on another. There were certainly plenty of times with Gene when I didn't want to do it, but though none of my friends ever believed me, he never forced me. Perry forced Joey, I feel sure, and I took no serious steps to stop it because I could see Joey more clearly during those times, perhaps because I knew it was going on and I was keeping a better eye on him. But the big change I noticed was in his playing. He made a huge leap, musically, in those months, and I felt Perry was helping somehow, even though I knew he was too aggressive, too demanding on his younger cousin who in love's architecture was a brother. I knew it couldn't be sustained, but I knew I could *hear* it, and I felt at some level that it gave Joey confidence. If Joey got out, which he did, he wouldn't have to worry about it, and that's what happened.

In those early years of his career, playing the piano and sexual energy were almost the same thing to Joey. It wasn't all that nonsense about "making love" to a piano that I occasionally read in some of those ridiculous articles or reviews, but he did connect with something elemental in the playing of music, all with an underlying fountain of elegance. I could give him my voice at the piano, but I couldn't give him anything else because I didn't have it to give away.

Giuseppe was so caring and tender on that first night in New York. When we didn't see each other for a while after that, even with all the turmoil gathering around me, I missed it. I missed him, of course, but what I actually missed what his touch. When we did finally begin to see each other again, our time was so limited and so special that I didn't think about my own pleasure. I wanted to be sure he was brought to full pleasure; I never worried about myself. But Giuseppe, true to every other moment we had together, wanted to find out if I'd ever experienced the fullest pleasure, and he took it upon himself to take me there. By the time he moved to Brenham, little Joey was nearly ten, and it was there on my family's ranch in Chappell Hill that Giuseppe became the first and only man to take me over that extraordinary cliff that others seemed to access so easily. It took, of course, our lifetimes together, not solely the contents of those sublime hours, but because he found a pathway to the most ecstatic tension and release available to a woman, and he took me there continuously for the rest of our lives. I felt disembodied, being slowly removed from myself and taken to the threshold of some unknowable abyss where I was both alone and with him. Yet I was always brought back safely into his arms just before I might have disappeared. I found safety in what was nearly dangerous.

Giuseppe might have had other women before he moved to Texas—I really don't know—but I firmly believe he was true to me. He never demanded that I leave Gene; we never talked about it. He was happy with what time we could have together, and it made it more special to him that it was rare. I had years of guilt, confessed to no one, over him moving to Texas when I knew it wasn't what he wanted. But Giuseppe was so gifted that he could be at home with his art anywhere, including a thoughtless little nothing place like Brenham. Our whole life together was in those few square miles, other than those weeks in New York when he trained Joey. Joey has never asked me about him again, and they were never knowingly in the same place. My great love was never in my Houston home. We never risked the lifting of our secrecy. There was so much that neither of us ever did. The love of my life was a melancholy thing. I am grateful for the great love, but it wasn't the type of love others would recognize.

Epiphany

JOEY

It was not by accident that Paul and Mary introduced us. They wanted me and Ben together, and the incident that separated us came years later, just a few months ago now, a decade into this new millennium. Did anyone notice the old one? How is it possible that Paul is the reason Ben and I are apart?

The distance from our split has only made it harder to understand. I think about it a lot, too much, as it is difficult to imagine that any friend could treat someone this way. Years after Ben and I were together, I was talking to Paul and Mary about their marriage, how it always seemed to happy and fulfilled, how they always laughed together about everything. I asked them how they dealt with the potential infidelities and crushes that Ben and I were both experiencing. They were incredibly helpful, open, so much so that I exposed myself further, especially to Paul, displaying my own insecurities and fears about opening my relationship and worries about raising a child. I made myself vulnerable to both of them.

Then I found a set of texts on Ben's phone while I was searching for a grocery list he'd asked me to find. Paul was in Sydney on business, unbeknownst to me, even though we'd known each other since I was a child, even though we had so recently been emailing and speaking on the phone of our mutual vulnerabilities.

Ben: "Did you cum yet today?"

Paul: "No."

Ben: "You're going to have a huge load churning in those balls after your long flight. I'll take care of that."

Another day, Ben: "Can I come over and let you fuck my hole?"

Paul: "Ruff."

Ben: "Joey would not approve of this, you know."

Paul: "Believe me, I know. It's hard to imagine a more high-maintenance partner than him. You need some carefree fun. And you know how to work a big cock; come over and ride mine."

Ben: "You bet."

It went on and on, text after text. Not terribly enlightening or interesting, just juvenilia. What ultimately hurt was not the sex but the deception of someone I thought a friend. I was, to my own surprise, tremendously aroused by Ben having sex with another, and we were certainly moving toward that most-common reality of gay couples. But when the other was Paul, all of the arousal quickly turned to pain. Paul wasn't just a hot fuck. He was someone who knew all of my intimate secrets and worries about Ben. Paul instigated my relationship with Ben; he introduced us with purpose, with the intention of us building a life together. He shared in the joy of it actually working out, and expressed the wonder at how rarely it does. He wrote me multiple letters about the pride he and Mary felt about my relationship with Ben—only to find out that he must have had some alternative purpose. Paul must have felt that having Ben close to me would increase his own opportunities to see him. That might explain Paul, but what about Ben? What was Ben's motivation? It was clearly more than just sex. Ben and Paul loved each other, in the same way I loved both of them, but as something they chose to find shameful and keep secret, they took it all a step further. I wasn't even gifted with being told that Paul was gay.

Mary and I have never spoken about it, and my long and close relationship with my loyal childhood friends came silently to a halt. They stopped talking to Mom, too, since I'm sure Ben and Paul talked about what to do, but for all I can discern Mary and Paul are still together.

Mom doesn't understand what happened and I haven't broken it to her. She has a high threshold of tolerance for things like this. We went from them giving me the most lavish and memorable party in the modern history of London to the tawdry and awkward silence in which we are all still engaged. Ben tried to make contact with me for a while, but now he has disappeared. We made arrangements for him to pick up his things from the Vaucluse house while I went to the Blue Mountains for a few days, but he never responded. When I returned home, one suitcase and a few items were gone. No other communication.

I reached out to Mary to see if she wanted to talk about it but, again, no response. We went from a clearly defined something to a nebulous nothing. With free and clear choices before us, we all accepted loss and mourning. I never mourned my career, but with this I was plunged into a profound depth that I can't define, something deeper and mistier than mourning. Mourning would imply closure and acceptance, neither of which I have. I can't accept what happened because it has never ended. I can't imagine what Mary has gone through during their marriage. Can it possibly have all been a lie? What was my relationship with Ben? What Paul did isn't even a human thing to do; only monsters play with people's vulnerabilities. For my whole adult life, I've complained bitterly about Gene's treatment of my mom—yet I walked right into it myself.

I wake early in the morning, prepared to be joyous, and by the time I get to this park everything has turned. I remember the Ben I thought of as mine, and I remember the precise moment when the past tense began. "You will always be mine," he said to me in one of those final communications, but I didn't believe him. How does love snuff out so quickly, like a candle in the lightest breeze? If I never really loved him, then *I* am the liar, and I know this isn't true. Ben made such verbal displays of affection after it happened, but they felt like they were meant for someone else. He was dismayed that I wouldn't allow him to live in the house, when it is clearly large enough that we would rarely have to see each other, and we could share our son. But all he really sought in that was a cure for his own sadness; he had no interest in mine.

Part of it makes me want to play again, just to use the sadness like a friend, the way an artist is supposed to. I circle the piano every once in a while but I've yet to pull any music off the shelf. How could I begin again, anyway, how could I start? Bach? Too difficult. Schubert? Too sad. Maybe Rachmaninoff, if I could manage to not physically hurt myself. At least with Rachmaninoff the sadness can remain at a distance while one tries to get all of the notes to sound.

I don't have enough to do, yet I am constantly too busy to get anything done. The end of our relationship with Paul was the worst, and I have no idea if Ben still has contact with him. Even as he tried to atone for the affair and explain it all to me, Ben missed Paul, and there was no discussion from Ben about him giving anything up. How odd…deadening, really…to think that we may live thirty to forty more years and die reflecting on our lives, yet we will never see each other again. Will we think of each other in the final moments, or will each of us fade away into just another distant memory, like high school friends: you know you have shared experiences but you ultimately cannot remember a single thing about them.

Paul and I had so many conversations about Ben before this happened, and they were always so intimate: I shared the deepest thoughts two people can share, and he used it for something he knew would hurt me, assuming it would never be found out. The strangest kind of pain wanders across me as I write this, here in Sydney with the winter wind spreading across the park, and western light shining through the downtown windows. I used to long for weekends in the Blue Mountains with Ben; how I loved it there. The days just after this betrayal and deception, when I went up there, were horrible—long and drunken days lost in a haze. He would call endlessly and cry and beg me to reconsider. I remembered long weekends he'd had in the mountains without me and it became a lie wrapped in a lie. He'd been in the mountain house with Paul. They'd been in our bed.

I used to obsess over Ben's every need and desire. Each time he looked twice at a boy, I tried to attain that boy for him, or at least tried to share some piece of the attraction. Ben was sexually voracious, which is one of the things I loved about him. How odd that the things that attract us are the things that end us. I tried to arrange so many three-ways with Ben, but it never worked; he didn't want to share me. He wanted his own sexual conquests, and I guess he got them. I hope they were worth it.

Ben died to me. And now, with no one saying it, I can feel his friends blaming me. Paul and Mary have intimated, in ways they knew would reach me, that the whole situation could have been just fine if only I had been more forgiving, like I had been the one having the affair and lying about it instead of Ben and Paul. What might have happened if I'd never known about it? Would we have all stayed together, with Ben just carrying it for as long as it lasted? Would he eventually have melted down from the pressure of it, or would he and Paul have just held it as a treasure between the two of them, something private and beautiful that they remembered in small exchanged smiles at dinners with the four of us? Some have opined that Ben ruined my life, that I stopped playing because of him, that I retreated after the heartbreak. They truncate and generalize what was for me drawn out over many years. I stopped playing because I stopped playing. It had nothing to do with Ben.

Gene, you fucker, you'd never be smart enough to know it, but you are the reason that my life tipped over at some point and I stopped believing that love was real. Your constant cheating with both body and mind was unbearable. Do you have any idea how much that hurt? You destroyed the most important woman in my life, and not only am I never going to forgive you, I'm going to be sure you pay for it, dead or alive. Believe me, I will figure out a way. If not for you, I would never have experienced the pain I am living right now, because you turned me into my mother: someone who discovers a cheater in the most painful possible way and has to wear it.

SALVE

ALTA

I turned to religion, to faith, as Joey got older, as I saw him move so much farther into the world than I did. I compressed when he expanded, and I turned to my church community to help me. Church was a habit from my youth, and it has only occurred to me recently that my beliefs didn't align with any religious traditions. I sought the ritual of attendance. Does anybody mind? It gives me something to do, something to search for. Most of the worst things I've ever heard people say have been in support of their beliefs, and I've learned that people are much more likely to rearrange their prejudices and call that a belief. I've seen parents destroy relationships with their children simply because they disagreed with some aspect of how they lived their lives. If a belief doesn't help you live, it is impossible to keep believing it.

I tried to lighten my teaching schedule so I could travel with Joey as much as possible. By 1989 his career had not simply taken off; it was beyond anyone's imagination what had happened since the Bicentennial summer. Joey absorbed piano literature like oxygen, and though I was his piano teacher through most of that time, albeit with some outside help, he needed very little from me besides the imparting of technical exercises to keep his fingers limber and independent. The rest was just me trying to keep up with buying piano literature for him. I had been in Main Street Music Store in Houston nearly every week through the early 1970s, searching their bins and ordering music that Giuseppe recommended for his son. And when little Joey was engaged with a piece of music, he learned and memorized it with frightening ease. As he approached high school, I wondered about sending him somewhere for more advanced training, giving him a few more years before he launched into a career; but by the summer of 1976, there appeared to be no stopping him. I took him to New York City that summer for the July Fourth Bicentennial festivities, wanting to give him a memory he would never forget. Mother, of course, was against the idea—"all that expense"—but that simply made me commit even more strongly to it. I booked a week in the Algonquin in a suite with a piano so Joey could keep up his studies. No train this time, but I did make Gene buy us first-class plane tickets.

And it allowed me the moment I'd been waiting for: to introduce Joey to his father. Giuseppe would be introduced simply as a piano teacher, since Joey was still too young to cope with the reality, and I was not ready to tell him because once Joey knew, Gene would know—and, more terrifyingly, Mother would find out. She would do whatever it took to stop me seeing Giuseppe, who came to meet us in New York and stayed with friends.

I don't think I had ever been so nervous in my life, awaiting the first time Giuseppe arrived at the hotel to teach Joey a lesson. I had prepared Joey for having some extra piano instruction from a renowned teacher in the city, and he was excited by the idea. Giuseppe was so eager to get into the same room as his son's fingers, because he'd been doing all of the instruction by proxy, which was proving effective but was naturally very frustrating for him. He wanted to see Joey's posture and particularly his finger and arm positions, to be sure he was on a safe track for the biggest repertoire he would play.

Giuseppe thought he would be able to control his emotions about meeting his son by concentrating on the pianistic elements. But once they got through exercises and a few technical ideas and started into repertoire, Giuseppe went into an emotional disbelief. The first thing Joey played for him was the *Moses* fantasy, which Giuseppe himself had worked on for years so he knew it intimately, but he'd never had Joey's level of technical ease. There was simply no struggle in the boy's playing. Music seemed to emerge out of him as if he was spontaneously creating it. Next came

Mozart's Coronation concerto, filled with all sorts of pianistic challenges that Joey sailed through with ease. Nothing exhausted him.

After a few hours, I sent Joey into his bedroom to watch television and relax before dinner. "Let your teacher and I talk."

"Alta, we have a phenomenon on our hands. This is going to be very complicated," Giuseppe said to me, holding my hands.

"Why complicated?"

"You've got to realize: there hasn't been a pianist like this in generations."

"I know he's very fine, but come on now…"

"It's true," Giuseppe said.

"We both love him. He is our son, and everyone thinks their son is the most amazing talent in the world." I disliked that I sounded like my mother.

"No. This is different."

"Then he will go to Juilliard or Indiana and have a normal college life. He's so young."

"He is, but he doesn't have to go through all the machinery I went through: conservatory, competitions, all that struggle. Look, I'm still struggling to book a couple of recitals a year. I teach in Texas and that takes all of my time. He's never going to have to do that. He's ready."

"He is too young…" I kept repeating. "Are you sorry you moved to Texas?" I asked him with sadness.

"Absolutely not, my love. I would move anywhere to be near you. You are my love and my life." He quietly sang his favorite line from *La Bohème* that he used to have me sing up in the country: "Sei il mio amore e tutta la mia vita." How he used to love to hear me sing those big phrases.

I took Joey to the unforgettable fireworks all around Manhattan the next night. And to see all of the tall ships. He would never forget the tall ships.

Thinking back now on those big years, like 1976 or most especially 1989, we didn't realize then was the year his career was more than half over. In 1989 Joey not only played recitals all over the world at the highest fees, he also released and recorded a dozen CDs, one a month, including several reissues of his earlier LPs, transferring onto the new medium but more lucratively. His July appearance on *The Tonight Show* was a rarity for a classical pianist, and his audiences exploded after he played the Liszt *Grand Galop Chromatique* as the last guest on a Friday night. He spoke to Johnny Carson for almost five minutes, and was charming and engaging. The world changed for him after that. Suddenly there was property being accrued: he bought a town home in New York City that shared a back garden with Katharine Hepburn and Stephen Sondheim. He bought an apartment in Hawaii.

Yes, in 1989 he went from being well known within the classical industry to being a rare household name. But I knew something shifted in him then, too.

ALWAYS THE HOURS
JOEY

I don't miss playing but I miss practicing. Everything that could be credibly defined as *me* loved my morning piano routine. Practice was fuel that needed no fire to consume it; I didn't need to transfer the exercises to anything. It was the only time of day in which my soul could talk to itself without the intervention of a composition. My morning routine was to make a big pot of green tea and take it to the piano. I would play ten Hanon exercises four times each, stop for a cup of tea, continue playing for another hour, then an hour of the Brahms or Liszt exercises, then more tea, then an hour of scales and arpeggios in various rhythmic combinations and tempi. How I loved that daily connection, just my own body and my own mind mirrored in the instrument.

My mind controlled everything about my fingers, of course, but the most truthful information of my entire life was *received* at the piano. The piano sits in silence, accumulating knowledge from somewhere, but it awakens in the daily practice. I am no closer to understanding it now than I was when I was a child being shown the same exercises I did every subsequent day until that last time in London on the morning of my last recital. On a little over seven thousand days of my life, somewhere around twenty-one thousand hours were spent practicing those faceless exercises. I know pianists who view that as a waste of time, that the bulk of their practice time must be spent learning the depth of the music. To me it now feels like practicing was the only time of my life that was fully of some use.

Music was available to me and I absorbed it if I had clear enough practice time, just my fingers talking to me, reading what had been there all along. As long I'd done that work, the study time was short when I got to the music itself. I could memorize quickly, and I could bring myself to it. I couldn't bring the music toward me if I hadn't done the technical practice. Now I sit in Sydney parks and wonder how I can choose to never think about the *Kreisleriana* but I can miss playing scales.

TERRE HAUTE

ALTA

Gene's reaction to Joey's career solidified my permanent seething anger at him. He never went to hear him play, never complimented him, never said he was proud of him. For Gene, if people were stupid enough to throw that much money at someone for playing the piano, then Joey should take the money and run. I could not believe that I could not arouse the slightest pride or admiration for Joey from the man who was, for all they both knew, his father.

Yes, for all I think Gene knew, Joey was his son. We never discussed any other possibility. I assumed for a while that Gene's parents had told him about Giuseppe and the New York trip, but anything was possible in those hasty days when we were forced together. It is absolutely possible that my unthinking parents decided to keep the truth from Gene. If he didn't know at first, to my mind he didn't deserve to know at all. He has treated Joey appallingly, and I will never forgive him for it. I do need to figure out a way to tell Joey the truth, in time.

It has been years since there was any relationship between Gene and me. We've occupied the same house but different worlds and bedrooms. Gene had unpredictable flashes of guilt about his treatment of me, and I could always tell when he was actively engaged in an affair, as opposed to a one-night stand, because he'd shower me with gifts. Single encounters with women tended to make him angry, as though I had kept him from some happiness, or had thrown him toward the affair by being so cold. My coldness to him, I've long known, was simply protection borne out of trying to trust him. Early in our hasty marriage, we did try to find affection for each other, but we couldn't. I did love him, strange to say, and I know that in some way Gene loved and protected me, too. None of this was visible to those around us, and certainly not to the boys, but there was something in the other that neither of us could leave.

I do love the feeling of really knowing Gene, much as I don't admire what I know. One loves him as one does a helpless child. Giuseppe and Millie are the only two people I've truly loved. I fear Perry and I think I feel more awe of than love for Joey.

SERVITUDE

JOEY

So perhaps I have to leave the Antipodes to discover why, or if, Ben did this extraordinarily cruel thing to me. And why is he gone now? Was Paul the reason or the instigator? Why does it matter now who started what and why?

If for no other reason it matters because the questions fill my hours in Sydney parks, long into the short afternoons of this July. I'm being asked for a record of my days; nothing to equal Queen Elizabeth's, but invasive and somehow humiliating. I try to write down some notes for a biographer who is interested in my career, yet few words seem to appear beyond what could easily be discovered from performance schedules in those years: I went there, I played that, I went back to the hotel, I traveled the next day and did largely the same thing. In retrospect it feels like the most difficult thing in the world, an accomplishment, but at the time it simply felt like the easiest escape from anything real. It didn't require a lot of work, since the piano was relatively easy for me. The thoughts hidden within the music I played were real, much more real than any description of them could be, yet every time I had to sit for a distillation of what I was doing and why, I felt diminished, like a bad servant.

Out There in the Dark
ALTA

Movies kept me sane over the years, and I held a small job with an agency in Los Angeles that hired people to track attendance and to separately report on the income-generating parts of the front-of-house. I realize I would like to have been a movie and/or music critic, because that's what I ended up doing with my life, anyway: I went to movies and concerts, and I taught my son to play the piano, acting as a proxy from the dad he never got to know. That's the big difference between Gene and me: he can see things for exactly what they are at the moment they happen. I can't. I only see my life in retrospect, and I'm always shocked at some of the decisions I made once I look back. I see now that I should have simply defied my parents when I got back from New York, especially when I found out I was pregnant, but at the time it happened, I felt I had no power, no choice but to submit to their wishes. Society had an importance at that time that it's never had again, and by the time I had the courage, I no longer had enough reason.

Even if I'd been unable to resist at the time, I should have left Gene long ago, should never have allowed him to sit in control of any part of my life. I didn't realize how it was supposed to be, what happiness felt like, until much later, until it was too late to really alter my life. Giuseppe made happiness possible, and at least I had the presence of mind to keep that absolutely my own. My parents taught me clearly that anything out of their control would be kept from me with totality. Daddy was too occupied, and then gone completely, and my mother too stupid to put together that Giuseppe got a job a couple of hours from Houston.

The worst thing to ever happen to Houston was goddamn *Terms of Endearment*. That film gave everyone an idea of an eccentric Houston lady of a certain age. Everyone in my life, all of the parents of all the children I taught, all told me I was like Aurora. Oh God, even that awful name: Aurora. I can't bear the painfully obvious symbols of so much entertainment. Awful. And was Aurora really such a ray of light? She was extremely protective and colorful and unbearable and loyal and without any kind of reality to me. Did she have to work? Did she have a husband who treated her like Gene treated me? She had a daughter who was exactly like her and they both heroically faced her cancer together. Sad story, and I'm terribly sorry for all the people who had to face it, but not one moment of it felt true to me.

I never wanted to be one of those irritating people who had to have something be "relevant" to them, who had to imagine something in a film actually happening to them. I think that attitude is the most joyless thing in the world. What kind of person are you if you can't put yourself in the place of another and feel what they feel? But every time one of those children or their parents said lovingly or jokingly that I reminded them of Aurora, I had serious thoughts of punishing them in some way. Not violence, of course, but perhaps teaching them nonsense and charging for it, and perpetuating their insensitivity in thinking I resembled that shallow character in any way. The problem was, the film was shot a few blocks from my house, and Gene walked by their trailers and crew every morning on his morning walk, so he never stopped mentioning it for the rest of his life. He thought it was of some import to the world that Shirley MacLaine had once traversed our street.

I loved a wide variety of movies, though, that were all many times more endearing than goddamn *Terms of Endearment*. Why does no one talk anymore about *The Shoes of the Fisherman* or *Inherit the Wind* or *The Apartment* or *La Dolce Vita* or *Lawrence of Arabia*? These were the master-pieces that defined my life. Now every looks back upon the inexplicable

1970s as the modern golden age of cinema, ignoring the glories of the 1960s. How can that be?

LIVING AGAIN

JOEY

I wish Mom would see a therapist but she won't because of Larry Mc-Murtry's book, *Evening Star*, as indelibly played by Shirley MacLaine in the film, the sequel to *Terms of Endearment*. Mom openly hates both films and particularly the character of Aurora, a hatred she extends to Shirley MacLaine herself, seeming to think they are the same woman instead of each an invented creation. We know nothing about Shirley MacLaine, though we did have a great deal of fun with her at a party in Malibu one night. Wow—haven't thought of that in ages. Mom was there. She must have met her. How can I not remember them interacting?

The party was a vast house, right on the beach at the far edge of Malibu, near Barbra Streisand's place. I can't remember whose house it was, but I know it was the weekend I played the Gershwin concerto at the Hollywood Bowl, and then played a house recital in Bel Air the next night. My agent always said that house recital brought the biggest fee I ever made, though I don't remember now how much it was. Two hundred fifty thousand or more. I played for two solid hours to about fifty people. The event was someone's milestone birthday, and I can still see Mom in her silver dress, looking radiant. We must have gone on to the Malibu party afterward. I hope I'm not mixing it all up. The Malibu party was super casual, and we arrived from the very formal Bel Air event. Whose house was it in Malibu? That's going to drive me crazy. I'll have to dig out the old diaries. I must have been after some boy who was there.

LABYRINTHINE

ALTA

Joey played an incredible few concerts in San Francisco only one time, ages ago, and I joined him: one full recital in the opera house and a set of concerti with the wonderful orchestra there across the street in the days that followed. I stayed at the old Huntington Hotel on Nob Hill, in a room near Joey. I would have thought he would love the Bay Area, as I did, but he always was out of humor there and not quite himself. The place made him sad for some reason, and he carried none of the typical romantic sentiment that most do about San Francisco. I, conversely, always had a secret wish to move there with Giuseppe, to use my inheritance for a little Nob or Russian Hill apartment where he and I could walk to restaurants, and the weather is so beautiful. All fantasy, of course, and I'm sure I wouldn't have liked it so much, but as usual, I waited too long in my life to make the change.

One morning while Joey was resting, I walked over to Grace Cathedral where I had a most surprising and interesting experience following a labyrinth on the cathedral floor. I'd never known of such a thing in a church, and it fascinated me. Labyrinths aren't mazes meant for games. On a labyrinth there is only one path and you can't get lost like you might in a maze. I entered the labyrinth slowly, not sure what I was to concentrate on, but I just found a few words that described what I was seeking on that day: peace, gratitude, even just a moment of satisfaction with myself that didn't involve anyone else, that wasn't Joey's or Gene's or Giuseppe's or

Mother's. And as I concentrated on those words, something subtle but very real in me shifted as walked.

San Francisco is a busy tourist city, so naturally there were others walking the labyrinth with me. That irritated me at first until I realized the lessons I was supposed to learn that day. So many lessons. The path of the labyrinth takes you near the center quite soon in your journey; you are given a glimpse of the destination before the path goes far from it. That was especially meaningful to me. One young Asian woman scuffed her feet across the labyrinth so rudely, completely unaware that some of us were engaged in a spiritual practice. She kept staring at me as if to say, *What are you doing? I don't get it*—and she sure didn't get it. She was disrespectful and rude in the face of potential beauty, which to me is unforgivable. Of course her dismissive concentration didn't last. She quickly got bored with anything but skimming the surface of the self.

Several others joined me on the labyrinth: a woman my age and a younger couple. What meant the most to me, after the rude young woman left, was that they all unconsciously took my tempo. Sometimes I found myself walking in tandem with them, and at other times we were walking in opposition. Inevitably someone had to get out of the way, and I made that an easy decision for each of them by quietly stepping aside and briefly pausing to let one of them pass.

Then someone came in who wanted to go faster than all the rest of us. He exhibited frustration and aggression because we were holding him back. I got out of his way, too. Once I achieved the center of the labyrinth, I wanted to spend some quiet and peaceful time there, so I sat down on the floor and just quietly observed. Despite five or six people meditating on the labyrinth, tourists would come into the cathedral and walk right over it, ignoring all of us. A man outside the great circle, aware of the spiritual practice going on inside it, said to his wife, "Pagan bullshit, isn't it?" I normally would have thought this incredibly rude, but it landed differently on that day, as something hilarious. And there on the floor of the cathedral I had to suppress great racks of laughter. I hadn't laughed that hard in years. The man must have thought I was one of San Francisco's crazy homeless people. I kept the laughter fairly quiet and private, but my insides were releasing a great deal of tension, I guess, because I felt twenty-five pounds lighter when I got up.

I loved that on the labyrinth I had to be aware of my steps, had to really think about them and make each one have purpose and direction. That is something my life has always lacked and I'm sure always will.

Why didn't the sadness or frustration occur to me in real time, as the sad and frustrating things happened to me? I could have rebelled against my parent's cruel and small punishments, but I didn't. I don't admire myself for that, but it does continually puzzle me.

PISCES

JOEY

Of all the places I've been in my life, the young guys I meet constantly now in Sydney are fascinated by where I'm from, by Texas. There's some strange psychic connection, I guess, between outback and cowboy. Even though I don't sound remotely Texan and never did, they find my nonexistent accent sexy. If I'm interested enough, I will occasionally pull out one of the great Texan sayings, for only Australia can rival us on word spinning, and that inevitably gets me several steps closer to getting the boy naked.

We had our first warmer day a few weeks ago, and I casually said to a boy interested in me that it was "gettin' hotter than a whorehouse on nickel night" with a full Texan accent. He blew me twenty minutes later. Where were all these kids when I was twenty-five? Now that I'm twice their age they're all over me. Since my relationship with Ben fell apart, I've managed to successfully distract myself often. There's been nothing like it in my life, to the point that I'm sure I'm smack in the middle of a problem, but it seems not to have tipped over into anything permanently bad. Yet. Where did Australia get these blond gods? Was the First Fleet packed with doe-eyed hunky blond boys? Our sexual desires are inherited, aren't they? Did mine come from Mom or Dad?

I went to Andrew (Boy) Charlton Pool the other day, the gayest place in Sydney, assuming it would be too cold for most of the boys so early in the swimming season. No matter how horny I might be, I *love* swimming alone. Having the pool to myself is one of the best feelings in the world. The rewarding contentment of an empty pool is one of the few universal feelings, and I've had it all over the world. The presence of another person in the water, no matter how distant, distorts its feeling, and diminishes what can be taken away. Water resists differently when it has to resist more than one person. Water can do whatever it wants because it has infinite time: there is the same amount of water in the world, just in different forms, as there has been for a hundred million years. We can't make more. Swimming puts us on equal footing with the water we are made of. We float in it and propel ourselves through it, but we ultimately can't win anything against it.

Appassionata

ALTA

Joey won't remember it, I'm sure. He was at the same party but occupied with his young admirers. Joey had played a private recital at a mansion in Bel Air or Beverly Hills, and I'd loved hearing him play in such close proximity again. He played for a long time so they must have very much sweetened the deal; usually his house recitals were thirty minutes at the most. This one went over two hours. The crowd largely was bored by even the greatest of pianists, but for me it was paradise to hear him play so much that I'd not heard in years. The four Schubert Impromptus, the ones I taught him. Then *Carnaval, Appassionata*—oh my goodness, he played it at such a speed, especially the fourth movement, which was breathlessly thrilling.

I thought we were going back to his Westwood apartment for the night, but as we were leaving he surprised me with the news that we were going to a party in Malibu. That home was another wonder; I don't know where those people got their ideas and money. The house wrapped around a huge pool in the front and was entirely glass facing the beach in the back.

Joey quickly got occupied with admirers, and everyone there seemed to know him. There was much buzz about the attendance of Shirley MacLaine, but I had no interest meeting the one woman in the world who might be most tempted to tell me I remind her of Aurora. Joey didn't play the piano at the party, so I guess we were there because he was interested in some boy. I couldn't really tell and didn't care, so I found a glass of wine and walked around. I noticed the only man older than me at the party seated by an inviting wood fire in a fireplace that looked like it was made of glass, so I greeted him. He was kind and felt a bit lonely and out of place.

"What are you doing here?" he asked me gently. I told him who my son was, and he looked mildly impressed.

"I live just up the road, in a much more modest version of this house. I have about one-tenth of this. I've lived in Malibu since the mid-'60s, the glory days."

The gentleman was easily in his mid to late eighties but young for his age. There was a beautiful sadness about him but I didn't want to inquire. He asked about Joey.

"Oh, Joey was destined for this career from his earliest days. From the moment he sat at our piano, we knew he was going to have a life there."

"Isn't that wonderful. I've always loved seeing people do what they were born to do. Where do you live, ma'am?"

"I live in Houston. That's where Joey grew up."

"I haven't been to Houston in years, since right after the war."

"It has changed so fast. It seems like they are forever ripping down some fine old building to put up some new horror."

"I remember Houston having marvelous old neighborhoods and gracious trees. I'm a walker, so all my life I've gotten to know cities on foot."

I told him I loved to walk, too, and he began to lighten.

"How do you cope with your son being so desired by so many?"

"What do you mean?"

"Your son is the most eligible of bachelors."

"He plays two hundred times a year at least. He doesn't have a lot of time for romance."

"Well, he could have who he wants, believe me."

I asked him if he was single.

"I've been single for a very long time, ma'am. Like so many of us, I started out marrying a girl I adored, and we quickly had a child. That's what you did in those years: we all thought that having a child and a gorgeous wife would make us normal. I stayed in it for a long time because

I adored her, but ultimately it was a lie and I couldn't continue to let her live so unfulfilled a life."

I didn't say anything. I couldn't.

"But I broke her heart. I've never forgiven myself. I lured her to California with great dreams of our life here. We had a son who sided with her. I left her the house and moved out here."

I took his hand because I didn't know what else to do.

"Look at all those young people trying to get to know your son. They have no idea how lucky they all are to be able to live openly. I wish I had been at a party like this when I was twenty."

"Would you have chosen a different career?"

"Oh, no. I would never have done anything differently on that front. I had the greatest job in the world. I mean, I got to choose talent for the studios. Got to make people's careers. Imagine the joy of that."

We sat in silence together until Joey was ready to go. I knew he couldn't be the man who walked from the Shamrock to our house all those years ago. But in the moments after he walked away, I thought it must have been. I couldn't speak. Why didn't I just ask him? Why did I allow everything in my life to wait?

Eros

JOEY

Late in my playing days, I loved the pool at the One Aldewych hotel in London, which was where The Savoy always sent me to swim since they didn't have a pool. This pool is all the way underground and really a beauty, with a strangely compelling video loop of manatees and sharks at the deep end. I went there dozens of times and almost never had company. On a couple of trips, there was an incredibly officious pool *meisterin*, for she must have been German, who was fanatical about hygiene. Before I changed she inquired as to what suit I would be wearing. I pulled my Speedo out of my bag and she grimly gave it a pass. She gruffly told me to shower for no less than four minutes in water as hot as possible, in order to ensure that the pool remained clear of infestations. I dutifully followed all her pedantry, but there were two French mothers with two unruly little three-year-olds who would probably have ruined my swim had they not been so adorable. The mothers were absorbed in conversation and the two little guys were running around, to the horror of the demon pool-keeper. Germania finally had enough and marched to the far end of the pool to discipline the mothers. The boys took their cue, going as far away as they could from both their mothers and the gorgon. As I swam toward the far end, they pulled their tiny Speedos down and let it fly, instantly turning the *piscine* into a *pissotiére*, and cackling with laughter.

I lived for my nearly annual swims in the Château Laurier pool in Ottawa, and I never had the heart to tell the orchestra there that I really only accepted engagements in their lovely city because of that pool. I swam there dozens of times, always alone, and those swims live in me to this day. But that was but prelude to the grandest swim of all, when I was given a private tour of Hearst Castle at San Simeon in California the day after playing a house recital, for which I was paid something like a hundred thousand dollars in Pebble Beach. I'd never seen the place and was thrilled to go. There were no public tours that day, so it was just me and the tour guide. The pools, indoor and out, are unbelievable, and I asked if I could have a swim in both. The guide wasn't authorized to let me, but he said he would wander off and leave me alone with them, so he wouldn't know if I swam or not. It was a beautiful morning that was warming fast, so the moment the guy was out of sight I stripped and jumped into the Neptune Pool, thinking that was the most dangerous because it was the most visible. I probably did thirty minutes of laps before transferring to the indoor Roman Pool, which was like swimming in a silky heaven. American excess, to be sure, but I doubt there are two more beautiful pools in the world, and I had them both to myself on that best morning of my swimming life.

The Boy Charlton pool is modest by comparison, even within the scope of Sydney's many amazing pools, all of which I frequent, but it is my favorite. It makes me feel like I'm really in Sydney. Just a few days ago, I immediately caught the eye of a blond, twenty-five at the most, who had the most stunning body I've ever seen on a man. He was floating on a raft next to the swimming lanes, probably not what he was supposed to be doing but no one came along to reprimand him. I suspected that no one would ever tell this kid *not* to do something. He kept eyeing me, smiling, his legs spread wide across the raft, his feet submerged on either side. He had on a tight blue suit, "bathers" as they call them here—not a Speedo, but one with short legs, and a white band that accented his tight frame. His legs were something out of a museum, and every time I swam a lap and sneaked another look at him, they seemed to be spread wider, a little too obviously, I thought, but it didn't keep me from looking. His torso was lean and rippled, and his hair, half wet, was tossed with a part. His suit had been chosen, obviously, to match his eyes, bluer than the pool or the sky over the harbor around us, and a wide inviting smile presented itself through his elegant lips. I don't think I'd ever even *noticed* lips on a man before, but his were set in a permanently enticing grin, healthy and new.

The boy was all over me. He put his float on the side and sat his six feet of gorgeousness at the end of my lane as I swam my laps. He made sure I couldn't mark the end of a rep without touching him. He followed me into the dressing room and had no difficulties with the clarity of his desires. This wasn't going to be one of those guys seeking to "go for a coffee" first. I told him I wouldn't play in public, so he begged me to take him home, which won't ever work for me because of Little Ben and Claire. He wouldn't give up, nor did I want him to. We whispered quietly in the dressing room for a while, and he kept turning it up, while I kept telling him he was too young for me, which seemed to turn him on more. By the time I was ready to leave, he was openly saying, "You are going to fuck me today," and I knew he was right. He must have still lived with his parents or something because he wouldn't talk about going back to his place. I didn't press it far because I didn't care—all I wanted was to be inside that beautiful body. I checked us into the Four Seasons at the Quay. We went up the elevator with just our gym bags and a nervous straight couple, which didn't stop the boy from pushing against me, driving me crazy.

Ben, goddamn you. I mean, I don't believe in God so there isn't anyone to actually *damn* you, but goddamn you. You made me feel safe enough that I couldn't imagine a future without you. We were a couple, and we were a family. I pictured myself old with you. I imagined walking on the forecourt of Sydney Opera House after a performance and gazing into the sensuous night of the most beautiful city in the world, the birds soaring above the downtown skyscrapers, warming themselves in the lights. Distant lights flickering everywhere. Other couples sharing the night. Time isn't time in Australia so we'd cherish it more, never wasting a moment. I loved making love early in the morning and sharing coffee over the sunrise. I know we will both be okay without each other, but why should we have to be? I've moved halfway around the world for you, and now I'm here by myself.

The boy was naked and on his knees before I could set my bag down. Beyond him, out the window, was the Sydney Opera House. He rivaled its beauty: you could see every muscle on him, and by the time he got all of my clothes off, he was as hard as I've ever seen a man. His cock looked like a limb, and he seemed to melt when I wrapped my tongue around it. He still tasted like the pool, and his skin was so perfect I could have licked him for days. I started kissing every muscle on him, driving him crazy. I laid him down on the bed on his belly and starting moving down his back, pinning him down. I remembered feeling Perry's biceps when he would get on top of me in the dark silence of our shared bedroom when we were kids. This boy's biceps were like strong and supple grapefruit. I made my way on down his back to his stupefying ass; you really just could not believe any man in the history of our species could be built like this. The boy had crossed a threshold of need by this point, so when I spread him out and started tonguing him, I thought he was going to pass out. He was begging me to enter him by that time, so I got the lube and condom from my gym bag. "Raw," he insisted. "I need to feel you fill me." I'd been incredibly rapacious since Ben left, but I hadn't actually been raw inside a guy since him—not just for health reasons but because it made me feel distant and lonely. By this point, however, I was going to give this boy what he wanted. I kept him on his belly so I could whisper filthy things in his ear. That's what people don't get about anonymous sex: it can be gaspingly intimate immediately because you don't know what will hurt them. He felt like tight silk. I'd never felt anything like being inside that boy. Nothing could have made me stop, and when I came it was as close to death as I'd ever been, a place I was unsure I could ever return from, and the journey back took longer than I could ever remember. My entire vibrating soul came, not just my cock. There was something visceral and unforgettable about this boy.

I texted Claire to tell her I probably wouldn't be home. She wrote back simply, "Be safe. X."

The remainder of the night with the boy was, with no emotion that I could discern, not safe, but it was febrile and thrilling. The boy was insatiable. I don't know how he could take what I was giving him, and for so long, but he did. I worried that we would be heard in the adjacent rooms. Then I worried that I was hurting him. There's no way, at least not for me, to have such complete intimacy with a man and not have affection for him. But I keep going back to the same well hoping for a different drink. Every boy, every orgasm, has hope built in.

He seemed to fall asleep for a moment after we'd both finally spent the forces that needed release. I stared at him, covered in sweat and every other secretion. I'd lost count by that point of how many times we'd surmounted ourselves. I surveyed his glistening body. Though he'd told me, I couldn't remember his name. He looked like a painting—beautiful and poised, and he was at that moment a satisfied body. Even asleep he looked like he was just about to burst into a smile. No one had broken his heart. He was just enjoying the physical trappings of love without any of the weight. Isn't that Mom's word, *carapace*, just the outer shell of something? Not me. I gazed at the sated naked boy next to me and I felt exhausted and unsatisfied, already feeling the beginnings of a new desire emerge, knowing I would seek him out somewhere. Sex fills in for love, like a language in which you are no longer fluent but can still pronounce the words.

I've heard myself decrying the promiscuity of gay men: slut-shaming. Yet I wonder now just how many men I've had sex with. I can't begin to imagine. A thousand? That's not improbable, and it's probably underestimated. What's the seating capacity of Carnegie Hall? Twenty-eight hundred or so? I have no doubt I could fill it with men with whom I've had orgasms. That's a lot of DNA. Straight people, especially those devoted to the cult of Jesus Christ or Muhammed, are constantly denouncing gay men for promiscuity. Well, you are right, those of you who believe in a magic creature in the sky; we are incredibly promiscuous. We have sex with impressive regularity, and we do it with strangers. We used to go to bars and try to figure out who was looking for what, which took several hours and made us drink a lot. Now we have apps on our phones that tell us what gay men are in our vicinity and what they will be willing to do and how soon. If you made the kind of money I used to make, before the convenience of apps, you just hired in what you needed because there wasn't time for anything else.

What, exactly, is the problem with promiscuity to all religionists? It isn't "natural" to them. Well, guess what? It is "natural" for gay men to give oral sex to a man whose name you don't know. It is natural to meet someone to whom you are attracted and immediately start role-playing. And it is incredibly exciting and natural to imagine what it is going to feel like to be inside a man, or to imagine what he sounds like while you are blowing him, because *sound* is by far the sexiest part of the act, infinitely better than the actual eruption. Why do you feel you have the right to decide what is natural? It is the assumption of supremacy that I hate more than anything else about the motherfucking Jesus freaks. Why am I supposed to seek your approval? Why are your beliefs considered to be the ultimate moral compass? You fucking condoned *slavery* a hundred fifty years ago. Slavery. Think about that: you couldn't get *slavery* right but I'm supposed to take seriously your thoughts as to how many feet of cock I sucked this year? And look at where the largest numbers of Internet searches of gay male porn come from: the American South, Mesopotamia, and Southeast Asia, the three most religious places on the planet. They want to look at it, but won't talk about doing it. The hypocrisy is unbelievable.

The religionists assume that promiscuity has no intimacy. First of all, so what if it doesn't? Why is intimacy or its lack any of your business? Second, sometimes the sex is incredibly intimate, even if the intimacy is temporary. And again, however it comes down, how is it any of your business? I have Ben inside me right now. He came inside of me hundreds, thousands, of times. He is part of me. No, having his DNA inside me doesn't create anything that *you* can discern, but it has created something between the two of us. Isn't that enough? And that boy asleep in the Four Seasons after hours of lovemaking, what about him? He has a significant amount of me inside of him now, and that's forever. I haven't given him a disease, haven't injected him with anything that can kill him—just a little perfectly joyous discharge of genetic material deep inside of his unbearably beautiful ass. And it was fulfilling in each of those fleeting moments. Why are you judging me for the overwhelming physical pleasure I'd just experienced? Is it because you've experienced that in some other way that you assume I have to follow your example? Or is it because you've never felt an intensity anything close to the orgasms I had with that boy? I know a lot of colleagues, or ones who tried to be colleagues, who got that high with drugs or booze. Don't I get points for never doing that? Sure, I drank a little but I didn't use it to replace myself. Sex? Yes, absolutely. I used it to replace myself. I still do. I will again.

I don't know how I managed to avoid the plague of AIDS, except to wonder that since I was at the height of my career during the height of the crisis, I was almost exclusively hiring in, I was always the top, and I always wore a condom. Sounds simplistic to say I don't know why I didn't get it, but it is true. By rights I should have gotten the virus and died, but I didn't. And that's not because I prayed or because Mom prayed. It was random luck. Timing is the only source of success in a rain dance.

I was working through the whole thing while so many died. So many beautiful and vibrant guys, brilliant musicians and writers. I used the plague to keep from falling in love. I said it was my career but it wasn't. It was the disease. I was hopelessly selfish. I didn't want to die so I didn't fully live. I waited on the sidelines of love until the plague was over. I fuck freely now without worrying about dying. But so many I knew died. I would play a concerto and return to that orchestra two years later only to learn that three or four members had died. Many rehearsals in the late 1980s began with moments of silence for someone who had passed on, and I bowed my head and I sent them peaceful passage but I never really involved myself.

I gave money to AIDS causes but I never did as much as I was capable of doing. I played for Classical Action. I wore my red ribbons. For some reason, I associate AIDS fully with San Francisco, even knowing it was everywhere. The plague seems to permeate the place. I find it sad that I can't muster the romantic affection so many have for the beautiful city by the bay. I told my agent not to book me there again.

I didn't get down in the front lines and fight, not even when Reagan and Bush and everyone in their deep state was ready to let us die in the shadows. This is an unbearable part of remembering my playing life, and how could I ever talk to a biographer about it? It's what any serious writer would want to know about, but that's the one thing I don't think I could talk about. My heart would just crack open. I think of all the friends I never got to meet, all the plays they would have written that I never got to see, all the musicians I never got to hear.

Voltaire Returns

ALTA

Gardening has always been my best way to pray. I never feel closer to my Creator than when I have my hands in the dirt, right here on South Boulevard or up at the ranch. There, in the earth, there is so much beauty, so much joy, and those two gardens keep me occupied. They require so much stewardship from us. I have some help with the large things, but I love seeing the fruits of my own labors every day, especially here in Texas where everything grows with such dizzying rapidity. One has to constantly be vigilant about predators and weeds, but that is not only true of gardening.

Compared to the joy of singing, though, or what I must now imagine the joy of singing to be, gardening is weak. Singing is what I've lived for. Opera and great songs. I felt old-fashioned long before it was fashionable to be so. Many people believe they were born in the wrong era but I know it is true of me, otherwise why put me through the constant frustration of not being allowed to make my own choices? There must be a reason that I will someday be able to discern, for if I wasn't allowed to sing in this life, surely I will in another. I have to believe that.

My parents could not understand my gifts, nor could they understand or countenance the passion with which I embraced them. To them I was out of balance in some way, and had to be constantly made more temperate. They feared for my future, not excited by possibilities. They believed in finding contentment on the sidelines of their lives, assuming I must feel the same. Anything that smacked of participation was a source of fear for them. They were like the fawns at Chappell Hill, always on the lookout for what might harm them.

I would have loved to live in an era when people didn't talk about everything so much, didn't feel the need to be so confessional. And everything now is so blindingly literal. I fear we have lost the ability to really hear poetry and feel the depth of music. This is what Joey, my dear son, has taught me more than anything, especially when he was young: that the passage of time is far too swift to spend on the literal or the small, yet my life has been so much smaller than I ever imagined it would be. What does it mean, to have a small life? It means that you were shown the full possibility of your destiny, only to have it taken away—that is quite a different act from being shown what might be and choosing a different path! No. My parents were too small themselves to realize what they were doing to me. And I allowed it all, realizing always too late the consequences of my choices. Why didn't I fight?

This is why I still garden. I consider gardening to be the earthly face of God because it allows me to see the consequences of my actions, or the results of my neglect. That is the only thing I've ever been truly free to do, and so I have embraced it by tending my huge gardens back to the earth each year, as a thanks to Him. Joey now, all these years later, finds my religious belief disconcerting and I understand why: it is a relatively new addition to my life, something I had to cultivate as surely as I tend roses.

HEXAMERON

JOEY

My life was all about repertoire, about memorization, about what I could offer audiences, about what I wanted to spend each of my days working on. I think people understand that we work hard to play the piano, as the clichés of practicing for hours run strongly through the culture, but I wonder if people can really conceive of the intricate and difficult work a musical career presents. I had an active repertoire, meaning major musical works I could present on a few days' notice, of several *hundred* compositions. I know why people have trouble believing that, because I can't quite fathom it myself. All of the piano sonatas of Beethoven, Haydn, Mozart, Brahms, Schumann alone, and they are only a start, amount to over one hundred hours of music from *memory*.

The plan was for me to record all of the Haydn piano sonatas, like I had the Beethoven and Mozart sonatas, but in the end I was barely able to even program them with regularity, much less record them. I used to play through them all in regular practice, and I love them very much. They are all such perfection. But I've been having dreams lately about pieces I hadn't thought of in years, like the Poulenc Improvisations and the Rachmaninoff *Variations on a Theme of Chopin*. Beethoven, the spiritual father of all musicians, hasn't been in my thoughts much, maybe because my own father has so recently departed. Did he, really? I never felt Gene to be my dad. I opened many recitals with the C. P. E. Bach A-major sonata; great way to warm up, but eventually presenters would ask for more popular things, like opening with Tchaikovsky's *The Seasons* and closing with octave after octave of the Liszt *Mazeppa*, which I used to love much more than the more-requested *Mephisto Waltz* or *Hexaméron*, which few presenters liked because it wasn't only by Liszt, it had multiple composers. *Funérailles* never failed for me, though I usually followed it with *La Campanella*, which would make them all scream louder, though I could never figure out why. It is pure athleticism, so maybe it is like enjoying ice skating competitions. But it hardly can be called music, all of those repeated notes. The public does like its repetitions.

Little by Little
the Pearls Become Real

ALTA

I should have tried to do the few community theater shows that I was asked for, which is as close as one gets to professional inquiries when one is only ever heard at church. The show producers always offered me parts that allowed me to use something close to my actual voice, like Mother Abbess in *The Sound of Music*, and Lady Thiang in *The King and I*. They needed me because I could deliver those. I couldn't stand "Climb Ev'ry Mountain"; what a cheap and tawdry thing it is, but I could sing it and bring the house down.

Lady Thiang's song, "Something Wonderful," is another thing entirely: it is literate and completely honest to its moment, a wife singing to someone her husband loves, who may well take her place. That was a feeling I knew well. Every word of the song is perfection, sculpted into truth, but it is the widely spaced melody that I love to this day. I felt those words, not about Gene, but about other men, especially my Giuseppe. My life was a mosaic of this song's words.

All would have been totally different if my mother had been able to understand this single song. Just *one* song was all I would have asked of her. The idea that a man needing you can be wonderful—is that too much to ask, Mother, that you understand even one *line* of this song?

I remember one show I did accept in Brenham at a church theater group in the 1970s. It gave me a small chance to sing and perform that

Giuseppe encouraged me to take. I was woefully out of place in that setting and had to rein in my voice—hide it, really—but it was enjoyable. I played Gabrielle, the third female role, in a little-known show called *Dear World*, Jerry Herman's musical of *The Madwoman of Chaillot*. How I loved that role. The show is a bit of nothing, but it mentions Voltaire; and the tea party scene is just heaven to perform. I would incongruously leave a discussion about Voltaire with Giuseppe and twenty minutes later find myself in a church hall rehearsing a mediocre musical with amateurs, using almost none of the knowledge I'd acquired, and having to tone down my voice so as not to falsely draw attention, but that was how I lived. To the theater groupies in Brenham, I was just an eccentric who was sometimes around in the summer. They didn't know who I was. I never socialized with any of them. Kept my distance. Still, it was fulfilling in some dispensable way.

REVOLUTION

JOEY

When I think about Ben, meaning nearly every moment of my conscious day, I'm still amazed to have to remind myself that Ben isn't his name. Ben was just his Western name. As a teenager he got a job in the Jin Jiang Hotel, where I met him. The big Chinese hotels of that era, probably still, made their employees take Western names so that foreign guests wouldn't feel alienated by seeing a difficult Chinese name on a name tag. He was actually Gu Shing Yen, and I should have always called him by his real name. How humiliating to have a hotel decide that your name is just too difficult, so you lose your identity to work there. Awful.

When I first encountered Ben, he was a waiter and I have no memory of it. I have searched endlessly through my life, through countless trips to Shanghai, and the Peace Hotel and the People's Park where I used to get propositioned, and all of the concerts and dinners at the Jin-An Guest House (one of the greatest restaurants in the world), and the many late nights in the bar of the Jin Jiang, and I cannot remember ever meeting him. He told me about it only on that first night we were together in London. Late that night, almost to morning, as the sun was starting to streak across the eastern sky, he told me that he'd waited on me in Shanghai fifteen years before, trying to spur me to remember. It frustrated him as much as it did me, and even now I can hardly believe what finally awoke the distant memory: The Carpenters singing "For All We Know." Even though Ben's English was accented, when he sang he could conjure the singular timbre of Karen Carpenter's voice; uncanny how he could exactly imitate the diphthong with which she maneuvered the final "know" in that unique way she had.

I don't know how he knew that song. Did I begin to associate him with mimicry from that moment? Did I unknowingly allow myself to assume that because he could copy her and sing about love perhaps growing, with that melting glance of his, that he somehow knew how to be false in other ways, that he would mimic the feelings of love and sex?

Ben was a great visual artist, one of the first of the modern era to break out of China. His art was subversive enough that he and Claire had to leave permanently, and neither of them will likely ever see their parents again. He emigrated to Australia, where he met Paul and Mary. I don't know when the physical relationship with Paul started, but maybe that's why he left. I long ago stopped asking.

Incredibly, the years between Shanghai and meeting Ben at my retirement party at Paul and Mary's passed without my giving him the slightest thought, yet he had thought of me constantly, and used me as a motivation to get out of China. To me he had been just another handsome waiter among thousands. I probably had a momentary attraction to him then, but I can't remember. I never would have acted on it in China, where we would have been watched or listened to in my hotel room. Yet from the moment I met him all those years later in London, I was instantly in love with him. I still am, as much as those words burn through this page as they leave my pen. He has an invisible thread from his eyes to mine that I can't forget, yet I forgot them for fifteen years. Did music do that? No. I simply didn't pay attention to him in China because he was a waiter, and I probably had to pack for a plane the next day or something. I was never in China for long. Did I really assume that any acquired culture was automatically false? I acquired everything from my mother—only the fingers were my own—yet I judged Ben for that very thing. I think I always assumed he was impersonating a person who could love me. Did I push him toward the entire situation with Paul?

FANTASTIQUE

JOEY

I'm amazed that, even now, almost no orchestra can play sections of the Brahms D-minor piano concerto with the precision it has on the page. There is some music like that, and I'm still amazed by it. In this case I was waiting to rehearse something in Birmingham in that gorgeous concert hall, probably my favorite-sounding concert hall anywhere, and they were rehearsing the Berlioz *Symphonie Fantastique*. What concerto must I have played with that? Saint-Saëns, maybe? Can't remember. Anyway, the conductor rehearsed a few things. It is an incredibly difficult work to play but orchestras know it very well because they play it all the time. Near the end of the rehearsal, as I was getting ready to join them, the conductor casually said about a particular passage, "Of course, the trumpets play offbeats here and the winds play downbeats, and I'm not sure we're doing that."

The principal trumpet said meekly, "Could you say that again, maestro?"

He did, which prompted the player to admit, along with his back-row colleagues in the trombones, "We've been placing those chords incorrectly for the last twenty years and no one has ever said anything. Do you mind if we do it one more time?"

They played it again, and the difference was amazing. Sometimes just naming things what they are is the most powerful thing in the world.

MIME
JOEY

The best conductors I worked with weren't the best conductors, in that they weren't the most renowned. Something happens to conductors when they get famous; they have to keep reinventing how they interact with large groups, which is a totally different art from any other exchange of ideas. Conducting is a much more mysterious art than playing an instrument, because a conductor's body is their instrument, like a dancer, but conducting isn't choreography or even physicalizing the music; it is a series of silent and thoughtful gestures that enable others to make the music. It requires enormous generosity and *lack* of ego. There are lots of great pianists, at least many who can put the requisite fingers down in the right place, and there are exercises and scales that if you can play them, you can play a lot of the piano repertoire. You may not be able to play the most demanding Chopin, Liszt, or Rachmaninoff, but you can play a lot of things and be very happy.

But with conducting, especially in the later part of my career, all the youngest ones, gifted and not, wanted to conduct the Beethoven, Mahler, Dvořák, and Tchaikovsky symphonies, long before they had done their time and learned their craft. No one should be in front of a Mahler symphony with a major orchestra until they are at least forty and preferably sixty-five or seventy. It takes a lot of life and heartbreak and a lot of mistakes before you are ready to confront what is in those symphonies. I played a lot of the biggest repertoire before I was ready, so I know about this issue. I should have played Bach, Haydn, and Mozart until I was forty, but the orchestras only want the big concerti now: Tchaikovsky, Rachmaninoff, Brahms, Saint-Saëns…most of them will even take the Britten concerto over one of the Mozarts, and I always had to fight to play the Haydn concerto.

The conductors who I found to be the greatest collaborators weren't the most famous, so they didn't have to spend vital energy tending the fame, they could just use it on the music. The best of them lived that music, knowing the brevity of our direct connection to it. The magnetism that I encountered in the most gifted of them didn't come from looks; it came from real musical sincerity and imagination. Yes, we all like handsome, but I don't need handsome in a musical performance. I need presence and connection. I don't need compliments and "help"; I need a temporary relationship I can trust that is grounded in the music we are momentarily caretaking. Ideally, we get along and we can do it again somewhere, but that rarely happened in my experience. The most inspiring conductors of my career didn't conduct musicians, meaning they didn't worry about how they were perceived; they conducted *music*, and if the musicians went along for ride, great. If they didn't, well, better luck next time everybody. No hard feelings.

The greatest of these conductors didn't fret over the relationships nor did they abuse their privileged time, but they certainly didn't try to pretend politics and personality were music. The great conductors I encountered were very few, because great conducting requires an enormous generosity of both spirit and knowledge, and that is naturally going to be rare. But conducting is also a profession that invites chicanery, because it can be faked and forced for a while, just as politicians stay in public life for decades because they have figured out how to inflame a base of people comforted by simplicity.

Donald understood this better than anybody. He made his career on simplistic messages. He derided me, always behind my back, of course, for being afraid of the famous conductors, and he found a message that resonated with his disciples: that only Donald had the musical intellect and gifts that would satisfy the famous conductors; whereas I, according to him, needed to have a lesser conductor on the podium so I wouldn't feel threatened. Donald was good at the surfaces.

UNKNOWABLE
ALTA

The tragedy of our family was the death of my sister, Sally, Perry's mother. I'm afraid to find out what happened to her. Probably only Mother really knows, and she's half out of her mind now, anyway, so who could believe her?

What I've always found exceedingly strange is that Mother never displayed any emotion about it, even when it happened. My memories from that time are foggy because my own life crushed everything around it, even the death of a sister. When we got the call, I was a pregnant newlywed, desperately unhappy, and looking for a way to contact Giuseppe since my parents had cut off every possible avenue to him. I remember horrendous wailing and disbelief from everyone around us, but not Mother. Sally and I were never close, and though I dutifully carried out my bridesmaid tasks that year, I barely recall her wedding—only the unspoken offense that I was not asked to sing. It was never talked about but understood that I would have sung at my sister's wedding.

Sally, as always, did whatever the hell she wanted, never a thought about anyone else. She was the picture of Mother. She got married at the lovely Palmer Glide Church in Hermann Park to Robert, a nice enough fellow for an oil man, but dull and already old in his heart for being so young. His local job in Houston took them off to Saudi Arabia as soon as their baby, Perry, was born, though I never understood what they were supposed to be doing over there. It can't have been safe. Sally didn't want Perry to go with them so he stayed with me, and she made me vow to take care of him if anything happened. It all sounded as shady and sad as it turned out to be. About a year into their journey, they disappeared and were never found, presumed murdered. How could Sally leave a baby in Houston and go off with her husband?

Every few years the State Department sent Mother and Daddy a letter about the ongoing investigation, but nothing was ever shared with us because I don't think there was much to know. Some of Sally's friends told me over the years that her few letters to them from the kingdom gave the impression that it was very difficult for foreigners in those years. The oil industry that has given so many so much was new to Saudi Arabia then, and I've always felt that they made so much money so quickly, and went from desperately poor before the war to unfathomably rich after, that the backlash against any non-Saudi must have been horrible.

I do hope they didn't suffer, though I've always felt they must have or we would have heard more. No one vanishes without a trace, even in the desert. I'm most ashamed to say, though, that entire months, probably years, have passed in which I didn't give my sister the slightest remembrance, not even a passing thought. I heard Mother say a few times that she found it so hard to think about Sally because the pain was so overwhelming, but I don't believe a word of that. Once Sally was gone, I don't think Mother ever thought a thing about her. That's how Mother was about everything: if you weren't directly affecting her, you didn't exist. Sally and Bob could have been brutally tortured before they died, or thrown into a vat of boiling oil, and I don't think Mother has ever thought about that. I don't enjoy thinking about it, and I'm ashamed that I often haven't, but I hate it when Mother says things I know aren't true.

Because of her, I've always loathed people who said what they thought should be said. I find that unbearable. Every member of my family has spent so much time lying to me—not calculated lies, but the deeper ones: the lies of omission. Even Daddy, when he put his will together and the inheritance of the store, I happened to be working that day. I was still a teenager, and it was before New York. He and a couple of lawyers went into the little office in the back to hash out his will, and they were in there for hours. When they came out, I was with a customer. Daddy greeted him and then looked at me and said, "Oh God, boys! We forgot Alta and Sally!" to which there was muttering about us getting married anyway and thus always provided for. Ultimately a few meager provisions were made. When the store was sold, most of it went to Mother's care, and who knew she would live so long?

But there was trust fund money that came from Sally's death, and the portion of it not used to care for the house on South Boulevard is protected until Mother dies. Daddy saw to everything. We've had plenty of money for the upkeep of the house and for taxes and most anything we wanted to do to the place, so the corpus must be a few million. I really don't know. Certainly small by Houston standards. Meanwhile Mother refuses to let go of life. She sits out there in Sugarland passing each day unaware of any havoc she has wrought. And she just won't die. Something is making her stay.

FLEURS

JOEY

O f all my old haunts, I guess I miss Paris the most. I guess that's a tad too predictable, for of anyone who has ever been to Paris, who does not miss it? It isn't playing in Paris that I miss, as the Parisian audiences never seemed to like music as much as they liked ideas about music, but it was the great glorious city itself. I felt particularly connected to Paris despite not understanding why, beyond the obvious dazzling pull of the place that everyone feels. Ben and I were planning our first trip to Paris together when we unexpectedly fell apart.

Paris was, for me, the George V Hotel, and I got to know more of Paris than I did most cities, because I played in various venues around town, most often the Théâtre de Champs-Elysées, which was within walking distance. Mom was with me on a summer night on one of my first trips there, which stands out beyond almost anything in my career.

I played the Bach *Goldberg Variations*, not normally the sort of program that would have appealed to Parisians, but I insisted on it. What a gloriously lonely work it is; just to learn it requires thousands of hours in one's own head, especially that desolate opening and closing aria, and the atmosphere one has to create to sustain that piece for that long. It is filled with myriad technical challenges. Inexplicably, the audience went insane for this piece. Theirs was the most passionate reaction I ever had in France.

After my recital it was still light, so it must have been summer. We went to Café de Flore and sat outside, Mom and several friends, old and new. There was a quality to the light that evening I can never forget, and which I could never re-create no matter how far I traveled and how deeply I tried. I think I kept my career going for years just trying to rediscover that experience, to bathe in that light again, to feel the warmth of that particular group of people. It was the happiest moment of my life, and I've never had it again. We are supposed to be able to just experience happiness, aren't we? We are meant to immerse ourselves in the majesty of each moment, vertically, as we move through time horizontally. But I am immovable: my energy hones into these specific moments of life and I can't budge them. They keep calling me back, but they're always just out of reach.

I sent Mom back to the George V so I could take a walk by myself. I loved to walk through cities at night as the darkness slowly descends. I walked all the way from the Left Bank to Montmartre. I just kept walking, and suddenly there was Sacré-Cœur, so I kept moving toward it. At the top of the one of those glorious stairways that feel like they will deposit you at the top of Mount Everest, I turned around to grasp how far I'd walked and to catch the last glimpses of light to the west. I had only a thin layer of myself that night, very little to hold me between my piano consciousness and something deeper. Bach had opened a passageway, perhaps. As I decided to descend the escaliers to find a taxi to take me home, I was struck by the most powerful image of my entire life. I'd never before experienced the true déjà vu, which is not a *slight* inkling of having been there before. Rather, it is the briefest of seismic moments, and it rocks every element of the spirit. I saw myself broken and barely living at the bottom of the steps, with people starting to gather. I had been thrown from the top, or I had thrown myself, I could not tell. But either I had died on these steps or someone close to me had died. That, also, I couldn't tell.

I carefully descended, and the vision eased itself back into nothingness. I taxied back to the George V and tried to sleep.

FUCKING AND SHOPPING
ALTA

I'd planned to have nothing in my life depend on the forgiveness of anyone, and certainly not their kindness. There's that horrid play again; I could never bear that one, with all those people screaming at one another all the time and professing things. How I detest this age of verbosity and confession. Blanche was mercilessly victimized, a cruelty beyond reason that most women have had to endure, so I do not understand why we should have to attend that lurid play and witness her go through it all over again.

Of course, I can't just ignore the infidelities Gene hoisted upon us all. He could be so cruel. But it was his nature. And he was so terrible at lying, just had no talent for it at all, yet he lied all the time, and I always knew when it was happening: his eyes darted, his brow lightly sweated, and he spoke in short phrases instead of his usual drawl.

He cheated on our honeymoon, for God's sake! We went to Pensacola for some reason I can't recall, for who would ever willingly celebrate a marriage in Florida? Well, that's where everyone went then. I went to the beach, which he had no interest in, and when a quick rain came up I headed back to the room. "Do not Disturb," it benignly said on the door, and I couldn't figure that out. When I inserted key, Gene yelled out, "No!"—and I came in to find him naked on top of the maid. They were mid-act and he had only ever fucked *me* once at that point.

Fucking. How I came to hate that word. Gene didn't like the word, either, but he certainly loved the act. He must have spent more time in search of orgasms than any man in history. That's all it really was to him, just those seconds of release, then he was on to the next one.

For a while, Joey kept asking me why I stayed. I always answered, "Why did you stay with Ben?" which never pleased him very much. Joey always wanted clear answers, but of everyone I've ever known he was the most incapable of accepting them. Joey could absorb anything, and he did, with incredible speed and a ferocious artistry that still frightens me. He said he didn't know where it came from. I knew where it came from, but I was never sure I could tell Joey in a way he could understand.

I now wonder why I stayed. I used to always wonder why Gene didn't just leave me. Our physical relationship didn't last very long, and after a few years, he didn't even kiss me. I could have lived without the act itself, which was never that fulfilling, anyway, but the lack of kissing cracked my heart. Kissing wasn't something I could live without, yet I could never bring myself to kiss any man but Giuseppe, not with a true kiss. A woman can lie about many things, but not a kiss.

I always wondered if Gene kissed the other women. He must have. He was a wonderful kisser, as I recall, but it was always just a way to get on with things. I don't think he ever kissed me to show affection; he kissed me to "get in the mood." Whenever I contemplated an affair, which was often, it was always just to get kissed. Every night I would lie in bed, usually waiting for him to get home, and hope that he would kiss me. After a few years, I knew that part of our lives would never return.

We had a very brief sex life. Gene would regularly come home and wait for me to get the boys to bed. I loved those nights, knowing he was in there aroused and aroused by *me*. One night he even waited in the shower, and pulled me in there with him and took me there for a while before ravishing me in bed. In those times it felt like it was me he wanted, but it wasn't; he really just wanted the sex. Still, we were together forty-four years. On our twenty-fifth anniversary, he sent me a bouquet of eighteen roses. "One for every year we've been happy," he said as he handed them to me, thinking his cruelty to be clever. I changed it to "One for every year I was there" for the boys, as I couldn't bring myself to repeat the words.

Gene seemed to get pleasure from humiliating me from time to time. In the first couple of years of our marriage, he went through a period of telling me how ugly I was, how no one else would want me if he left. It was during an affair he was having with one of his co-workers, one of the more serious affairs. They were seen around town having dinner, and he bought her flowers. It was a romance and he made sure I knew it.

I've never told the boys this, but during that time I got work as a model for Sakowitz Christmas catalog. I never told Gene, either, but I used the extra money to get especially lavish Christmas gifts for the boys. I used to hate Christmas morning with Gene, because he would overspend so wildly on gifts, always out of guilt, of course. The fur coat was potentially the most humiliating, but ultimately I thought it was humorous. It was so blatant, so him. But the acres of clothing over the years were the worst. He would buy clothes he thought I should wear, stressing what I *should* look like, not what I actually did, with never a consideration of what I actually liked. He never bothered to find out what I liked or what I felt I looked good in. We never shopped together. I spent hours buying his work clothes and keeping him supplied with ties and cuff links, as he had a phobia about repeated wearings. But he never returned the attention. My closet is filled with clothes I've never worn; the only things I will wear, I've bought myself.

I probably could have survived financially without Gene, but I felt I couldn't. I could easily have sold the South Boulevard house, especially during the boom times in Texas, but it was my home, my whole childhood, and I felt the need to have a home for the boys. Little Perry never even knew his own mother. Although I taught music, I only ever really taught Joey, and used that money as wisely as I could. Joey made a fortune from what I taught him, and he's certainly been very generous in sharing it, but he's also pissed it away in ways I can't imagine. What's happened to the money from those houses?

Elvira Madigan

JOEY

The fights with the agents over repertoire became more oppressive as my career took off. I *needed* a whole season of Mozart concerti. I longed to play concert numbers 18 through 27 in successive concerts, to really immerse myself in those final ten concerti, and then perhaps record them if I could find a great enough conductor. It was hard to bear the endless conversations about this, the hundreds of e-mails, the complaints from orchestras saying this or that pianist had played one of them in the previous five years, all underlain with the argument that they wouldn't sell, that audiences wanted only the big romantic concerti which told them what to feel and think, which practically knocked them in the head with when to applaud. Oh, I enjoyed those concerti, too, but they didn't require the discipline of the Mozart concerti, and I wanted to see what kind of pianist I would be after a year of memorizing and playing those ten concerti. The idea never came to fruition, though I eventually got to program a few of them. I played the Coronation concerto twenty-four times one season, and wish it could have been twice that, because in addition to having all of my favorite pianistic challenges, it is *such* music. I made three recordings of Mozart concerti, and I love them so much I'm tempted to get ahold of a copy and listen to them again.

The Angel Mozart

ALTA

Joey playing the Brahms Sonata was soul-changing for me as well as for him. But there was never more giddy joy in my heart than hearing him play Mozart's 25th concerto, the great C major. He insisted on playing all the Mozarts, 17 through 27 at least, but this is one I love the most. It is the most ingenious and moving. The orchestra seems to present something like my mother: immovable blocked chords, a series of problems in search of help. The piano constantly quells and softens the orchestra's arguments until they finally find peace in the second movement, and complete dancing joy in the third. How I wish my life could have been like that concerto! There are peaceful and loving ways to fix the world, and Mozart heard them fighting. What an instinctively childlike tour guide he was.

Quaint

JOEY

I miss the struggle of imagination, that thrilling gap between expectation and the articulable reality. My lifetime has corresponded with the apex of a huge decline in the art, and I've merely responded to it, even as my few regular commentators insist that I am part of the cause, spurred on by Donald, of course. The idea that a mildly popular pianist could have an effect on national culture is quaint. Art is devalued now only in proportion to the devaluation of everything; for what, now, *is* meaningful? If we are meant to hold dear the most precious moments of our lives, how do we decide what those are?

Friends all around the world tried to get me engaged in social media, and I tried it for a brief time, but there is nothing true about it. It doesn't "keep us in touch"; it distracts us from conversation and engagement. For the few days I explored it, I received hundreds of requests for my "friendship," always from people who were not friends at all, but who bought my records, or wanted their piece of whatever morsel of notoriety I might supply.

It isn't just happy hindsight: the few weeks before what happened with Ben were among the most blissful of my life. I remember them with great clarity. That is what happiness looked like: awakening early, and I would fulfill a morning routine with no stress or anxiety: reading the paper, making breakfast first for myself then for the family as they awoke in order: Ben, Claire, Little Ben. I would have time and energy with each of them, time that feels incredibly tender to me now.

The routine hasn't changed, but the feeling about it is altered; now it is a yoke. Joy has been translated into burden by the discovery of something I need never have known about, yet would my ignorance have altered anything? Ben and I used to wake early and hold each other, often using that earliest time of day for our pleasure. "Best way to start the day," he used to say, even on days that I now know he later spent sexually with Paul. "Spent"…hell, I can't even write down truthful words anymore. He didn't "spend" those days with Paul. He fucked him. They fucked each other.

AUGUST

ALTA

The infinite thought of Augustine has made me a richer person, knowing that he invented Christianity. The symbols within symbols are how I have lived my life. Each day is a symbol of another. Music has been my theology, St. Augustine my city of God.

I know when I pray to you, as I have since I was a child, that you understand the luminous nature of music as the only earthly way to see eternal love of which you preached. You want our faith to go completely to Jesus Christ, but this cannot be, St. Augustine. Our faith must not go toward political whims and things that men have propagated (all respect, Saint), but with that which is higher and more exalted than words, and there are very few pathways available to us. Music, of course, and a certain type of sexual communion, which I have felt a few times. Please, St. Augustine, don't judge me harshly for aligning eros to your theologies, but I can only pray from what I have personally experienced. That must not sound like a woman of strong faith, but I assure you, music and sexual union have both given me faith in faith. Without them I would be doomed, so I pray you to allow these fleshly symbols to serve as nobly to your wisdom as have generations of scholarly honor.

I am only interested in what is true, or true for me. The Neoplatonic has no interest for me, given my parents' insistence on it for my entire life, relieving me of the decision to participate in my own choices. Mother was so furious that I enjoyed sex that she tried to be sure I never did again. In that she was a failure, which I will make absolutely clear to her before she dies.

THE ARMS

JOEY

Implications: there are various classical music websites now that occupy a great deal of artistic energy, at least they did during the end of my playing days. There was a particularly crushing busybody who was forever exposing stacked-competition juries, as if competitions had any influence over careers. They were, and are, money magnets, and he was right to expose that particular hypocrisy; but his obsession was always on the qualities of the judgments inherent in the juries, how they couldn't possibly be partial because a teacher, as judge, would favor their own students and sway the cherished competition toward their own, enhancing their own success. There is enough *actual* corruption in the world without wasting reading time on the supposedly foul classical music competition world. A major win would garner a half-dozen recitals for most, and then a teaching position. Those are valid prizes, but the idea that a huge career would be made by one of the many competitions is willful Cold War nostalgia. Ticker tape will never again precipitate for a classical artist. It only happened once, anyway.

Every era needs its heroes, especially now that we have clearly defined our foreign enemies, especially Russia, and having allowed the world to project many of its invented ills upon us. At the outset of my career, as Russia and the U.S. reached some facade of agreement and cooperation, both countries turned inward and started fractioning among themselves instead of each other; it can only end horribly for both. I barely noticed politics during my playing days, and now I only view them from afar. But it feels like what used to be safely foreign is now nastily domestic.

My greatest audiences were Russian. I gave fourteen Russian recitals in my career, and played only one concerto, the Rachmaninoff No. 3, all in Moscow. I couldn't say they applauded the most, nor that they were even effusive, but they were real. They listened. They sent back the positive. I was somehow able to convey something to them that didn't need to be spoken, and almost everywhere else in the world seemed to require words.

I can't say that to a biographer, not because it is xenophobic, but because I expect a biographer wouldn't or couldn't understand what I was talking about. They would make it nationalistic or a reverse-cultural cliché, but it isn't either. The crushing website used to talk about my "political hold" on Russia, as though it was some calculation on my part. We simply connected, art to public and public to art, nothing more. I knew almost no one in Russia besides the few presenters I worked for, and I've never had a quiet meal with someone else in Moscow, never had to dine with patrons. The few restaurants I visited I went to alone, and though I was a regular at the Café Pushkin, I never had that experience with someone else. Every year I wrote postcards from there with a quill pen, part of their many expensive offerings, but as far as I know not a soul ever received one.

MURALS
ALTA

Some months after he left Houston to return to London, the trip that would eventually end in Australia where he has remained, Joey called me looking for some papers that he knew were boxed in the garage apartment. The cleaners had been up there since he left but I hadn't. It was an overcast day and difficult to see much in there. I could tell that large canvases lined each room, and I was incredulous to find that Joey had painted them all with incredibly colorful and intricate abstracts. I couldn't believe how beautiful they were, and each was so different, like little movements of highly contrasting music. I put on as many lights as I could, and it took me too long to notice the obvious: Joey had also painted every inch of what had formerly been solid white walls. He had turned the entire apartment into a mural, and it was now a living work of art. I could instantly see it becoming a place of pilgrimage, with all those hippies who frequent the Rothko Chapel just swinging by here when they are in the neighborhood. The intricacy of what he painted was astounding. It must have taken months of solid work to achieve it all, yet he'd never said a word the entire time he was here. He went running nearly every day, occasionally saw friends, went to cafés, and did who knows what else, but he spent most of his time up in the apartment alone creating this extraordinary thing.

I immediately called Paul and Mary to show them and get their assessment. They wanted to show Joey's paintings as soon as Joey would allow it. He has never responded to them. And now something seems to have transpired that has kept them from talking.

Camera Obscura

JOEY

Invisibility is a gift I've given myself, willed it upon my life, and it is the one thing I sought in my career. What I consistently learned from great conductors—and there were only a few of them—was the utter necessity of invisibility, of complete sublimation. I left the plethora of self-serving charlatans to Donald; they were more his speed. Great directors of plays and films, great conductors of wonderful works of art, all have an ability, indeed the *need*, to make themselves invisible. They create worlds that unfold naturally and honestly. So much of what I felt coming from a conductor's baton was fear. It is so uninteresting to write about concerti that begin in one tempo and end in another, and that's about all I have to say at this point. Isn't that ridiculous, coming from someone who has played every major piano concerto ever written? Was it all just about what they lacked? Throughout my playing life, there were scattered moments of awareness, little glimpses through a keyhole into some larger room, but I could never grasp it for long. What was it I was looking at?

Paparazzi still take my picture from time to time, usually walking around Surrey Hills or Glebe in the winter. They love for the photo to have autumn leaves for the northern spring papers and websites, as it deepens the sense of distance. The coincidental change of the seasons helps the narrative they have decided should be attached to me: an artist in the springtime of his career choosing the days of autumn.

Even after ten years of retirement, I'm amazed that I still get calls to play. My former agent will phone every few months with a list of proposals, none of which I have ever accepted, but he dutifully conveys the requests: Carnegie Hall, Vienna Philharmonic, the London orchestras, Berlin, and especially from Houston—"money no object," as if that has meaning to me now. They are constantly reminding me that I'm a Houston boy and I never played with the orchestra there. There was no malice in my decision; there simply wasn't time. I did do several recitals in my hometown, but, as they also constantly reminded me, "It isn't a recital town." Indeed it isn't: Houston is one of the few places I consistently couldn't sell out, despite having no problems filling the Musikverein. But they have been kind enough to ask, anyway.

Artist's Life

ALTA

That single night in New York, all these years later I can still hear it, and it means more to me now: Giuseppe soaring through the grandeur of the Goldowsky Fantasy on *Künstlerleben*—music about the life of an artist. How, I have always wondered, even as I've known, is music "about" anything? And how could it ever portray an artist's life, especially Giuseppe's life, and our son's?

I embarrassed myself deeply in Vienna with Joey the year he gave a January recital in the Musikverein in Vienna. We went early to Europe for Christmas so he would be fully rested up and over the jet lag, which never seemed to bother him, anyway. But since we were in Vienna we went to the New Year's Day concert with the Philharmonic, and they played *Künstlerleben* near the end, unexpectedly. In all of my years of hearing it, I'd never heard an orchestra play it; I'd only heard Giuseppe play Godowsky's artistic translation of it, a feeling about a feeling. I didn't recognize it at first because of meeting it in a form I didn't know. Translation is the most important art in the world.

But over the years, having heard him play *Künstlerleben* many times, I've come to realize it to be the perfect organization of the feelings we've had for each other, of the cavalier way my parents treated things that should always be treasured. Did my mother imagine that I didn't love Giuseppe or that I didn't have the personal strength to cope with the life I knew we would have? This musical work says it all much better than I ever could.

Versions

JOEY

With all this time on my hands, I realize how much I don't know about Mom's life. The "trip to New York" she talks about changes slightly with each telling, so I'm not sure what actually went on there. I know she sang for a coach at the Metropolitan Opera and/or Juilliard. I know she met a guy. I know she was taken there by Millie, her voice teacher from Houston, and I know she was in epic trouble when she got back. It feels like a black-and-white movie. What really happened?

She's right when she says she sacrificed everything for me, in that she taught me everything I know about the piano. I never had another teacher, never went through the traditional routes of conservatory and competition. I was such an anomaly that I found entrance into musical circles sometimes based solely on my rarity and not my playing. Who knows what gains you interest these days? But my playing wasn't mine; it was hers. She used to sing every phrase of Chopin, Liszt, Beethoven, Schubert, and Mozart. When I played the big Schubert sonata, the B flat, it was her voice in my ear that I heard. You should have heard her sing that opening tune! People were amazed that a fifteen-year-old pianist could play with such depth. It wasn't amazing. I was just displaying, mimicking, *her* longing. I had an unusual ability to move my ten fingers; it was nothing more.

In my playing days, I knew every major city in the world through the viewpoint of the concert hall, my hotel, and, because of Mom, the opera house, which usually meant my radius was rather small. But they were home to me. The staff of the Bauer au Lac in Zurich knew me by name, and I knew the names of their wives and children. I would walk the distance between the Bauer and the Tonhalle, despite the pleas to take me the short distance in their car. At night after concerts, the staff of the Tonhalle would worry about my safety, which always made me laugh. If they only knew what I got up to after concerts along the shores of Lake Zurich!

My memorable nights were not concert nights, as those weren't really mine. They were for the public. The nights I recall from my playing days were operas, thrilling to me because I'd never have to be responsible for them; I could simply go there and lose myself in a composer's world. In almost every opera, I imagined my mother's voice, and I imagined the life she could have had if she'd had the courage. Was it really only courage she'd lacked?

It is hard to imagine my mother afraid. She tried so hard to control every aspect of Gene's life; I can barely call him Dad. She was so controlling she chased him away. That would always be her story, but it's bullshit. She didn't chase him away. He never loved her. He fucked the maid at their honeymoon hotel. On their twenty-fifth wedding anniversary, he sent her eighteen roses—"One for every year we were happy." He loved that kind of cruel joking.

All a biographer will ask me is, "Do you miss it?" I miss the physical connection to the instrument, but I miss the physical connection to Ben, too, and no one will ask me about that. I miss the crackling intensity of my fingers working with limber dexterity, capable of anything, able to sing the poetry hidden behind the notes. That's what I really miss: what is behind and around and underneath the notes, the spiritual part of playing. I miss the feeling of having energy, and that came only from hours at the instrument each day. I miss having an entire week to practice. All of my energy now, that mysterious inner motor, has ebbed away. I wander around inner Sydney as I used to wander the entire world, but now I arrive at the end of each day unaware of anything I've done or accomplished. Is this retirement? I don't have presence in my own energy any longer; I have to remind myself that I am, in fact, alive.

Gene lavished Christmas gifts on Mom, and every year they got more elaborate. You could always tell how many women he'd screwed by how expensive the gifts were. The year of the fur coat was the worst. She opened a huge box Christmas morning to find a fox fur coat, a beautiful one, too, but a size too small. Thinking nothing of it, she took me down to Sakowitz with her the next day to exchange it. "Oh yes," the idiot saleswoman said. "Your husband bought two coats and he must have mixed up the boxes."

So I would go to the opera. *La Traviata, Le Nozze di Figaro.* How could I hear the Countess sing "Dove sono, i bei momenti?" (Where have they gone, those beautiful moments?) and not think of my mom? Did my parents ever have those moments to reflect upon? I can hear Mom's voice in that aria, those two gentle undulating notes on either side of each other, trying to find a center, rising with each phrase. I used to hear her singing it in the shower at the other end of the house. In later years that was the only time of day when she would sing. Years of Gene's dismissals silenced her voice, and with each passing month I heard less of her, and I got more and more angry.

But she put her voice into my playing. I swear she did. I don't really know how, and anyone interviewing me for a book is going to put their own spin on it, try to make it a big revelation, and that won't work.

FAITH

ALTA

How anyone can refuse to believe in God is beyond my comprehension. Who could be so arrogant? I can certainly understand being dubious about religion, but about God himself? That simply boggles my mind. There is no religion that can contain him. Only music can truly express the wonder that must be God, or that God must be. I have come to believe it strongly, and I've needed that strength in the trials of my life. I've not been proud of very much. I've been forced into situations and decisions that I could not have foreseen, and I've done my best with them, but I have unquestionably gotten more wrong than right.

But I know God is watching me and will help me atone someday. I have two sons, really, though only little Joey's heartbeat was ever a part of mine. Perry was my sister's son but I raised him. There was no choice, really, since the boy was staying with us and both of his parents had disappeared in a crime that remains unresolved. I feel that a lot of my life would have better if I'd known what happened to her, but it doesn't matter now. Too many years have passed.

One of the ways I know there is a God is by looking at the differences between Perry and Joey even though they were raised together and in the same way. They were close in age. Joey was, is, a great musician and he was from a very young age. There was nothing whatsoever to raising him; it was just a matter of giving him the right amount of care and attention and waiting for him to grow into his talent, which happened early on.

Perry, though, was constantly in trouble. He just couldn't make the right decisions about anything. He still doesn't. He was a larger version of his father, and they both let sex guide everything about their lives.

Winter Dreams
JOEY

If anyone is still writing obituaries when I am carried off, they will probably write that I played both the Brahms concerti in one concert. Actually, I did it several times, as it was an easier mental night for me than most, though physically very challenging. A pianist must separate the temporal from the mystical, and thus the physical from the spiritual. My preparations for the Brahms evenings were not at the piano or in commune with a score, but in a gym, strengthening my core, not the sort of thing one teaches in a conservatory. And of course I couldn't have played anything without a pool, where I learned more about musical line than thousands of hours at the piano. The first time I played both concerti together, with the National Symphony at the Kennedy Center in Washington, D.C., I ran three miles in Rock Creek Park. Whenever I look back on the most joyous days of my career, I think of those late-winter runs in Rock Creek Park, so isolated from the world, but with the city looking in every few hundred feet. Sitting in this Sydney park now, far from there, it seems there were quite a few happy times, more as time goes on. Happiness accumulates as memory fades.

THE ROMAN HILLS

JOEY

My agents are still calling. Why can't they believe my decision was final, or right, or mine? They want me to write a book, which I'm not about to do. These are the very people who tried to control my "message" for years, believing the thoughts of a concert pianist were of some great import to the world.

They didn't want me to say this because it didn't fit their booking agenda, but: Cincinnati is the best place in the U.S. to play. It's not the message they wanted to hear, because one never got a very high fee in Cincy, but it is true: they are the greatest U.S. audience. I played in Cincinnati probably a dozen times, and I still think of those audiences. Everything about the city felt like another era to me, which was reason enough for me to love it. Not like the old European cities, of course, but old, and with a particularly beautiful type of decay. The whole city, at least the downtown area I knew, the space between the dear old Vernon Manor and Music Hall on Washington Square, seemed to be aspiring to live up to its illustrious history. It failed, but somehow with great beauty.

I always felt myself not quite deep enough for the place, not because it was of such a high standard by itself but because it knew that some greater thing was somehow encased in its many hills and vistas named after the great Roman Cincinnatus. The city is beautiful, and one never knows where the seemingly immobile Ohio River is going to suddenly come into view. The look of Cincinnati, despite a lot of progress and development, is still the brick buildings of the late nineteenth century, and the many abandoned and dilapidated versions of them that dot the downtown and long-forgotten industrial center to the city's west. They have an aspirational beauty. No doubt even at their zenith they were utilitarian; and though their original dreams and the housing of their early passions and obsessions are long dead, there remains in them an essence of American memory. I never tired of walking or driving among them, sometimes late at night after a concert.

Cincinnati always seemed smaller than it actually was, while San Francisco seemed larger. Still, in the U.S., there was something to selling out the War Memorial Opera House for a recital. But selling out was the not the primary thing, you must understand; it was just being a *part* of that building. Less so in Minneapolis, where the building isn't up to much, but I loved playing in that community, too, for they knew great music when they heard it. Denver. Seattle. Chicago. Cleveland. Pittsburgh, Baltimore. Boston. Atlanta. New Orleans. Dallas. Houston. San Diego. All of them vainly wanting to distinguish themselves from the others by making themselves more like the other. It is not much different in Cologne, Manchester, Birmingham, Rotterdam, Toulouse, Milan, Bologna, Ljubljana, or several dozen other cities—they are all trying to be the best version of themselves. I do miss the striving for distinction.

Heart Belonging
ALTA

I loved seeing Mary Martin in so many shows over the years; I feel like I grew up with her. She always made every word so meaningful, and you could feel how much she loved to perform, how responsible she felt to everyone present. I can still hear her saying lines from *Hello, Dolly!* and *I Do! I Do!*, two shows I adored. Mind you, the great artistic loves of my life were to be found in the greatest operas or, unexpectedly, in the most challenging piano music ever written, but I could also be very moved by a song like, "My Cup Runneth Over" or "It Only Takes a Moment." Martin's voice was husky on the *I Do! I Do!* recording, but oh, how movingly she sang it. And I can still hear her saying certain lines as Dolly Levi.

That is what I miss most about singers these days: individuality. Now nearly everyone seems to sound alike to me, if they can sing at all. The singers like Martin had real voices, distinctive and artful. They sang dynamics and colored words and made music out of them. There is such a disconnection now between words and music. I should not have read Mary Martin's book, *My Heart Belongs*. I was hoping to glean some knowledge about her artistry but instead found page after page of gushy and syrupy nothingness. I could hardly believe it! How could that great artist have so little to impart in what would be her only book? That is my terrible fear about a book about Joey, that he will erase the one opportunity he has to leave a lasting testament to his musical gifts, and possibly pass them on to someone else. Of course, I have a huge shelf full of his recordings that will exist forever, but I want the story of his playing to be told without diminution or dilution.

One book I do remember loving, about the same time as Martin's, was Rudolf Bing's *5000 Nights at the Opera*. First, I so loved the title, for how I longed to have five thousand nights of my life at the opera, mostly singing in them myself but having the opportunity just to experience the performances of others, as well. When I look back on my life, I am shocked by how little opera I was able to attend. Naturally I went whenever I could when I would travel for Joey's concerts, but so many nights were taken up with his playing that it limited my availability to do anything else. Rudolf Bing could well have been my boss, had I been able to follow the path that was put before me. I loved his book because it was filled with the joy of greatness, and I know that my era, my exact contemporaries, were a summit of the history of opera. The 1960s and '70s, exactly when I should have been singing, were a time of so many glorious singers, and I loved every one of them. I was critical of singers I personally knew, like those I met at church who thought they could actually sing, but those great professionals at the Met and elsewhere in those years, before the fake singers we have now, the ones with modest talent who cuddle up to a microphone but have never sung in a real opera house.

In my heart they were my colleagues, even though they never heard of me. I carried on a secret, silent career during those years, even keeping a performance diary of my fantasy nights. I found it a few years ago and destroyed it, because anyone who found it would think me thoroughly crazy, since not a single date in it was true! I would write, "Violetta... Metropolitan Opera" or "Gilda...Royal Opera House, Covent Garden," complete with dates and times and rehearsals—imagine! Not a single one of them actually happened. But I would listen to the Met broadcasts and attend what live opera I could, and I never once felt a pang of anything. That is strange to me now: how I could not have felt jealousy or at least regret when I attended some of those performances, yet I loved hearing them so much. They brought me back to life many times.

That all seems another life ago, really. Soon after, I was helping Joey tend to his very real performance diary, particularly when he was young.

The Center

JOEY

My playing was a simple extraction of a resource: I possessed a unique ability to independently organize each of my ten fingers into an enormous variety of combinations conceived by much more incredible minds than mine. And each morning, positioning myself over that tiny space between E flat and E natural, I would not control but simply *notice* the weight and balance of each finger. On some days, depending on my level of rest, the median of my body would have moved, and the piano practice would slowly bring it back, like a telescope being moved into position to notice its object.

And I mined the resources of the art, the full range of repertoire I could find that best aligned with what I could play at a high level. My bookshelves in New York were lined with charcoal-gray scores of the Henle editions of so much of piano repertoire, though for the pieces I studied I owned every available edition, and I separated my bookshelves accordingly: by edition, not by composer. I had most of that music shipped to Sydney, and it is on a shelf in my den as I write. I expect I will give most of it away or sell it to the nice shop in Glebe that sells used music. Isn't that an amazing thing to think about? All the music I played all over the world will be farmed out through in a sleepy corner of Sydney and taken home by someone unaware of the journey they've acquired.

SEPULCHER

ALTA

I had a terrible phone call with the newspaper about Gene's obituary, one of those frustrating things that must be done quickly after a person's death. I refused to print the word *burial* because he wasn't being buried. Gene was to be cremated and placed in a columbarium, so I insisted they print that he would be interred. The silly woman told me it was not their practice to use words their readership had to look up in a dictionary. I informed her that I was not interested in their traditions. I was paying for the obituary and it would say what I wanted it to say. It would be accurate and elegant. And if they had to look up a word, good...they probably needed to. Then I slammed down the phone.

Is my voice so silent that simple instructions cannot be followed? Perhaps not, for they printed *interred*.

When I thought back on it, I should have realized what was wrong with Gene. Our bathroom cabinet was filled with over-the-counter stomach treatments. He was clearly suffering but, as usual, he didn't communicate anything to me. His cancer didn't surprise me, but I would not have predicted cancer of the stomach for him; lots of other places he had misused and life might have singled out for excess growth.

He'd said he was sorry for all the trouble he put me through, for all of the sadness he caused. I cried when I told Joey, and he reacted strongly. I cry when I think of it now. It is perhaps the only thing in life that makes me cry. I used to cry at certain musical phrases, and when reading speeches from the great Greek tragedies, but that was in my younger days. No created work of art is now capable of bringing tears to my eyes.

Joey was the creative voice of his father and of me, and once he silenced himself it was a wound so deep in me that I have lost the need for tears. I used to love to be so moved by a work of art that the joy made me weep; that was how I'd planned to spend my life, engaged in creations. And I was, in those few brief years when I was teaching Joey to play, but then he left, and I had to let him fly away. There was no choice. I couldn't keep him from the world.

THE CHANCE

JOEY

Mom keeps looking for meaning in the long arc of my career, in all kinds of art, and now, most scarily, in religion. She looked for meaning in Gene finally kicking the bucket. I still see that man Millie talked about from RKO walking through the oaks of North and South Boulevards, whether or not he was real, being diverted by Mom's voice. I can see him approaching the great windows of the house in which I grew up, and having the scene come into focus: a few dozen people politely sitting around our huge living room. Christmas decorations scattered around despite the warm weather, the dark-brown gilded piano that sits there still, the piano on which I would eventually have my childhood, and in the center of it all was the blond and statuesque girl who would grow to be my mother singing. Just singing.

I've heard the story so many times it now assumes my presence. The moment is vivid in the lore of our family, because it is how she has chosen to define her entire life: an event that may or not have been true that may or may not have had an effect on her future. She has transferred the weight of this single moment onto every moment of all of our lives. All I know and feel about music is due to her, and that love of an art has become the confusing love of a mother. I know, of course, that she loves me separately from my ability to sculpt keys into sounds, but having now given up playing, there has been a shift in us. I'm in retreat from everything, feeling the imminent arrival of an end. Absent the performance of music, I am in most measurable ways more alive than ever, yet some indefinable thing has died in me. I long to see Mom again but I'm also fine here in Sydney knowing that I may one day get a call that she is gone.

Mom thought I possessed something elemental, if for no other reason that she felt music to be so. *She* was the musician. I was her product. I mimicked her and tried to please her, and I was, with all modesty, gifted at doing both. But that didn't make me gifted at being a musician.

What Mom won't, or can't, understand is that musicians don't want to be *musicians*, we want to be *music*. I just knew that she could do it and I couldn't, yet I was the one who did it and she didn't. What no one wants to talk about, the awful truth underneath it all, is that music is as dead as God, as dead as Gene. Obviously, people continue making music and propagating a worldwide industry, and all the arguments for its strength and importance are now financial. I extracted upward of $30 million from the industry in my career, most of which is now gone, so it will sound inauthentic for me to say that it was a falsity. People's interest was in my *performance* of music, not the music itself. We musicians are feeding people who aren't hungry. The world has consumed classical music, recorded it, put it on YouTube, and moved on from it, already immersed in their next obsession. But the musicians haven't noticed yet. Oblivion is terrifying. I know all of the optimists who say it has been dying for centuries, but now it actually is true. We are keeping a critically-ill patient alive for no reason. Let it go.

But then there are people like my mom for whom music is completely alive, because music is the only thing that keeps them alive. I've been all over the world, played thousands of concerts, learned hundreds of hours of music from memory, but I'm a cipher. She is the musician because it is a true language to her. Music is her Jesus, her Muhammad, her Buddha—but she projects belief onto them instead of it. *She* is the one who absolutely believes that there is me, you, us, and *something else* between us that great visionary artists have created as proof of it. I didn't create anything, and I had a limited ability to re-create. Her talents were, are, total because she believes. I don't believe in anything.

MY SON

ALTA

Isn't life about discovery? What do you do with something after you know about it? Joey learned so much repertoire. He absorbed it faster than I could ever imagine anyone doing. He amazed his father every year with more and more music. All of the Bach *Well-Tempered Clavier*, all of the Beethoven sonatas, so much Brahms and Schumann, fifty concerti, the *Goldberg Variations*, *Gaspard de la Nuit*—which he strangely didn't like—this entire world I was the first to open for him. I quickly went from being proudly joyous at hearing him play to being unable to keep up. Recordings would arrive in the mail or reviews from the clipping service, and they involved music I'd never heard him mention, much less play.

Giuseppe, before the end, would call me about various details in recordings, as though I retained some power to change what had already been set down. I didn't know Giuseppe was slipping away. I hadn't seen him in some months, which was a sad reality of our lives together, and though his final communications were unquestionably strange, I didn't understand them until it was too late. He must have spent his final months listening to Joey's recordings.

GANT

JOEY

My northern summer was the same for almost a quarter century before it became a winter in Australia: idyllic and privileged places that were preternaturally beautiful, and the hotels where we all stayed while being there: the Hollywood Bowl (Hotel Bel-Air), Tanglewood (The Red Lion Inn), Aspen (The Gant), the Edinburgh and Salzburg Festivals (the Hilton and Goldener Hirsch), and right at the end of my career, Verbier (Hotel Royal). Each shared certain qualities: the white jackets, the decreased formality, the ability to program works you'd never be able to do in the winter. But beyond those surfaces, there was the connection of music to nature, and the hope of giving a vacation to musicians they could not otherwise afford.

The audiences for the summer festivals are generally more relaxed than the rest of the year, and they are largely, again, incredibly wealthy. Even the least affluent in Aspen, those who live in condos instead of houses, are accustomed to privilege, and the summer audiences are mainly rich white people, no matter how hard they try to claim otherwise or sincerely try to change it. Diversity is every noble goal in the arts world since I've stopped, and it should be, but it isn't working. The audience isn't more diverse because the music isn't.

Agents and presenters used to nag me about diversifying my audience, but in the end, I was a privileged white guy playing music written by privileged dead white guys for audiences that were just like me except they couldn't play it. And let's face it: even as a leading classical artist for twenty-five years, my audiences were very small compared to my pop music contemporaries. Tony Orlando and Dawn or Captain & Tennille, for example, who were the major pop artists during my heaviest years, sold twenty times what I did, but they lasted at the top for less than two years while I stayed for two-and-a-half decades. It's just that my top end never each reached their lowest point. Perhaps it evens out.

I will never understand why some make it and some don't, and I cringed every time a journalist asked me this unanswerable and lazy question. Obviously only a few are defined as the top pianists, but what does that mean? There were hundreds of pianists over the years who played rings around me, but they couldn't sustain it for some reason or they didn't catch on with the public, or they didn't want acclaim, or they wanted it too much. I understand only that I had it, whatever "it" was. It was not a burning desire in me that I could ever identify. I wish I had wisdom to offer to those who want it, but I don't. Maybe I could just advise them, "Don't say no all the time." Only the cynical say no to everything, to save them from having to be wrong. Say yes to ideas because yes invites knowledge. This is why I loved to collaborate with the slightly-less-famous, for they were able to avoid cynicism, and working with them allowed a feeling of wonder and romance to live in the music.

The Woods

ALTA

It was only through Joey's playing that I noticed that he was in over-drive. Offstage he was the same calm boy he'd always been. After the Tanglewood opportunity, things happened quickly. I took him out of school and starting tutoring him myself, which let us concentrate for hours a day at the piano. My own school schedule suffered a lot in those years from the traveling, but I managed to hold on to that job somehow.

So much attention was paid to the turn into the twenty-first century, to releasing old recordings of Joey's and making a fuss about the arbitrary construct of the millennium. I found no joy in it except that we were all in New York together in Joey's house, and he played a Carnegie Hall recital around the 28th of December. Little did I know that he was contemplating ending his career. Not long afterward he made his decision in London, the first major milestone in his career that didn't involve me. Not a word. I read about it online and was forced to ask him about it myself. In those millennial days in New York, there was no hint of him retiring. He was loving his house, the feel of the light in the late afternoons, and he seemed genuinely joyful in the presence of his family, even with Perry. They seemed to be at peace during that trip as they never had been as children. I now know that not only can single days be epiphanic, but so can the smallest moments. I recall forever an instant around the dinner table at Joey's house in Turtle Bay, when Joey and Perry looked at each other in the middle of a huge laugh about something. Both of them were convulsed in the pleasure of life, confessing with a look some secret between them. I found overwhelming joy in that moment, as I have each time I've thought of it. Whether or not they noted the importance of it, I've never known. I wanted that evening to stretch out just a little longer. The days with Joey became so short.

When Giuseppe died, I had no one to mourn with. I didn't attend his funeral, of course, as I couldn't have. I was the widow who couldn't mourn. There was nothing. Our life together just stopped. He was living and then he wasn't. I did my crying in private following his death. Back when Gene died, I had people around to comfort me, and I sobbed on every single one of them, but with Giuseppe's death, I was totally alone. Through it all, there was Mother. I was not about to cry on her!

I would go to the Chappell Hill house, sometimes for days at a time, just to hear the wind in the trees. By that time, I was able to think back on the years with Giuseppe with some joy. I was so fortunate to have that man at all, and I must remember that for the remaining time I have.

Choices

JOEY

Ben left me with a large amount of his money, a reality that has set uneasily with me. It must mean he is back in China, but I don't know. If I had real integrity, I would have left the money with Claire and Little Ben and moved somewhere else to start some version of life again, but I didn't. I couldn't leave that little boy. From some unsupportable place, I thought Ben owed me the money for all the pain he caused, as if people can repay those things. But I took the money, and I accepted Ben's wish (why?) that I help to raise Little Ben and support Claire with the money. "You are better for the little guy than I am," he offered. It pissed me off no less for being true.

The Vaucluse house is big, and Claire still lives in the small guest house near the front of the property, while I am still in our bedroom suite off the pool. It all happened with my knowledge but has flown by without my participation or consent. It is strange to admit, but I'm living in what should be a blessed and happy time, yet I feel completely stuck in it, unable to make my own decisions, and unable to move forward.

I could choose to play again, to go back into that life, but that feels paralyzing, too. I could commit to this potential book I'm diarizing for, to at least talking to the biographer they want to send here, but I don't want to paint my life quite as unhappily as it is. I would end up just lying to a writer, or lying to myself, and I've engaged with enough liars.

Claire is stuck, too. I know she'd like to pursue a life with one of the men she sees. She is such a figure of joy, so ready to face every day happily, and I don't know how she does it. She works in the family courts and sees the worst of humanity: children who have been abandoned or neglected, incredibly violent relationships, a parent who has killed their spouse *in front of* their children. Inconceivable stuff. But she doesn't bring it home or carry it around. She is amazing with Little Ben, always gentle and patient, exactly like Ben used to be with me. I've missed seeing him as a parent, and I've resented being a parent myself. I am terrible at it: I feel this great intrusion of time from our son. Our *son*, Ben. I recognize the joy he brings into the world, yet I view it from afar. I don't feel it myself. How can I say the truth of that to a biographer?

Ben didn't mean to hurt me. That is truth. And he won't be waiting on the other side to tell me otherwise someday. It is entirely possible for Ben to have loved me *and* loved Paul. I accept that. But what feels forever irreconcilable is the lying, the simple pain of discovering that I thought one thing and then had to suddenly think another. It was only a great imposition on my life because I made it so.

But others seem to think the most important thing in my life was being a great pianist. They wonder how I could I say good-bye to something so central to who I was. But that pianist wasn't me. I was a fraud.

Yes, I played all the notes, and yes, I memorized all the piano sonatas and concerti, and I played to thousands of people and recorded with renown and success. Yes, I had homes all over the world and was sought and lauded and interviewed and photographed. All of *that* was real. I actually did those things. But the person doing them wasn't me. It was a creation of my mother's that I willingly did to please her. I wanted, for even one day, to feel what *she* felt about music, and I could make her feel it by playing. I engendered feelings in others that I didn't have myself, and I don't know exactly how. I didn't have a regular story, didn't take the established paths, so that became the nodal point of my life. Reporters asked me thousands of times: how did you learn all this without a famous teacher? *I don't know.*

FIFTY PERCENT

ALTA

I loved New York City at it grittiest in the 1970s, and I always needed the break from Houston in those years. I'm one of the few people who saw *Ballroom* and one of even fewer people who loved it. I thought it was the masterpiece of that time. The song "Fifty Percent" was written with the contents of my soul. It summed up my relationship with Giuseppe, and I sat there stunned when I heard it. It was not a song I could have sung for many reasons, but it was *mine*.

It was just us girls on that long weekend, so I could share my feelings about the shows. None of them knew about Giuseppe. No one but Millie knew about him but I could walk the same streets we walked, which I always did on every trip. One of the girls came up with a plan to get us into Studio 54, saying I was a famous opera singer…and damned if I didn't look like one at the time.

My voice was never the same after that mid-1970s trip to New York. It was huskier and couldn't quite gather the top notes anymore. At least I have the knowledge of having had a discernible peak; most people don't even get that. Unfortunately, I was the only one who knew about it. My voice was momentarily appreciated at church services, but since I was a fixture for years on the Houston church scene, by the 1970s I was considered passé, I'm sure.

HIGH TIDE

JOEY

W hen I decided to stop playing, my agent concocted a story about a hand injury, "because it will be more plausible for people." An injury, he said, would allow public sentiment to be on my side and allow for a comeback should I ever desire one. "It leaves you with an option."

I read the proposed press release, which gave a date and time, and a doctor's prognosis—elegant and regretful prose about the injury affecting my left hand, which sadly ruled out the left-hand repertoire dominated by Ravel's *Concerto for the Left Hand*, still held in romantic adoration in popular culture as something that could be remembered about classical music. I refused the fake story, not only because I didn't see any reason to lie to the industry, but also because I was sure some gimmick would arise to write me a right-handed concerto or sonata.

Paul Wittgenstein's fame as a pianist who lost his right arm in World War I led to the fame of Ravel's concerto. While I have no doubt there are a comparable number of right-handed pieces that simply never achieved the same level of fame because there was no famous pianist who lost his *left* arm, I didn't want to falsely become that person. I rejected the marketed fabrication of why I stopped, but it is indicative of the art form I left: trying to sculpt a facade for fear of unmasking something, anything; a lack, a hollowness, the sense of wanting depth but knowing the business of the art is as shallow as any other business.

I quit. Period. I didn't quit because I was physically injured. No, I quit because I loved it so much that I couldn't keep watching the talentless wordsmith hacks sabotage it. I quit not simply because the music critics were laughably bad, but because even for the few who could connect what they heard to what they wrote, no one cared enough about them. I trained for a world that would value what I loved, only to find a world that just valued what it already knew.

I told the literary agent who keeps phoning (whose name I resolutely refuse to remember) that I'm not going to write another score-settling memoir, because no one would or should care about that. Yet…as I pore over my memories, trying to decide if I should respond to him, I feel so much anger toward a world that I simply tried to make more temperate and beautiful. In trying to do that I was hurt, probably mortally, and I lashed out at others trying to even the pain. I certainly lashed out at Donald. At the time I thought my hatred had principles, that I was the real art and he the fake, but now I see I was just jealous of a rival who had talent. Donald is no talentless hack. He is a self-promoting boor of a person, but he can also play. But who cares? The high tide lifts all boats.

UNDONE
ALTA

Wilfred Owen, one of my forever poets, spoke of the "undone years." But my years weren't at all undone. I *did* them, and I now do this, this journal, because they feel done to me now. Joey has years ahead of him, and he's put an end to being remembered. Every year, as each holiday passed with Gene and we continually put on the robes of happiness, I noted the passing of what had been done, what was missing, what was gone forever. At a certain point you have traveled so far in one direction that you can't alter it. It becomes its own engine—you control it for a time, but only in hindsight, after it has traveled far in front of you, do you notice the engine no longer needs you. It is powered by itself.

Giuseppe is gone now. I will never see him again. Our relationship passed so fast. It feels like we just met. What happened to those years?

The thought is surprising to me now, but I have so much for which I must atone. It never occurred to me until recently that I might not be forgiven for the many wrongs I've done, and no one can compare their wrongs to others. I've seen the most horrendous behavior all around me all my life: mostly just a profound rudeness. Is someone rude if they simply take no notice of you? It is more than that. It is an epic misunderstanding of how quickly our lives flow by us. Will I find redemption anywhere?

FIRMAMENT

JOEY

We share everything with the stars, and all we are ultimately trying to do is find our way back to them. It is an extraordinary thing that we call famous musicians and actors *stars*, as if they were a firmament. But we are made of desires and flaws and hurts and expectations, qualities difficult to imagine in the cosmos. The elements surely have desires, but they have none of the cruelest qualities of sentience, those pressures and delicacies of time. I constantly felt imprisoned by time during my playing days, and I suppose I still do. I find each late afternoon to have arrived with unimaginable swiftness. My former routine seems impossible to achieve now. I would begin each day with finger exercises between breakfast and lunchtime. In the afternoon I would work on music for a number of hours determined by whether I had a recital that night. But I would sometimes practice eight to nine hours a day plus play a recital, because the recital was the easiest part of the day. The constant confrontation with myself during the practice hours became far easier than presenting my ideas in front of an audience.

ANTIPODE
ALTA

Despite Joey's conjectures, I do not have a problem with letting go of the past. It is letting go of a possible future that terrifies me. I want to hold to a life in which my son is one of the greatest musicians in the world. But even though he undoubtedly still is, he is also a formidable visual artist, and I can't believe that these pen strokes convert themselves to these words on the page of this diary: but he doesn't want it. I'm turning *my* desires for his fulfillment into useless fantasies. I know it is wrong to try to control his happiness, and I know that whatever joy he extracted from making music is his alone. But he brought *me* a profound joy, as well, and that is now gone, blurring forever what is and isn't mine, and I've never lived in fantasies.

There is nothing to prevent me from going to see Joey. It is clear he will never leave Australia, never meet me in Europe or Hawaii again, as we've reminisced about and toyed with on the phone every few weeks. He is deflecting me by making plans, always pushing them further into the future, pretending there is enough time, or that I wouldn't notice he's not serious about any of the plans.

But there is no more time. I must go to him now. I will go to Australia to see my son. My son has lost his father. There are things Joey needs to know, and I have to make the journey to tell him. How have I allowed this sin of omission to go on for so long? Oh, Mozart, Schubert, Schumann—help me! He might understand that you played a role in it.

Oh, my dearest love, Giuseppe, I should have kissed you longer. Why did I waste so much time? That is why I cannot bear to watch our son waste any of his. We loved, as Poe said, with a "love that was more than love." We had a love that no one saw, but why should that make any difference? Why should a sunset or the Grand Canyon care whether we are there or not, care whether or not they are seen? They are beautiful with or without that knowledge. They just exist.

There is some kind of noble divinity in learning to love yourself while you are sad. Gene gave me every reason to leave him, but I stayed. He taught me how to be alone, and now I am. Giuseppe taught me just to be, not to be haunted by what I didn't get to do, because he showed me that I'd enabled that in our son. Giuseppe and Gene shared one quality: they both invited me to leave, and I didn't leave either of them. Oh, how confusing I find it all now. Why can I only see things clearly after they happen?

That is Joey's great gift: he sees things exactly as they happen. No one hears him now, but he is no less a pianist for it.

SILENCE

JOEY

The staff of the Hotel Bel-Air never thought I was an eccentric, never found it strange that I wanted silence. It all just elegantly and seamlessly happened: I would check in, and they would escort me to the quietest room in the place, and there was never a problem. They just took care of me. There was a valet boy there, I can't remember which trip, and I knew the morning I arrived that he would somehow end up in my room. He did. He brought my luggage and touched me several times: just a tap on the shoulder and particular glance. He wasn't a rent boy; he was just attracted to *me*. That wasn't so rare, really, but he could easily have been fired for coming on to a guest.

"What time are you off work?" was all I had to ask him.

"Five," he said. "Are you playing the piano tonight, Mr. Joey?"

"I'm not." *Mr. Joey?* I thought.

That was our entire exchange. I tipped him for the luggage and he left.

I spent the afternoon catching up on correspondence and managed a halfhearted swim that was unsatisfying and too loud. Shortly after 5:00, there he was at my door, delivering a bottle of water in the distinctive uniform of the hotel: blue pinstripe pants and white shirt.

"I thought you stopped working at five," I said.

"I did. I hope it is okay that I brought you some water. I don't want to get in trouble."

"How will you leave here and not be discovered?" I laughed.

"My car is off-property. I've never done this before, but I'm a piano student and just have to meet you."

I realized it wasn't actually me he was interested in.

"You want to talk about the piano?" I said, moving toward him.

"Yes," he said, grabbing me as I came close to him.

I kissed him lightly, holding his head, and after a short time I felt his hands caressing my back. I kissed him deeper and started down his neck. He moaned and made his desires clear, moving my hands to where he wanted them.

He didn't leave until after midnight, an interval that included a room-service dinner for both of us, delivered by one of his friends. He hid in the bathroom while it was delivered. Before Ben, I had never been in a relationship with a man. The career simply didn't have me in one place long enough to cultivate one. This valet boy at the Bel-Air, that piano student, was one of many. They were often my connection to something that felt normal—sex—and at that moment there wasn't anything deeper to it than just acknowledging that he was beautiful. And he was: he was just a beautiful man. I wonder if he is still playing, and if he is, I wonder if he takes any part of our encounter into his music-making.

He was extraordinary at sex—second only to Ben at his best. This boy, this anonymous valet (I can't for the life of me remember his name), was so hungry for all of it, for the whole experience, for the precision of certain sensations, for being entered, and for the powerful driving into something that can never be reached. I have no idea of any placement of our encounter in his own memory; perhaps he had sex like that regularly and it was just a part of his life. For me, though, it was something rare, a real union of bodies and minds. I never took my eyes from his while I fucked him, and we talked through dinner about various pianistic subjects. He was erudite and interesting. I can actually imagine us together still, waking up with him, fucking, talking, holding each other as Ben and I would do for a time. And I wonder how different my life would have been if I had called him the next day. Would I be sitting in this windy sidewalk café in Sydney writing about him? Does he ever think of me?

He asked me about chamber music, what I most liked to play, and questions of that sort. I remember telling him something I'd never thought about until that moment, which was that one of my most memorable times was playing the Mendelssohn D-minor piano trio at the Metropolitan Museum, in a specially arranged concert. The violinist, cellist, and I weren't a regular trio; we only met to rehearse that one piece, and I don't remember the context. It must have been a benefit with many participants or we would have played something else. I remember we were the finale of the concert, as so many others joined us for the final applause.

I told valet boy how the great arching tune of the first movement, the one that begins on the cello, then the violin, and is then repeated and completed by the piano, had accompanied all of my most precious memories—a confession I'd never realized until the moment the words came out of my mouth. The whole trio is a handful. There are more notes per bar for the piano in that trio than almost any other, but I loved it, and when I was still playing, I would often pull that out and go through it, singing the cello and violin parts, missing them. If I could have played more chamber music, I might have been able to stay in the career longer, but it wasn't what the public wanted from me, I guess. What *did* they want?

That Mendelssohn melody…was there ever a more beautiful tune, a more beautiful idea of music? There were greater and more serious composers, but in terms of sheer beauty, I sometimes can't believe the overwhelming joy of being able to play that piece. It was worth all the years of self-doubt and fear, the quests for silence and the travel and endless amounts of money made and spent on my career, just to play that melody well. For the violin and cello, it is probably the second movement that is the nodal point, and I loved that, too; but for me it was all about the opening movement. The third and fourth movements are about physicality and fingers—great fun.

That Mendelssohn connection is something I never told Ben, who would have completely understood it. But the only person who knows that about me is the valet at Bel-Air, a man whose name I don't even know, who may well be married now, and I was his sole male encounter. Ben inhabits all the unfinished business of my life, all the music I no longer play, and the confessions I have yet to make.

PLANET
ALTA

The church and I do not see eye to eye on many things. I go there for comfort and solace, but those are in short supply when the church tries to put forth theories they best stay out of. At Bible study a few days ago, someone railed against evolution: "I did not evolve from an ape!"

I finally could not contain myself. "You do realize, don't you, that no one has ever said we evolved from apes. You are exhibiting a basic refusal to understand evolution."

Chaotic indignation ensued. I continued, "We did not evolve from apes. We share a common ancestor with apes. We evolved separately from simians but our DNA is ninety-nine percent the same. That is very different from 'evolving from' apes…so when you ask these idiotic questions like, *If we evolved from apes, why are there still apes?* and other such nonsense, do you realize how terrible it makes Christians look? How backward?"

More chaos. I could not stop. "Don't you notice that there are many different types of simians? Chimpanzees, orangutans, gorillas? There isn't a single ape; there are many. We are among them."

I don't know why I was so vehement. I felt like I was trying to get something through to Mother, and that is worse than talking to an ape, for it is difficult to believe my mother evolved from anyone. Never have I known a more obstinate woman, incapable of hearing anything, refusing to accept the clearest truth presented to her, always preferring to hold to her own version of events, no matter how improbable or provably false.

The women in my Bible study are just as bad, but I hang in there with them, hoping I can make a dent in their reductive minds.

FAREWELL

ALTA

I know I'm jealous. Jealous that Gene pursued fleshly pleasures with such openness while I felt the feminine need to hide my desires beneath cloaks of secrecy. I'm jealous of my son because of his talent; he could do things I couldn't hope to do, and he did them easily, or it looked easy to me. I'm jealous that he had his dreams fulfilled at their earliest possible convenience, thanks to his parents, yet now he is giving up those dreams. I'm jealous that he got to live with the love of his life, a gift I was never allowed, and that he's also given him up because of some silly affair. Oh, if only he knew what I endured to keep his life going!

I feel the sunlight on my skin because I am broken into so many pieces; each little fragment gets its own moment in the sun. So many people hate the heat, but I love the Texas sun. I want every pore to absorb the heat of our greatest star, which we feel so powerfully in this enormous state. Aren't we all in an enormous state? My wonderful Giuseppe, not only the love of my life, but the love of life itself...I have to imagine we will meet in some other place, where we will wonder how we could have ever squandered the scarce time we had.

Sehr Innig und Nicht zu Rasch (Very Inward and Not Too Fast)

JOEY

Vienna was the city I played the most but probably knew the least, because in Vienna I always stayed at the Hotel Imperial, which had backdoor access to the Musikverein, the only concert hall I ever played in the great city of music. I once wandered out to the Naschmarkt, and had a wonderful time, but I had little experience with the city beyond that, for my time there was all work. The Viennese musical culture is an extraordinary thing, but it is also stifling for foreigners. One of the great truths of Vienna—really for all of Austria—is an assumption that there is a code for music only they understand, particularly if Mozart is involved. Your success there is not based on what you bring, certainly not in presenting any challenges to the code, but in how closely you can hit the bull's-eye on what they've known all along. The Viennese are not, like other musicians, awaiting your approach to Mozart, not even to discern your tempo; rather, they measure what you present against their collective memory. The process isn't inherently creative, but it has its own joys.

Beyond music, my Vienna experience always included a couple of hours at the Kaiserbründl, a unexplainable gay bathhouse that sits on an ancient site in the middle of the city, inside the Ring. Only a few forgettable times did I have sex there, as that was never the point. Mostly I walked around the place and relaxed. It is an otherworldly experience, filled with old-world nooks and crannies, little corners of sunken baths, Moorish arches, and tons of prowling men in towels. There are dozens of rooms where men go for sex, but it is the social areas that are the most memorable. You cannot believe that any establishment has so much room in central Vienna, and it feels like it goes on for blocks.

Von den Freuden und Leidenschaften (Of Joys and Passions)

ALTA

I was not ready to say good-bye to Millie. I'd been visiting her regularly, and each time she had lost more life force and strength. So many in a short span of time: Gene, Giuseppe, and now Millie…but Mother soldiers on.

Gene's was a difficult passing solely because of the waste and pain he symbolized. He always tried to love, and we did enough laughing together to make it worthwhile, I suppose. He apologized at the end, at least, which was more than I thought he would do. I've not fully absorbed the pain of Giuseppe departing the world, and my heart would simply crack were I to ever truly accept that I will never see him again.

But Millie had been a second mother, much truer and dearer to me than my real one, and I've never known life without her. The last time I saw her, she told me she was refusing treatment. "It is time," she said. "I've had a wonderful life." I worried that it would be unbearable to see Millie for the last time, but as I drove over to River Oaks I felt so privileged to have known her, and grateful for all I learned from her.

"Oh, my dear, I'm so happy to see you. I know it is hard, but please don't be sad," Millie said in a voice surprisingly strong.

"I'm fine. I'm glad you told me," I said to her gently.

"Have you been to Brenham much since Gene died?"

"He prepared me very well to be alone." That made Millie laugh, which I thought odd, since it was more sad than humorous. I went on, "You are so fortunate, Millie. You got to know *real* love."

"So did you, my dear."

I stared at her. Millie couldn't have known anything about Giuseppe living in Texas or his influence on Joey, could she?

"You think I didn't know?" She laughed. "I always knew. I followed him through mutual colleagues in New York after our trip, and I knew when he moved to Texas. I never said a word when you took long weekends. I figured you were with him and were happy."

"I can't believe you knew all this time and didn't say anything."

"I didn't want to know in case your parents ever asked me."

"I wouldn't have minded you knowing. But why would my parents frighten you like that? Why would you care what they thought?"

"Oh, I just didn't like to live like that, having people fight and be offended. I was afraid, I suppose, that they would somehow put a wedge between us. I saw them do that for years to others."

"Why? Why do they do that?"

"Fear. Your mother was afraid that you or anyone else would find out she wasn't as pure as she put on."

"What?"

"I've said too much. It's these pills. I never could hold my mind-altering substances."

"What about Mother? Tell me."

"It's hers to tell."

"You know she won't. Tell me what you know."

"You've been through enough with her. I don't know why I didn't tell you…I think now it might have helped, but it was just impossible at the time. All the rumors when I arrived in Houston were that your mother had an affair with a pianist who came to play with the Houston Symphony, some years before the war, but I never believed them. But when everything happened with Giuseppe in New York and your parents reacted the way they did, I confronted her with it. I told her about the rumors I'd heard, right in front of your dad."

"Was it true? Did she have an affair? What did Daddy say?"

"They were very angry that I brought it up. Your father stood up for her, saying something about that all being behind them and they weren't going to relive the painful past."

"So it was true."

"Yes, I think so."

"She could have told me and made everything go a different way."

"Yes, but it's pointless to try to imagine how something might have been different. It wasn't different."

"Who was the pianist?"

"I think she is the only person who could tell you that."

"She's so out of her mind now that she probably can't tell me, anyway."

"I don't know why I told you. It doesn't matter now. But the incident with the agent, then Giuseppe, once I put it all together did paint a certain picture of her. How is Joey?"

"I don't know. He is in Sydney and seems to never want to leave. I don't know what he does all day. I don't think he plays at all anymore. What agent?"

"I've told you before. The agent who wandered by your house shortly after the war, the night you sang, 'O Holy Night,' just after I got here. Oh, you were so young…"

"Millie, you may think you've told me. But am I forgetting something?"

"I told you on the way to New York."

"You didn't. I would have remembered. Mother used to talk about it, but how did you know about it?"

"But have you heard from Joey?"

"Yes. He's had everything I dreamed of having and he's given it up like it doesn't mean a thing to him. I'll never understand."

"Maybe Joey just needs to collect himself. Oh, my dear, my head is swimming, and I've already said more than I should."

"I seem destined to live my whole life with her. She just won't depart, no matter how grim the reaper. Tell me what happened at the Christmas party, Millie."

"Maybe you just both lived life so differently that you can't possibly see each other."

"Are you dispensing all your lessons now?"

"I've had a good long run, too, Alta. And yes, I can feel it ebbing away. The motor is winding down. One morning you wake up and you know there are only a few mornings left."

"You always loved the mornings. Even in New York."

"Oh yes. The very early morning, before all the horrendous machines start. How I love that time of day, even now. I sleep so much on these pain medications, but I've stopped all the other barbaric treatments. I'm not going to waste away being held to life by the thinnest thread. I want to have these few days where I can still talk and the pain is at bay, then I'll slip away. It's absolutely fine. I think it will be wonderful to just not *be* anymore."

"I'm glad you are at peace with it. I'm not ready for you to leave, though."

"No. You're not. But you'll be fine. I think you should just pick up and go to Australia. It will take your mind off of my departure and you can see that wayward son of yours. The agent came from RKO and wanted to screen-test you. Child stars were big. Your parents had me there for the conversation for some reason. Your mother refused, and they sent the man away. He was at the Shamrock and he went home the next day. They made me swear never to tell you. Oh, I'm so sorry."

I hugged Millie for the last time.

I held my tears until I pulled away from the house, and then what felt like years flooded out of me. Not simply because of losing Millie, or Giuseppe, certainly not Gene. I mourned all the missed opportunities, and the power I've given away to Mother, to time, to not causing a fuss, to trying to live as others expected me to live.

When my tears dried, I turned the car onto the freeway instead of toward home and headed to Sugarland.

Mother was alert that morning, but physically very frail. "Hello, Alta!"

"Hello, Mother. How are you today?"

"Oh, I'm fine. How are you?"

"I've just seen Millie for the last time. It's been a hard day."

"Millie the voice teacher?"

"You know exactly who she is. And I want to know: Why wouldn't you let me do a screen test?"

"Not that again. You were too young; I barely remember it."

"You do, Mother. A man who worked at RKO was coming through on the train from New Orleans. He checked into the Shamrock and took a walk and wandered by our house on South Boulevard when I was singing for one of your parties, the one when the cousins all came back from Saudi Arabia for the holidays. Child stars were big then: Deanna Durbin, Shirley Temple, and Judy Garland."

"Did you want your life ruined like Judy Garland?"

"I should have known about it at the time and had a choice in the matter."

"You were six years old or something."

"I was ten."

"What does it matter now if you were ten or twenty? It wasn't right for our daughter. It was no kind of life." As always, Mother was trying to move *her* life back to normal, where difficulties were not discussed.

"Not this time, Mother. You owe me an explanation of why you took my choices away. I might have had a chance in Hollywood, a chance for something different."

"Child stars were done by then. It was a fad that was already ten years old."

"How could you make a choice like that for me? And then with Giuseppe."

"That wild boy raped you."

"He did not rape me, as I've told you my whole life!"

She did not reply. After a long pause, I said, "Mother, are you there?"

I could see that she wasn't yet gone. I held her hand and could feel her heart beating. She looked frightened, looking to me for comfort. I leaned into her. We hadn't been so physically close in years. I could feel her breath.

"Can you hear me?" I asked. She didn't answer, so I kept going. "You probably thought you were doing the right thing, but you ruined my life.

Can you hear me? You ruined *my* life. You wouldn't let me live with the only man I ever loved. But he lived in Brenham and has since Joey was a little boy. He taught Joey to play the piano, using me as a proxy. And I spent all the time with him I could in Brenham. Every time I went to the ranch, I was in Brenham and we slept in the same bed together. Hundreds, thousands of times. You did not keep us apart. You did not win. You did not make me love Gene."

Mother tried to speak but couldn't get the words out. She struggled to breathe. She wanted to tell me something.

I pushed harder. "What happened to Sally? Who was my father? Did you have an affair with a pianist? Were you forced to marry Daddy? Who is my father? Tell me!"

It was like snuffing out a dying candle at the end of a night. She was close to the end, anyway, so I hastened her to the other side by perhaps a few days. I could see comfort in her face to finally be letting go. At the moment she passed, she looked at me like a child to a parent, trusting, helpless, and small. I realized how few times we'd actually looked at each other. Liberating tears finally came. I had just quietly killed my mother. I whispered her name and told her good-bye.

I rang for the nurse, a sweet and enormous black woman, who came in, saw what had happened, and hugged me. "I'm so happy you were here for the privilege of her passing. She brought you into the world, and it is a great gift to witness her leave it." The words felt true in that moment.

I stayed for a short time, filled out the necessary papers for this sadly common occurrence in this particular building. I moved slowly through it all, flooded with memories of my laughing and smiling father, and so many unexpected small remembrances of my childhood, little glimpses that came quickly as I walked back to her car: snowfall in Brenham when I was about six, early-morning dew, the first time Joey's hands were placed on a piano, Mother at the train station in Houston to see me off with Millie to New York. Life changing forever upon return. How had it all happened so fast?

Gaspard de la Nuit (Treasurer of the Night)

JOEY

One of the saddest comments I ever overheard was outside of Carnegie Hall the last time I played there. I had departed the stage door after finishing a solo recital and twenty minutes of curtain calls, and was going to an apartment in the Ansonia for a party. Heading up Broadway just past Columbus Circle, I passed a group of people who had been at my recital. One of them said, "Forget Joey. You've got to hear Don Sherman in this repertoire. There's just no comparison. Tonight was all about line but had none of Don's visceral thrill. Too bad, really...he used to be so good."

And on it went. Ten years before, it would probably have made me angry, but all I felt then was nausea. After a few minutes, I got so faint I had to pause around Lincoln Center to align myself. *Forget Joey*, the man had said. While being forgotten doesn't worry me, all I could think about was Donald. Why wasn't it possible for both me *and* Donald to be remembered? Why did one of us have to be forgotten in order for the other of us to be remembered? Were those the only options?

Within minutes I was flooded with feelings that replaced what had been me up to that moment. In an instant I was at the center of this world so privileged and shallow that it could bear no responsibility for facile judgments. In an instant I saw how denuded and worthless my time as a musician had been. I was Siddhartha on the river. I'd always considered myself the temporary guardian of a long line of pianists, and I'd considered

Donald that, as well; but in that moment something new was unleashed, and whatever force was within me started its slow draining away. Death was unlocking itself, from just a few overheard verbs and nouns. It wasn't overhearing the opinion that undid me, as my mother would undoubtedly diagnose. No, it was the emptiness of the whole enterprise. I'd contributed nothing to the world but a few hundred hours of distraction to people waiting to be distracted by the next person, and I'd spent tens of thousands of hours for the privilege. Although I didn't realize it at the time, that moment began my decline.

Oddly, my playing actually improved afterward, but the will to play, the cantabile spirit, started to ebb. The week after the comment, I played the Brahms Concerto No. 1 with the Berlin Philharmonic. Minus a portion of my poetic impulse, I was found by the conductor, one I really respected, to be more visceral and less self-aware, which meant to me simply that I was less aware of the music and more of the audience. Naturally they liked that. They expressed their feelings about themselves as observations about me, and with that other floodgates began to open. It didn't matter what I felt as an artist. It didn't matter any longer what I did as an artist. I had become an expectation, and for those who sought to have their expectation fulfilled, I delivered. When the balance tipped in my audiences toward those who arrived to see me fail to meet what they had been built to expect, my energy started to fall away.

For my pianistic voice, though, nothing changed. I didn't love the music less nor did I play it differently. It was the encasing materials that changed, not the jewelry. And diary, please understand: it is not *I* comparing myself to jewelry. These were sentiments expressed by my colleagues at the time—that I was the "crown jewel" of the form, that my playing was the "diamond" they'd all been waiting for—all that hyperbolic nonsense. Most orotund of all, one of the major critics in the United Kingdom declared that he'd always thought the world didn't need more artists until he heard me play. Everything changed, he mused, "when I made him forget everyone else he'd ever heard play Schumann."

This was, I was supposed to accept, a world that didn't need more artists. In that moment on the street, the "forget Joey" moment, all my memories, all the misinformation, all the inane surface judgments coalesced into a realization that I was immersed in a music world that had lost its reason to exist, not because of *me*—the last reason in the world was me—but by the reckless and mindless deterioration of possibilities. Artistry was always escapist to a degree, or so I'd always thought. I escaped into painting until painting became something just as corrupt and petty as the music business had been.

I still think and breathe and dream in terms of the piano. In the between-hours in the early mornings, with the house still quiet, my mind still plays entire works, all the great sonatas, and the Chopin etudes and the Schumann *Symphonic Etudes*—all those incredibly challenging piano works are still in me somewhere. Where are they? They are no longer at the piano and they no longer sing from my body to others, yet they are here, or there. They are somewhere.

In real pianism, that which has *cantabile*, the fingers create an obvious diction, one that puts certain ideas to the fore and subsumes others. Every single note on the piano, exactly like the words we speak, dies away. There is no way to sustain a tone on a piano. Isn't that an eternal frustration? Poor organists: they can't make any single tone die away—they all have to die away together. How awful. But so is the piano: trying to get a tone to begin the same dynamic as the tone before it, and the one before that and the one before that…unbelievably stifling and imprisoning.

Mom says I'm angry about something in my career and just don't want to admit it. It's like she thinks I went in search of something anarchic to say about my career or to blame someone for the decisions I so clearly made. I can go back at any time, or assume I can. The industry has undoubtedly changed a lot in the last decade, but I still get calls. My poor agent. Though he made a fortune off of me at the time, he now makes very little—just ten percent of a few recordings, sales of which would spike quite a bit if I were to die. He still calls once a month or so to tell me who is inquiring after me, and even how much money is offered for me to return to this hall or that, to this orchestra or festival. While I am interested and grateful, at this point it is simple terror that makes me refuse. I am not afraid of the piano, but of having to explain all over again not only why I stopped but why I started again. I longed for obscurity and found it, so I can't change the rules again. Obscurity it is.

I'm like those random pathways worn down by children in playgrounds or by students on college campuses, and which pavers or others who decide those things decide to make official. I'm suddenly what I never expected to be: bohemian, and to prove it I live in an exclusive neighborhood named after a closed valley, and even my part of town has no real provenance. It is named after something named after something else.

I was once described by a presenter in London as having "become routine." It was a classic music industry insult: entitled and arrogant all at once. The presenter invited me to his concert series every year, and my agent was always ready for me to accept because the fees were high. I spread out the engagements so the London public wouldn't tire of me, yet here was the most routine of managers describing me as routine, something he only understood because it described him. I had the pleasure of hearing this delightful comment moments before walking onstage to deliver a recital, which is the inevitable way of these things, as the beginning of a recital is the only time managers and agents tend to have time to talk to one another. They are rarely around for the end. I always understood that: when you present concerts and recitals every night, you can't spend each evening at the hall until 11:00 and be back in the office the next morning. But it is also fair to say that I had much less sympathy for this manager after he called me routine. I played five to six different solo recital programs a year for twenty years, and I took great pains never to repeat a concerto in a city. Only the Coronation concerto got played more than once in some places, and I never felt remotely bad about repeating such a masterpiece. All that can't be routine if I was one of the few pianists who did it.

So many people, even budding pianists, think playing the piano is about fingers. It isn't; it is about the back and spine and the breath. It is from there that all musical ideas originate. Pianism now seems to want more and more technical mastery: quantifiable numbers of notes per beat, and lack of errors as a sign of perfection.

I never felt I was exceptional. I simply felt I was doing what the music required. My mom was the ultimate mirror. She gave me the greatest gift and greatest prison all at once. Making music requires urgency, and that must begin with the performer. I could never achieve from Mom the one thing a teacher must provide: total independence. Students have to be taught to teach themselves, and even though I learned a vast amount of music without her, I could only learn the pieces in which I could hear her voice.

George Bernard Shaw said that feeling is what sets a man thinking, not the other way around, that thought sets him feeling. This idea begs the major question about my career: do we learn to play the piano to protect the legacy of the music, to perpetuate the long line of musicians, or do we do it for maximum exposure and notoriety? When I could go on the spiritual journey of the music at the piano, there was never a happier person, but ultimately I was deceived by distractions: all the things required of me by fame. I could fulfill the music or feed the career, but it became impossible to do both, so I gave up the part that felt expendable.

I still have the Beethoven sonatas memorized. Thirty-two of them! I play them in my memory, amazed they are still there. I am part of that legacy, whether anyone hears me play the sonatas. As well, I played fifty concerti in my career, and they were by far my preferred repertoire to the recitals because I got to work with others. Ten Mozarts, five Beethovens, two Chopins, two Brahms, five Rachmaninoffs, five Prokofievs, one Tchaikovsky, one Haydn, one Grieg, one Schumann, three Saint-Saëns, two Gershwins (the concerto and *Rhapsody in Blue*), two Liszts, plus his *Totentanz*, the Strauss *Burleske*, one Samuel Barber, two Bartóks, one Ravel, two Shostakoviches, one Benjamin Britten, one Stravinsky. That's fifty concerti from memory, and it wouldn't take much to work up any one of them again. Do people realize what kind of work that is, and how many hours it takes to prepare the brief performance?

ONDINE (WATER)

ALTA

I confess my fears to my oldest friend, sadness. We sit down together every few days. Will sadness someday remember me and wonder what I was going on about?

Ophelia sings invented songs and hands out flowers to the court. Do her parents ever look at her with disgust? Did they punish her for wanting to love the man she wanted? Did Gertrude and Claudius ever say to each other, "Maybe we were wrong"? I'm convinced Ophelia isn't mad; she is driven to it by unfeeling men.

Scarbo (Goblins)

JOEY

A few weeks ago, I started noticing posters around Sydney for an appearance by the Vienna Philharmonic, a rare event in the Antipodes. Then the subject starting coming up with friends at the various coffee shops I frequent around Darlinghurst. Had I noticed, they would ask, that the Vienna Philharmonic was shortly to arrive in Australia? Surely "you can't wait" for them to arrive, they would offer. Even Claire mentioned it, though it was something she normally wouldn't notice.

I wouldn't have given it much notice, either, even though I played so many times with that orchestra, and knew so many of the players in that shallow way guests have of knowing one another. Shallow, yes, but simultaneously inordinately intimate, for when the moment of performance happens and it is truly special, no one talks about it, for pronouncing on it negates the very thing that made it so. I would be happy to see some of them again and to hear that extraordinary sound, but I know I won't go. The reminders of what was and what might have been are just too great.

All the people around me now, the ones I encounter every day, know I won't attend but they bring it up anyway. Why? I suppose for the same reason they tried to connect with me when I played, to connect *them*, not me, to some noble grandeur or romantic notion. Nothing could induce me get in a cab and instruct the driver to deliver me to the Sydney Opera

House, possibly be recognized, and then wait for the auditorium to darken and to passively sit for a concert. I know my heart can't take it.

My phone rarely rings now, but as I busily tried to ignore the ubiquitous Vienna talk and stick to my routine, two calls came in rapid succession: first was Donald asking if he could see me while he's in town playing the Brahms Concerto No. 1 with the Vienna Philharmonic. Fuck that. Not only is the great orchestra coming to my city, but the *one* pianist in the world I never want to hear again is coming with them, and I'm unlikely to be able to get out of seeing him. I don't even want to have a conversation with him. What can I say—"I'd rather chew my own fingers off than hear yours"? How, in all of the intrusive inquiries I've had about the imminent arrival of "the Phil," did no one mention that Donald was the soloist?

As it turned out, Donald and I spoke for over an hour. All the old times; all the mutual friends; all the perceived hurts, accusations, and apologies that longed for sincerity were exchanged between us. Conversations with Donald always take a long time, because he never speaks directly about anything, and he is the subject of most his sentences. He speaks in a code I used to know well, as it is the way of communication at the top levels of the classical industry: everything is inferred but little is actually said, and assumptions and equivocations are meant to be accepted as genuinely informative and fascinating.

I have a few weeks to prepare for hearing his concert, and he even got me to agree to dinner afterward. I guess life isn't finished with me yet. What started as a few fantastical notes for this diary during the lonely winter months must have created some opening in the world for this unwanted series of unwanted realities. An hour after hanging up with Donald, Mother called to tell me she's coming to Australia *next week*. After years of refusing to make the trip! There was no reasoning with her, no persuading her this isn't the best time. She insisted that she had already made the decision, bought the ticket, and was unsure how long she would stay. My choices, again, were removed.

There must be some reason for coming that she won't share with me. I've been here in Oz almost ten years, and the only thing she's mentioned is that I moved so far away to prevent her from visiting. I'm sure her reason will become apparent within hours of her landing. When I asked how long she would be staying, she answered, "A few weeks." Holy fucking shit! It had better not be about this autobiography, and it had better not be about trying to get me to play again. As much as I hope her trip is motivated solely by motherly affection, I know it can't be that.

So I'm suddenly forced out of years of peace and quiet and have no choice but to make plans. I will have to get to the Blue Mountains house as soon as possible in case she wants to go up there. I'm having to face several things simultaneously that I'd hoped to avoid indefinitely, including walking back into that house in Katoomba. Yesterday there was nothing to burden me; today there is Vienna, Mom, Donald, possibly Perry, the mountain house, even getting Little Ben and Claire prepared for my mom...all unexpected and yet, strangely, I also want to see them all, though I could live without seeing Donald.

What Mom doesn't seem to understand about my life—one of many things—is that every time you travel, every time you aren't home, not all of you returns. Performing music is the same. Every time I played one of those extraordinary pieces, I couldn't ever quite get back to who I was before I played it. She would hear that as music being "transformative." Oh, it is. But transformation is often a terrifying, violent, and chaotic thing. Bach, Beethoven, Liszt, Brahms (so dangerously close to the word Brahmin!), Chopin, Schumann, Schubert, and so many others...so many translators who all altered the journey. Or are they the journey? The subject is travel. But the objective is also travel.

Ben transformed me, and everything he was when we met was all I ever needed. But what happened with him and Paul transformed me, too. I can't shake it. I'm not jealous of them. In fact, embedded somewhere inside all of the pain, like a fossil, is some magnetic erotic impulse; I'm turned on by the two of them together. Ben isn't dead. I made him die in my life because I couldn't figure out how to live with what happened. Why have I let everything die? I have a life force that for twenty years I poured into the piano. I clearly still have it. But where is it? Literally, physically, where is it?

I look at this empty page every morning in the cafés and parks of Sydney, and I know every one of them and the casts of characters who people them, and I often think the best solution for my life right now would be to leave Australia and go back to New York. Do all the American Christian things: rebirth, resurrection, forgiveness, then let everyone know I've done it. Yeah, like that will ever happen.

I know now that I overreacted to the Ben-and-Paul situation. But it isn't possible to go back and underreact. The screaming, the sobbing, the bargaining with Ben in trying to understand it, even as he apologized through oceans of tears followed by days of silence, didn't go anywhere near resolution. His silence just enraged me further, since I wanted to see the passionate tornado of a man unleashed again, wanted to see that he didn't want to lose me. I knew he had been volcanic with Paul, knew he had found that energy to make something that was solely his. But when did I ever get the benefit of that from him?

Schubert, Chopin, Schumann, and Liszt were *mine*. Yes, others played them, too, and wonderfully, but the way I did them was solely mine. I was not better than others, but the way I played was *mine*. Having had them, I didn't need them again. If I were to travel back to Schumann now, or to any of the later Schubert sonatas, I'd never be able to get back.

LE GIBET

BEN

There is so much Joey cannot understand, and I've never blamed him for this. He has much force, so much *xi*, and it never tires in him, no matter what he thinks. He doesn't realize that I can feel the *xi* at our most intimate. He will never understand what happened with Paul, and he may always see it as betrayal, but I've never loved him less than epic—is that the word?—the epic love I've felt for Joey since I first saw him in China all those years ago. It bothers him that I abandoned my Cantonese name for a Western name, and over time he has classified that as a symbol of oppression. But I want to leave it behind me, except in art. I want my artistic name to be Gu Shing Yen, and so it has been.

Joey does not know where I am, nor does Claire, and so neither does Little Ben. I abandoned my son, our son, but unlike my own father, I know my son is better without me for a while. Maybe he will understand someday. My sister Claire—her Chinese name is Lian—has given us this great gift from her body, our son. What a miracle of medicine it is that the man I love more than any in the world has been able to make a child with the sister who shares my heart. There were no twins without punishment in our China. It is somewhat different now. My sister is a barrister here in Australia. She's lucky to have a father who taught her to read so many languages that she could study when we came to Australia and learn to be such an important woman. It would be impossible in China, which is a sadness.

Since I became an Australian by the grace of the government, and since I brought such shame on myself with Joey by my friendship love for Paul, I took myself to Arnhem Land in the Northern Territory to try to understand the country where I will spend the rest of my life. I had to understand the painting of the land, so different from my painting before. I have been in the desert with no contact with Joey, Claire, or Little Ben. I had to learn the new Ben, for the old Ben has died. Paul was so good to me, and Joey cannot understand my background, that when one is so good, when one saves not only my life but that of my sister, that no matter the horror, I am a person who can only turn to love. I should have told the truth to Joey always, and this is my forever shame. But in Arnhem Land I have learned that I can tell him the truth now. I saw no possibility in my life, ever, to show love to a man. Then my art gave me the possibility to leave China and show my love to Paul for all he did. But what Paul did is not like my love for Joey.

Joey thinks sex is like his art, something to be practiced. For me it is not like art. Art confines. Sex is liberation, and Joey has never felt anything to be a prison. He thinks he has, but he has not. He has no idea of the oppression we faced in China, and I have never bothered him with it because I want my love to be an escape for him, like it was for Paul. I caused a great pain by trying to be an emperor for both of them. After Joey learned about us, Paul and Mary disappeared, I guess forever. Joey told them, though I wish he hadn't. It would have been better if he'd let me handle it, but he was in pain and I understand that great pain costs. Joey lost Paul and Mary when he lost me, but my loss was greater. Paul and Mary still have each other. Joey still has Claire, Little Ben, and his beautiful mother. I have no one. No parents, no sister, no son, no Joey, who was everything to me.

I don't expect I can ever make my life right again, but I have made a great amount of art during my years in the desert. Perhaps it has changed me and made me better at knowing when I have hurt Joey. I cannot imagine how much pain he has endured because of me. I can only offer my life to him again and hope that he will hear me, hear my voice. Paul was about giving thanks. It was simple and young and very stupid. Joey was different. It was everything—like Bach, as he would say. There is a life for us, if he will have me again. I hope it is possible. I love him more than any sunset.

The Wanderer

JOEY

There was something about that old man in Malibu that has stayed with me. He was so present somehow, so...totally with me, in a way I can recognize but almost never feel. Ben had that. When Ben looked at you, you were the only person in the world. This old guy, talking about talent scouting and living in Brentwood, and Kenter Canyon, and trains. It reminded me of Mom's story about somebody scouting her by accident, a guy who was taking a walk from the Shamrock Hotel. She must have thought of it, too. I've never thought the story was true, but what if it was? How would he have found his way to Houston? He probably had to change trains and wait overnight to get to LA, and waiting a night to take a faster train would have been worth it. The Shamrock was new and famous, so that would have been worth it. He would have arrived from New Orleans, maybe, late morning.

It must have been the days leading up to the Christmas of 1949.

"I had the greatest job in the world," he said to me at that party, and I felt competitive when he said it. Isn't that stupid? I was the one with the greatest job in the world! He searched for talent for the film industry, just then recovering from the war, to feed the insatiable need for novelty from a public that still went to the pictures two or three times a week. Unlike my job, there was a hunger for what he selling. Everywhere he went, there must have been talk of hard times, about the recovery from economic depression, and the aftermath of the war. Did they just feel like films to him? That wasn't *his* life. His life had been weeks in the Waldorf

Astoria and European resorts, and trains back to California. His wife and son probably picked him up at the Pasadena Terminal and drove back to the perfect weather in Brentwood.

Did he love the Atchafalaya Basin? Was it raining that morning? He must have thought it a place his studio could never set a film in, because you'd never be able to re-create it on the back lot.

December is so beautiful in Houston. I wonder if it was beautiful that day? The Shamrock must have had a green car waiting at the station to drive him the four miles south. Traveling straight down Main Street, they would have passed through the modest downtown, with its fine department stores, restaurants, and movie theaters—a lot of bustle so close to Christmas. Then they would have come to a more verdant area, packed with live-oak trees, and the Main Street south of downtown was filled with palatial homes spread out like in Beverly Hills, without the hills. This was a city trying to impress, he must have thought, yet there was a quality about it that wasn't quite real. On the right just a few minutes down Main was a beautiful Art Moderne Sears store that he probably wished he had time to go into but he'd already purchased all of his Christmas gifts and had no time.

The green car would then have passed a small and beautiful Beaux arts museum off to their right, followed by an expansive park on the left filled with families. Maybe the man asked about the small cluster of buildings to the left, and the driver would have said "Hermann Hospital." Did he say it with pride? Was he wearing a green uniform and matching hat?

The car would have pulled into a small opening in a towering hedgerow, the monolithic Shamrock and its newly famous grounds. He would have seen every shade of green imaginable. Would he have thought it overdone? Texan braggadocio, or just another movie set? His suite might have over-looked the enormous swimming pool, more of a lake than a pool. He might even have seen a small boat moored near the diving area. In the distance he could have seen the area he'd just traversed in the green car, with the hospital quite close and the small group of downtown buildings beyond. The land was as topographically flat as anything he'd probably ever seen, but the blanket of trees must have comforted him. In Brentwood, did he look down on beautiful canyons of trees? A bellman probably brought his bags to the room and asked him if he needed anything. He must have told the boy he was going to nap and then take a nice long walk. The bellman would have told him to be careful about water moccasins.

He must have walked north from the Shamrock, through streets named after famous authors: Dryden and Shakespeare. Did he find delight in literary names? Rice Institute would have been sparse of students in those days before Christmas, but he must have walked through there. Did he notice the symmetry and studied beauty of the buildings, the attention to how it might look in a century?

The late-afternoon winter sun would have been rapidly descending to his left, and Christmas displays were beginning to be turned on in the neighborhoods beyond Rice. He wouldn't have known where he was going, but the organized grid of streets would have assured him he wouldn't get lost. That was the first postwar Christmas to fall on a Sunday, so that Tuesday would have been an obvious choice for many parties. It must have looked like a movie to him.

Somehow he found his way to the house I grew up in, the house Mom grew up in. Did he love the cathedral of live oaks through which he had to have walked? Did he find it amusing to cross a Sunset Boulevard, just like the thoroughfare that took him to Brentwood?

What song was it that mother was singing that made him stop? What was the sound that caught his ear? Was it "O Holy Night," "Ave Maria," or maybe "O Divine Redeemer," the songs that would remain her party pieces on the few occasions when she would sing as an adult? I think the last thing I heard her sing must have been "Care selve."

He would have looked through the living room window, and from there a young girl could barely be seen from behind the huge Steinway piano, just a tuft of blond hair accented with a red-and-green ribbon. She must have been nearing the end of the song, about to ascend the climax of "O night divine" maybe, and when she did, the man would have felt the vibration even out on the street. Her voice was mature beyond her twelve years. He would have entered the open front door of the house, the wood of the house still ringing, like he had entered an enormous cello. A polite applause would have followed the girl's performance.

What happened then? Was it like mother always said it was, that he entered the house and demanded to see her parents? Had he explained that Deanna Durbin and Judy Garland were then aging out of their childhood status and he needed a new young singing star? Did he really tell Grandma and Grandpa that he'd been all over the world and never heard a voice like hers? Was her voice really as pure, radiant, and silvery as has always been told in the story? Did he need to leave for his train the next day and so demanded to speak to them right then and there at the end of the party? Did he say he couldn't wait to screen-test their daughter?

BLUE MOUNTAINS
JOEY

I needed escape after hearing Donald's voice again after so many years, so I drove up to the Katoomba house. Hadn't been there in years. I'd forgotten how much I love that drive. It is always too short to absorb the uniqueness of it. As I keyed in the code on the gate, the light to the west caught my eye and suddenly I was back at Hollywood Bowl, surrounded by hills that are verdant and dry all at once. The shape of the valley around the Katoomba house was similar, and the near invisibility of neighboring houses that I know are there always brings Los Angeles to mind.

By the time I unloaded the car and opened the patio, the light was just achieving the Purkinje shift that Ben used to love to recognize whenever he had the opportunity. It was the time of day when the sun's angle increased the luminescence of nature's bluest colors. Purples and blues in particular were brought into relief as greens and darker colors faded into the background. I know why Ben loved this time of day, when the darkness faded into the background and that which was happiest and brightest came to the fore, because it was nature's version of how he tried to live. I wish I could have just let him have that color and never questioned it. I liked the darker colors, and I didn't need the brightness to show them to me. But Ben loved knowing things; his governing light would not allow him to notice the darkness unless he chose to do so. Why did I always try to quell his light?

I pulled some piano music off the music shelf for the first time in ages. The shelves of piano music in the mountain house were in alphabetical order by composer, and they weren't my main copies of anything, just second or third used copies I'd collected all over the world. All of my music that I really used, the first copies, were boxed up in the garage apartment at Mom's. The first thing that caught my eye was Schubert, the Impromptus, so I played through the eight Impromptus and the *Six Moments Musicaux*. Occasionally I had to stop to remember the intricacies of a passage, but largely the music poured out of my fingers with ease, like I'd had a good night's sleep. I grabbed the Bach *English Suites*, which were considerably busier for the fingers, requiring a totally different set of masteries from the Schubert. I spent four or five hours that night on the *English Suites*, the longest I'd played anything since the London recital. Although I'd never stopped playing exercises, simply because I loved them, I rarely could bring composed music off the shelf.

When done, I felt tired, and my fingers actually felt strained.

The light the next morning was perfect—welcoming and vibrant. It had been so long since I'd been outside of Sydney, outside of anywhere urban. Ben was somehow everywhere for me in the Katoomba house and the surrounding little mountain towns. I love it up there. The only way to silence Ben in those days was to play the piano, so I finally brought out the two Brahms piano concertos, even though none of my fingerings and reminders were in them. They were clean copies. The opening thirds of the first concerto came more easily than I thought they might; I wished I could play them with such rhythmic elasticity with orchestra, but there were just enough instrumental interjections put there by Brahms to make that almost impossible. Both Brahms concertos were often played but rarely rehearsed, and the type of rehearsal it would take would be too boring for the types of orchestras who regularly programmed it, except with a conductor I have yet to ever find. People don't realize how rare it is for a conductor to be able to get an orchestra to think outside of their perceived comfort zone for a work they know. I spent days up there that trip, longer than I imagined. Claire didn't seem to mind. She was probably happy for the break.

Late on one of those nights, the ringing phone came crashing into the complete silence of the mountains. It had been so long since the phone had rung in the Katoomba house that I had to remind myself where it was. I ran to the kitchen wall phone, hoping I wouldn't miss the call. It was, of all people, Perry. I couldn't imagine him having the initiative of finding the number and calling, so I immediately figured something bad had happened.

Mom was in the air, he told me, and arriving in Sydney at dawn the following morning. I explained that I was at least two hours from the airport. No sympathy with that. He just said, with no emotion, "Well, just be sure you go get her; I promised I would call." The conversation took no more than five minutes.

There was no time to deal with anything. I couldn't even pack to go back to Sydney. I tried to sleep, but by 3:00 a.m. I gave up and just got in the car and drove to the airport, expecting some kind of feeling of homecoming and reunion in the airport's arrival hall, but mostly I just felt relief that she had made it and I was there to retrieve her. It had been ten years.

I drove immediately back to the Blue Mountains house with her, unable to introduce her to Claire and Little Ben at the Vaucluse house just yet, a decision I made impulsively, unable to immerse her straight into my life.

Jet lag was on my side. Mom slept much of the journey to the mountains, and upon arrival she was more exhausted than hungry, so we exchanged niceties that any visitors might, and we each retired to our rooms.

Tempest

ALTA

Negotiating LAX alone was like a war zone to me. What a horrendous place! All the sections look alike, leaving no landmarks to help you remember where you are. I slept much of the endless flight, so although I was slightly dazed at the end of it, I wasn't so tired as to not notice the profound changes in my son. Joey looks gaunt and devoid of his former playfulness. He used to view life lightly, with his father's (the actual one) dry humor. I am going to have to find an appropriate time during this journey to come clean about his father. I've left it far too late, and I'm deeply sorry for that, but I can't continue this particular secret; there are secrets enough.

Joey assumes that because I have flown halfway around the world and am doused in exhaustion that I will not notice the obvious, that he is just as unhappy as I've expected all these years, and I should have come sooner. Not only should I have come sooner, why in the world did I not get him out of this place that is so far from anything he's ever known? Oh, I knew he wanted me to stay away, and I knew he had to get his life with Ben settled. But Ben is nowhere to be found today, not even in small talk, and he obviously didn't greet us at the airport. Joey decided not to even take us to the nearby Sydney house, where we might have been resting as I write. No, he drove us miles away into the dark, to his beautiful and elegant house in the Blue Mountains. It is a lovely spot, to be sure, but it isn't his. It doesn't feel or smell like Joey. He hasn't even bothered yet to drive us to a promontory from which to see the Sydney Opera House.

"You'll see that easily from home in a few days," he said, as if it's the most routine thing in the world. No doubt it is for him, but not for us.

Pour les Tierces

JOEY

There was a fairly awful-but-popular film early in my career, *The Competition*, that briefly popularized the playing of piano concerti, and brought to life the struggles of being a young pianist trying to build a career. Many people thought the character Richard Dreyfuss played, Paul, was based on me. But the only thing I shared with the character was an instrument, which didn't stop a lot of people speculating about it to this day. The movie was unintentionally hilarious: the twelve, quickly six, finalists of the piano competition were all facets of the same person: the good-looking dude who checks how his muscles look while he plays, the Russian prodigy whose teacher defects, the nerd who can tune his own piano, the token African American, who practices in the nude, while the two leading contenders fall in lust. And poor Lee Remick as the cynical piano teacher, forced to say the most risible faux-serious lines: "Ludwig *van* Beethoven taught Carl Czerny"—(puff cigarette)—"who taught Leschetizky, who taught Schnabel, who taught Rinaldi, who taught me. And now the sixth pianist in a direct line from Beethoven is standing here staring at me in her Jordan Marsh mix-and-match," et cetera.

The film gave people an impression of the seriousness of piano competitions, including lots of judicious shots of juries evaluating the pianists. Sam Wanamaker had the impossible task of playing an egotistical conductor. "What I do see is allegro ma non-fricken troppo." God. But he does get to lie around listening to "sensual" new music, "more modal than serial," in the company of one of the more lithesome contestants.

All post–*A Chorus Line* films or plays about any kind of performing ended up simply being *A Chorus Line* retold in another medium. *The Competition* was no exception. But the movie had one sincere scene, and it often came back to me during my playing years. Richard Dreyfuss and Amy Irving, and presumably the characters they played in the film, are in bed together after a night on the town getting to know each other. The two can't really know each other, in the conceit of the plot, because they are in competition. (That an actual musical career involves competition solely with one's self was lost on this film.) He kisses her. He cries (from relief?). He releases a lot of tears from the tension of trying to be heard as a pianist. They confess their beginnings in music. "Music is a hard enough trip without any distractions," says one of the interchangeable and forgettable characters. Dreyfuss plays an artist from a working-class family, guilty about what they've spent on his musical education. Irving's character comfortingly Hallmark-cards him with, "You're not stealing their money; you're letting them love you."

Finale

JOEY

I wanted to be sure we didn't have too much time at the Vaucluse house before we'd have to turn around and leave for the concert. I needed Mom to meet Little Ben and Claire but not have too much time to pry, so I timed our journey down from the Blue Mountains back to the city very precisely. Ninety minutes after we got to the eastern suburbs, we had to leave by taxi for the Sydney Opera House, and that was pushing it for the late-afternoon traffic.

As Mom and I were being seated for the concert, about twenty minutes before the downbeat, one of the administrators of the Vienna Philharmonic, somebody I recognized but couldn't name, came right up to our seats, I assumed to go through the ritual Viennese niceties, which he quickly did, adding, "Joey, could I ask you to come backstage with me, please?"

I told him it was nice to see him and I thanked him for the invitation, but I had no need to go backstage, no one I needed to see. I told him I would call Donald the next day rather than greet him backstage. My anxiety rose at just the thought of walking into the green room of the Sydney Opera House, with its great photo of Joan Sutherland covered in streamers, and everyone sitting around talking.

But he was forceful. "Please, sir. Come with me." So I went.

As I remember it now, I know Mom realized something was happening well before I did, just as she always had.

I reluctantly went with him. We only passed to the side of the green room, so well known to me, before he walked me through a labyrinth of hallways to a conference room with a view of the Sydney Harbour bridge. I must have been in there before through the years but I couldn't remember it. A group of musicians, all in their tailcoats ready for the performance, stood as I entered. I knew many of them. They motioned for me to take the one empty seat so I did, perplexed and nervous.

An older man at the far end of the table spoke, with only the slightest Austrian accent. "Dear Joseph, Joey, we recognize how unorthodox it is for you to be brought before the musicians' committee of the *Wiener Philharmoniker*, when you were planning to simply be our honored guest in the audience tonight. We revel in many memories of you playing with us over the years."

I thanked them. I could tell by their faces that something was wrong with Donald. I glanced at my watch. Ten minutes to the top of the hour. I said, "I cherish the many concerts we had together at the Musikverein, so far from here and in my former life." I hoped *former life* would easily translate.

"Donald got to the hall this evening and collapsed in his dressing room."

"He's had a heart attack," I said, for reasons I did not understand. Some deep impulse in me knew he had, but I had no idea if it was true.

"Likely so, yes. He has been taken to the hospital, of course, and we do not know his prognosis. But it is obvious that he cannot play the Brahms D Minor tonight. Naturally, we have a number of works we can substitute for it, but the musicians' committee of this orchestra, assembled secretly in this room, remembering some of our most cherished performances of the concerto, respectfully ask that you consider playing it tonight."

Even as I knew it was coming, hearing the words quietly fill the room took my memory back to The Savoy, when I was the one who collapsed and Donald took me in. Strangely, I didn't feel anxious. I needed silence. I listened to my own breath, then I was hearing their breathing, then the slightly out-of-tune buzzing F sharp of the only light in the room.

"Gentlemen," I said, for they were all men, "I am overwhelmed that you've asked, but I have not played professionally in a decade, and we all know how taxing the Brahms is. I'm very sorry."

"We understand, of course. It is the finale of the concert, so you would have some time in your dressing room while we play our first half, plus the intermission," the man said, seeming not to hear me.

"I have retired from the piano. There must be someone else you can find who can play it."

"We are, as you well know, at the far edge of the world. If you do not play the Brahms, we will substitute a Beethoven or Brahms symphony."

"But there is no time even for a rehearsal with the conductor, as he will have to perform the first half of the concert."

"That is true. But in our experience as an orchestra, some of the greatest performances come from either copious rehearsal, or none. Please…Joey."

There was tenderness in the way the old gentleman spoke my name. I slowly and silently looked at each person sitting around the table. They were all probably wondering if I actually could make it through the concerto. I knew I could. I had played it just a few days before in the mountains. Thoughts came rapidly then: would this mean the end of my retirement?

No. I would not play again after tonight. That would give the orchestra an exclusive story that might break out of the classical bubble. Would Mother take this as some kind of vindication, something she caused by being there? Yes, I figured she would accept such a trite explanation, but so what? She deserved whatever would make her happy about it. Then I decided I wouldn't do it. Before they were all onstage warming up, I would simply say to this group of musicians that I appreciated their request but it would be impossible. Then I realized it was too late. I could hear the First Symphony of Brahms starting over the tannoy. Two men came to show me to the dressing room I knew so well. It smelled of Donald's unmistakable cologne.

I sat in the dressing room amid a type of silence I used to know well. It is a loud silence, always aware of dwindling time. I began a few of the Brahms exercises. I didn't want to tire. I tried the first phrase of the concerto, the calm D-minor undulation with lots of thirds and sixths in the outer right hand. They were secure. I cursed myself for doing such a bizarre thing. How was Donald, I wondered, or was he even still alive? I knew Mother must have known I would be playing, since the concert had begun and they must have made an announcement or an official of the orchestra had told her. The dressing room speaker had been turned off, so I couldn't hear anything said from the stage and I didn't want to hear the first half of the concert. As if no time had passed, I was in my old world again: a dressing room, waiting, doubting, hoping, waiting.

I was surprised by the thunderous and warm ovation I received for simply walking on stage. I first turned to greet the orchestra, as well as the audience members wrapped around behind them. I went to the piano, hoping it would be an instrument I would like, it having been chosen, naturally, by Donald, and we always had very different tastes in keyboards. I sat down, but the applause continued. I stood back up to acknowledge it, mustering solemnity, but the length of their greeting choked me, and I held back tears I wasn't expecting to have. I found Mom in the crowd. She was smiling but not applauding.

The conductor started. During the long introduction, I noticed many new members of the Vienna Philharmonic, and a few of them nodded toward me, smiling. Part of the Philharmonic's mystique is their non-chalance in all circumstances, an acceptance that only the exceptional is their due. The introduction to the concerto was somewhat ponderous and slow, I thought, something the concerto sadly invites in conductors. It didn't quite crackle with energy, but I knew I could alter the tempo imperceptibly when I began, and the musicians would go with me. I was somewhat cautious in the opening, but by the time I got to the soaring F-major chorale, my old stride was back. The audience faded from my awareness. The hundreds of trills in the first movement of the Brahms concerto all sparkled like they had when I was a boy, and I loved how they felt. I didn't feel bad having a score on the music stand, since it had been so many years since I'd played from memory in the front of the public, but I never opened it. The Brahms has handful after handful of notes: widely spaced chords in rapid succession, antiphonal octaves for bar after bar. It is among the busiest of concerti, but I remembered it as if no time had passed since I'd last played. It seemed happy to see me, having lain dormant within me all those years.

The first movement drew applause, as it nearly always does. Brahms made it nearly inevitable, ending the first movement with great crowing strokes, like the end of a Verdi aria or Beethoven symphony. I always loved the spontaneous acknowledgment of the grandeur of the first movement, because it so perfectly invited the idyll of the second movement. That second movement of the first Brahms concerto was where I housed the entirety of my life; all of my memories, painful to joyous, were contained within its brevity, in something that felt like a third person, something outside of me.

The second movement had been almost unbearable to me for so long, but I was able to find joy in it that night. Was it because Mom was there? Was it because my own emotional remove from the cascading beauties of the movement allowed the *real* intentions of the music to come forth? How I detest all those heaven-gazer pianists, pretending to make music by showing their audiences how much it means to them. Don't *show* them; make it as easy as possible for them to *hear* it.

ALTA

My mourning fell away in the exciting improbability of it all: I had arrived in Australia for the first time only a few dozen hours earlier, having not seen my son in a decade. In this far corner of the world that I'd only begun to explore, the last place I'd expected to visit, was a concert hall in which I was hearing my son play again. How was it possible?

Yet there he was, roiling through the profoundly long phrases of the Brahms concerto. I hadn't heard anybody play this music in years because I could not bear the sadness of it once Joey stopped. Maybe, I thought, some portion of the faith I walked through was present in this music, or present on that night. It felt like the answer to a long-forgotten prayer. I hoped that Giuseppe might be somewhere on the other side, even hovering somewhere listening if such a possibility existed. I was transported back to a night in an apartment in New York City, when I first heard Giuseppe play, and the beauty of the memory, as well as the pain that followed, all of the confusions and regrets, made me think I should cry. But the tears didn't come. I was too crowded with thoughts and memories to have room for feelings. Many needs fell away that night.

Joey conjured an energy I never knew he had for the final pages of the concerto. He pushed the conductor into finding that energy, as well, and I could palpably feel the might of each musician in the orchestra. It felt like the old days, like no final London recital had happened, no painting, no decisions, no Ben, no pain. Just playing. The ovation was volcanic.

The same man who found Joey came to take me backstage after the concert, where it was pandemonium, as seemingly each member of the orchestra wanted to greet Joey, which was unusual in itself. The executives of the orchestra, along with the conductor, came to Joey's dressing room in an official delegation to thank him for saving the day "in this farthest corner of the world." Joey inquired about Donald, but no one had any news. A group of the older musicians congratulated him and brought him champagne.

With no forethought that I could discern, he invited whatever members of the orchestra who wanted to come to the Vaucluse house for a party, saying he was texting Claire to warn her. He told me she'd sent back a smile and the words, "I heard; good idea for a party."

I finally got through the crowd to my son. I hugged him and held him. Nothing needed to be said.

ABSHIED

ALTA

I stayed with Joey at the concert hall until all the guests had been greeted. Joey relayed to at least a dozen people that Claire was preparing for the unexpected guests by calling a local restaurant and explaining the situation. Food and waiters awaited them once they got home. Joey handed me his phone and instructed me to text with Claire as he continued to everyone who was waiting to see him. Claire relayed that they were setting up buffet tables in the largest single room of the house, the downstairs pool area—"where the cheap piano is," Joey joked with a few people. I knew that he kept his great piano, the Steinway that was made for him, upstairs in a room overlooking Sydney Harbour, but there was a piano by the pool as well. Claire noted in a text just how long it had been since anyone had been in their enormous home and how happy she was. She said taxis were already arriving with musicians still dressed from the concert. She feared Little Ben would be spooked by the crowd, but he seemed to be enjoying the energy of so many people.

I imagined that Claire needed our help at the house, but were we still at the opera house, though we were at least able to see the end of the line of people assembled to greet Joey. I gathered his things to go home.

"Mom, we should get moving. I imagine there are a lot of people waiting at home," he said, gathering a few flowers that had been left for him. As he had arrived at the theater not expecting to play a piano concerto, he didn't have anything else to take with him.

"Yes, we should go. This was quite a night, my dear." I wished I could find more to say, something to match the occasion.

"It was like the old days," he said. "And thrilling to tackle that monster again."

I told him I thought he should do more of that. But the laughter didn't last long. He quickly amended, "I'm not going to start playing again, Mother."

There was a timid knock on the door. Joey opened it.

"Good God," Joey said breathlessly, like he was going to faint.

The man spoke quietly. "I thought I was coming tonight to hear Donald play Brahms, so imagine my surprise." The moment he spoke, I knew it was Ben, because I recognized his voice.

"I, uh, are you still living in Sydney? I…haven't heard from you."

"You haven't wanted to hear from me. I've returned for a few weeks to wrap up at the gallery," Ben said.

"Were you going to call? Maybe see Little Ben?"

"I probably wasn't, to be honest. I thought it would just upset everyone." Ben looked over Joey's shoulder to me. "Alta, it's nice to meet you, finally." He entered the dressing room and hugged me.

"I seem to be the only person in this room without a clue as to what's going on," I said, nervously.

"No, that would be all of us," Joey said. "Listen, Ben, we're going back to the house where there's a big party. I'm sure Little Ben is long asleep, but you should come and see Claire."

"Too risky, I think, for the little guy to see me in case he's still up."

"I'll call Claire and make sure he's in bed. Really—you really should come."

"Are you sure you want me back in that house?"

"Why don't we meet you there?" Joey said, sounding like a compromise, as he turned to me and gestured for us to leave.

"Could I ride with you? I walked here from the hotel…and, if you are going anyway…"

I thought I would help, saying, "There are a few things I need to discuss with Joey."

But Joey was having none of that. We were coming down off of our cloud.

"Of course you can come with us, Ben. The orchestra has arranged a car," Joey said as he gestured for Ben to accompany them.

The car was waiting for us, incredibly, inside the opera house. Since the performing spaces are high on the pedestal of the building, meant to echo a Mayan pyramid, it was possible on certain occasions for a car to be waiting right at the bottom of the stairs on the street level, not in the public thoroughfare. They walked us to the car and we drove out the loading dock area near the stage door, but another crowd of people was waiting there to see Joey. The police opened the way and shortly we were heading up the hill and down Macquarie Street for the twenty-minute drive to Joey's house. There had been so many sensations and feelings in such a short time that I felt all I could do was listen.

"You do realize, don't you, that I've never heard you play, except on recordings?" Ben said, trying to break the ice.

"What did you think?" Joey asked him.

"It was extraordinary, Joey. Where did you learn to play like that?"

"That's a longer story than this car ride, Ben," Joey said, lighthearted again, looking at me.

I knew Joey had traversed the South Head Road thousands of times, but that night he seemed to get a thrill from it as though he'd never been there. They passed Rushcutters Bay on the left as the view opened out to the harbor, and then the ascent around Rose Bay as they neared Joey's house, and the two men stared at it with wonder and joy. Joey seemed to be collecting memories everywhere that he hadn't thought about in years, particularly with having Ben next to him again.

"I've never seen this many cars in this part of town." Joey said.

As we parked, Ben said, "I don't know if I can do this."

Joey took his hand for the first time since they'd seen each other that night. "You can."

JOEY

We entered the party, which had spread through every room and balcony. Neither Ben nor I had seen so many people in our home before, but we got quickly separated, since I was inundated with visitors and Ben went to find Claire. I mingled in each room upstairs, and on the upper balcony, where members of the orchestra were admiring the view all the way down Sydney Harbour where they'd just been. The lights of Manly Beach were visible to the north, the very lights I used to watch late at night from within a quiet house, imagining that the lights themselves were playing the *Goldberg Variations*.

I went downstairs, greeting so many along the way. I half expected to see Paul and Mary, as the party reminded me of their amazing party years ago, the one that had started it all. My heart ached with the memory of that night, and everything felt suddenly heavy. Would I ever see Paul and Mary again? And what of Ben and all that had passed between them? How could it ever be possible for them to stay together?

Yet I knew Ben was in the house somewhere, presumably reconciling with his sister. I ran upstairs to check on Little Ben, who was safely tucked in and asleep, unperturbed by the milling crowds downstairs. I kissed him, and he barely stirred. When I turned to leave the room, there was Mom.

"You didn't want him to hear you play?" she said.

"I didn't want to break his routine. He's still so young," I said.

"Yes," my mother whispered. I assumed she was going to bed, having been through quite a lot that day.

I heard somebody playing the old piano down by the pool. Mom liked that I called it the cheap piano, because it assured her I still cared for my custom Steinway. As I made my way down the back stairs, I heard someone playing jazz, with a bass joining in. Clearly the major party had moved downstairs, and members of the orchestra were taking their turns with several different pianists, each extending the joy of the evening into their unexpected selections.

Before I got downstairs, I stopped by the packed kitchen to get some water, only to hear, "We are so glad you're back!" I knew I wasn't back. The tectonic plates had only momentarily shifted, releasing a pressure that was already slowly building again. The orchestra turned into an improvised band, with members joining together to step outside their disciplined norm. I entered the room where I'd spent nearly every late afternoon for a decade alone, swimming. But on this night, it was filled with people drinking, laughing, and making music. Compliments flowed toward me from all directions, before each person went back to their own lively conversations. I was surrounded by admirers even though I was alone, and someone nearby handed me a glass of white wine.

Out of the crowd, for the second time that night, there was suddenly Ben, this time accompanied by a tearful Claire, who presented Ben to me as though introducing him for the first time, and the three of us embraced. We stood together for a few minutes, saying nothing, before I took Ben gently by the hand and led him to the far end of the pool. Despite so many strangers around, and potentially so many cameras, I slowly undressed down to my underwear, and after some confusion, Ben did the same. We walked into the pool and began to float on our backs, just as we had often done when we first owned the house. A few musicians followed their lead and quietly entered the pool. I floated, thinking of Little Ben upstairs asleep.

Music was all around us: musicians played and danced as Ben and I floated into the night, each of us fixed on the small lights overhead that were pretending to be starlight. Through the water distortions, I heard the room grow quiet, a change of the focus of the sound. Was it really what I thought? The pianist, playing my own piano, intoned Handel's "Care selve," and for the first time since I was a child, I heard my mother's voice.

www.ingramcontent.com/pod-product-compliance
Lightning Source LLC
Chambersburg PA
CBHW030646020726
47493CB00006B/1891